THE
HEIRESS

ALSO BY RACHEL HAWKINS

The Villa
Reckless Girls
The Wife Upstairs

THE
HEIRESS

Rachel Hawkins

HEADLINE

First published in the United States by St. Martin's Press
An imprint of St. Martin's Publishing Group

First published in Great Britain in 2023 by
HEADLINE PUBLISHING GROUP

1

Cataloguing in Publication Data is available from the British Library

Trade Paperback ISBN 978 1 0354 0960 0

Offset in 11.20/16.7pt Sabon LT Std by Jouve (UK), Milton Keynes

Printed and bound in Great Britain by Clays Ltd, Elcograf S.p.A.

HEADLINE PUBLISHING GROUP
An Hachette UK Company
Carmelite House
50 Victoria Embankment
London EC4Y 0DZ

www.headline.co.uk
www.hachette.co.uk

For Vera Etheridge Blake East Hobbs Haynes

It would probably shock the average American to learn just how little we know about those who go missing in the wilder parts of this great nation of ours. A tangled knot of jurisdictions and separate government agencies means that there is no singular place to collect that data, no easily searched resource that tells us just how many of our fellow citizens vanish into the thick forests of the Appalachians, the cold, stony reaches of the Rocky Mountains, the dense mists of the Pacific Northwest. And when someone is swallowed up by these elemental places, our brains struggle with the sheer vastness of both the land itself and the overwhelming myriad of possibilities. Did they vanish on purpose, seeking some kind of freedom from our plugged-in, switched-on existence? Was it an accident? If so, what kind? After all, there are so many things that can kill you once you've left well-traveled paths. Something as simple as a broken shoelace can lead to a stumble which becomes a fall, hands scrabbling over slippery rock. Wild animals are not the lovable cartoons we grew up with, but genuine threats. Did the missing person meet up with one, finding themselves plunged into the primal nightmare of becoming a food source?

And of course, we can never discount that most dangerous of animals, our fellow man. Lord Byron wrote, "There is a pleasure in the pathless woods / There is a rapture on the lonely shore / There is society where none intrudes / By the deep Sea, and music in its roar." But we know all too well that sometimes, society does indeed intrude, and we picture the lonely hiker, their excitement at seeing another human slowly curdling into terror as they realize that this is not a friend, not a fellow seeker of peace and tranquility.

This is why these stories have such a hold on us. So many questions, *too* many possible answers, and the reminder that the woods may be "dark and deep," but what can happen to you inside them is often far from lovely.

—"Without a Trace," by Bill Naracott, *Outside*, May 2017

LUMBER BARON'S BABY GIRL VANISHES, SEARCH ON FOOT, BY AIR UNDER WAY

By THE ASSOCIATED PRESS

Tavistock, North Carolina

On Sunday, September 12, an afternoon constitutional in the Blue Ridge Mountains of North Carolina took a tragic turn when the three-year-old daughter of Mr. Mason McTavish of Tavistock, North Carolina, seemingly vanished into thin air. The family, consisting of Mr. McTavish, his wife, Mrs. Anna McTavish (née Miss Anna Ashby, formerly of Wichita, Kansas, daughter of the late banker Mr. George Ashby and his wife, Mrs. Amelia [Thorpe] Ashby), and their young daughter, Miss Ruby Anne McTavish, were accompanied by the family's nanny with the intention of having a picnic in the mountains surrounding the McTavish home, Ashby House.

The child was discovered missing at approximately 2:30 P.M., and after a brief search by the family, the sheriff's office was alerted. A thorough search is now under way, involving authorities from multiple jurisdictions as well as civilian volunteers, several of whom have offered to fly their personal aircrafts over the site where the child was last seen as efforts on the ground have been hampered by torrential rainfall overnight.

At this time, the Tavistock County Sheriff's Department says they have "no reason to suspect criminal activity" involved with the child's disappearance, but Mr. McTavish is among the wealthiest men in the state of North Carolina, and, as such, kidnapping has not been conclusively ruled out.

The Atlanta Constitution,
Monday Morning, September 13, 1943

Changeling (change-ling): **Noun**

> **Definition: 1) A child put in place of another child. In folklore, various magical beings (witches, fairies, trolls) are often responsible for the switch.**

RELATED LINKS: BRIDGET CLEARY
1928 WINEVILLE CHICKEN COOP MURDERS
DISAPPEARANCE OF BOBBY DUNBAR

Internet commons entry for "changeling," accessed October 4, 2023

CHAPTER ONE

Jules

There should be some kind of warning when your life is about to change forever.

I don't need a siren or bloodred skies or anything, but I still think there should be just the littlest bit of . . . I don't know, a *frisson*. A feeling under your skin and inside your bones when something fundamental shifts, when the ground underneath your feet grows suddenly unstable.

And you should *definitely* not be wearing a fucking bonnet when it happens.

But that's exactly what I'm wearing the September evening I come home and Camden drops the bomb that's the beginning and the ending of everything.

Not just a bonnet, I should add, but also a black dress and white apron that are supposed to say "pioneer woman," but instead just make me look Amish, plus a pair of stiff leather boots that rub my ankles raw and pinch my toes. It's all part of my costume at the living history museum where I work in Golden, Colorado.

You know the place.

I mean, even if you don't *specifically* know Homestead Park, you know the *kind* of place. Beautifully constructed re-creations of old farmhouses, barns, general stores. Docile farm animals in pastures, the mountains rising around us, with only the whooshing of cars on the nearby highway and the black rectangles of cell phones lifted to capture anything even *vaguely* Instagrammable as signs that you haven't somehow time-traveled to the nineteenth century.

Manifest Destiny Disneyland.

That's where I work Tuesday through Saturday, playing the part of "Mrs. Hiram Burch," a farmer's wife who tells school groups and tourists about the hardships on the Western Fron-tier, how people lived Back Then, all of that.

All in all, it's not the worst job, and it's certainly one of the few that actually lets me use the few semesters of the-ater classes I took nearly a decade ago, but it isn't without its drawbacks.

"Do you have any idea," I call to my husband as I enter the front door of our little house, a house we'll leave in just a few days and never see again, "how hard it is to talk about churning butter without saying the words 'cream' or 'pole'?"

There's no response, but I know he's here. I saw his car in the driveway, and this house is so small it would be impossi-ble for him not to hear me. "Three entire junior highs at the park today. Like, nine thousand prepubescent boys, and there I am, trying to figure out how to do my job as an 'interpreter of the past' without getting sexually harassed. Real banner day for Mrs. Burch!"

Still no answer.

Frowning, I hang up my keys on the little hook by the door and move farther down the hallway.

There's nowhere to hide in this house. It's more or less a box. Front door opens onto long hallway. Directly to the left? Living room. Across from that? A small closet where we've managed to store most of our winter gear. Just past the closet is the kitchen, and if you keep going down the hall, you'll find a tiny bathroom and, finally, our bedroom.

I'm beginning to wonder if Cam is sick and laid up in bed, but as I pass the kitchen, I spot him sitting at the small wooden table we picked up from a flea market last year.

His back is to the door, but even without seeing his face, I know something has happened. Cam never hangs out in the kitchen, and never like this, sitting stiff in his seat, his elbows on the table, his hands clenched in front of him.

That's when I realize it's Wednesday, the day Camden usually tutors at the junior college until seven. It's only just past five thirty now, and there's real worry in my voice when I lay my hand on his shoulder and say, "Cam?"

Camden turns, his hand automatically coming up to cover mine, and while there's still a trio of wrinkles over the bridge of his nose, and the knuckles on the hand still on the table are white, he smiles. It's quick and distracted, but it's something.

His gaze moves over me.

"If I'd known Goody Proctor was haunting this house, I would've tried to rent something else," he says, and I tweak his earlobe.

"I didn't feel like changing at the park," I reply, moving past him to the refrigerator where I take a can of Diet Coke. "And I *assumed* I would be free from mockery in my own home. I take enough shit from the eighth graders, you know."

Another half-assed smile, then his eyes drift to his phone.

It's nearly on the other side of the table, far enough away that he'd have to get out of his seat and really reach to retrieve it.

I sit across from him, the phone just inches from my soda when I set it down, and I study the man I married in a California courtroom nearly a decade ago.

You need to know that I'm not one of those people who constantly puts up gushing Facebook posts about my husband. You've seen those, I know you have. Probably talked shit about them to your friends.

Molly from high school, her arm around some dude named Rushton, lips smushed against his cheek, a long caption about how happy she is to be "doing life" with "this guy."

That's never been me.

For one, Cam doesn't even have social media, and for another, there's always been something about him—about *us*—that feels private.

Special, even.

It's been that way from the moment we met.

You don't expect to meet the love of your life at 25 Cent Wing Night at a college bar. Or hell, maybe you're more optimistic than I am, and so you go to every "BOGO Beer Wednesday" and "No Cover Charge For 36C and Up This Weekend!" special that's advertised assuming you're going to meet the One.

Me, I just really wanted some cheap wings. I'd moved to California from Florida after three semesters of community college for the usual reason pretty girls leave small towns and head west—to be a star. Thing was, the only person I knew out there was an acquaintance from high school, Emma, and since she'd lived in San Bernardino, I'd landed there first.

Bloom where you're planted, people like to say, but they

ignore the fact that *planted* is sometimes just a nice way of saying *stuck*, and I'd definitely fallen into that category.

So I was juggling two jobs back then, waiting tables at one of those nightmare chain places that makes you wear a lot of buttons on your black apron while also spending a few afternoons every week watching a couple of kids who lived in my apartment complex. I didn't charge their mom much, given that she was working just as hard as I was. Sometimes when I watched her come in with greasy sacks of fast food, already cold from her long drive over from the next town, I wished I were able to say, "Hey, it's fine, you don't need to pay me."

But that wasn't my life.

So I took her twenty bucks and tried to make it last, and that was why I was at Senor Pollo's on a Thursday night when I was just twenty-one, the same night that Camden was tending bar.

I'd ordered a water—couldn't afford wings *and* a beer, even when the wings were cheap—but from the way my gaze had followed a couple of pints of Stella he pulled for another table, he must've known what I really wanted.

A few seconds later, a frosty and perfectly poured glass was sitting in front of me, and he'd flashed me that little smile I would come to know so well, the one that could almost be a smirk on another guy. "On the house," he'd said quietly. I'd noticed then, as he'd looked over at me, that his eyes were two different colors.

One was gray-blue, the other a clear golden brown that made me think of high-end bourbon. It's a genetic thing, heterochromia, and because Camden was adopted, he has no idea if he got it from his mother or his father. Sometimes I wonder if any children we might have will inherit it, too, will look at me with that same patchwork gaze that always seems to see everything.

That first night, I noticed more than his eyes, of course. He was tall, a little too thin back then, brown hair longer and shaggier than he wears it now, and I liked the way he moved behind the bar, liked how his hands looked when they held a glass or opened a bottle.

He was cute, yes, but it was more than that. There had been something about him that was so calm, so still. So sure of himself, even though he was just barely twenty-two and, as I'd later learn, going through his own shit.

We kissed later that night beside my shitty car. He spent the next night in my even shittier apartment.

And that had been that.

I don't know why I'm telling you this part now. I mean, it probably doesn't even seem all that romantic to you. Cheap college bar, my heart won forever by a free beer and a cute smile, sex on a mattress I'd gotten from Goodwill and suspected someone had died on.

But it *was* romantic. More than that, it was *real*.

And I guess I just want you to know that, before you hear the rest of it.

I'm getting ahead of myself, though.

For now, we're here, in our little rental in Golden, Colorado, a place we've lived for the past five years, where Camden teaches ninth- and eleventh-grade English at an all-boys prep school and I churn butter on a make-believe farm. We're happy with each other, if not exactly with the lives we're leading, and later, I'll realize it's because we knew eventually this moment would come.

That we were waiting for this.

For a cool September evening, a random Wednesday that shouldn't have been anything special at all, when Camden nods at his phone and says, "It's my family. They want me to come home."

HEIRESS, PHILANTHROPIST, ONETIME KIDNAP VICTIM, RUBY MCTAVISH CALLAHAN WOODWARD MILLER KENMORE DIES AT 73

One of North Carolina's most famous (some would say infamous) women has passed away peacefully at her legendary mansion in the Blue Ridge Mountains, Ashby House.

Ruby McTavish was born on June 1, 1940, the oldest child of lumber magnate Mason McTavish and his first wife, Anna Ashby McTavish, in the town of Tavistock, North Carolina, a once-sleepy hamlet transformed by the power of the McTavish fortune.

That fortune came at a cost, however. In 1943, when she was barely three years old, young Ruby McTavish vanished on a family picnic in the mountains surrounding Ashby House. The disappearance held the nation in its grip for nearly a year with the McTavishes offering what was, at the time, the highest reward ever for any information leading to her safe return.

Authorities had assumed the child had succumbed to exposure in the thick forests of the Blue Ridge Mountains, and were stunned when the private detective hired by Mason McTavish found the child alive and well, living in Spanish Fort, Alabama, with a family by the name of Darnell, eight months after she first disappeared. The return of "Baby Ruby" was a balm to a country still locked in the Second World War, and the joy at seeing a family reunited overshadowed the grubby and sordid end of her alleged kidnapper, Jimmy Darnell, who was killed while attempting to escape the local jail before his trial could begin.

While the kidnapping had a happy ending, it would not be Ruby's last brush with notoriety. Married four times, Ruby seemed singularly unlucky in love, losing her first husband, Duke Callahan, to a shooting on their Paris honeymoon, her second to an electrical accident at Ashby House, the third to a lingering illness, and the last, Roddy Kenmore, to a boating mishap.

It was this last husband that gave her a nickname people in North Carolina barely dared to whisper: "Mrs. Kill-more."

However, no charges were ever brought against Ruby McTavish, and those closest to her insist it was not in her nature to hurt anyone.

"If you ask me, she just had bad taste in men," one confidante said. "Duke was reckless, Hugh was stupid, Andrew had always had health issues, and Roddy was a [expletive] basket case. I see where it looks bad, but I promise you, that woman was a saint."

Saint or not, Ruby McTavish—who reverted to her maiden name after the death of her last husband—did devote a large part of her life to charitable works, most involving disadvantaged youth. It was through this work that she met and eventually adopted her only child, a young boy she named Camden, who, with her death, becomes sole heir to a fortune rumored to be in the high eight figures.

In addition to Camden (20), Mrs. McTavish is survived by a sister, Nelle (69), a nephew, Howell (49), a great-nephew, Ben (23), and a great-niece, Elizabeth (17).

A cause of death has not been released.

—*The Asheville Citizen-Times*, April 2, 2013

TO: CAMcTavish@goldenboysprep.edu
FROM: BHMcTavish@AshbyLTD.org
SUBJECT: [FWD] Ruby's will/house issues

Cam,

By now, I guess you've heard about Dad. Nathan Collins said
he'd get in touch with you and let you know, so I assume he did
that. Nana Nelle thought it was "tacky" to let your lawyer tell you a
family member died, but I reminded her that you'd made it pretty
clear you didn't want to talk to any of us.

Honestly, I don't blame you, especially after the last email Dad sent
to you (hope you don't mind me attaching that message, by the
way, but I wanted you to be sure I wasn't bullshitting you about
knowing what he said). If it's any consolation, you weren't the only
person to get an email like that. His drinking had been bad for
the past twenty years, ever since Mom left, really, but the last six
months of his life were particularly rough. Probably sounds shitty
to say, but me and Libby both felt like we'd already lost him by the
time he wrapped his car around that tree last month.

Anyway, it doesn't look like you replied (and, hey, I can't judge since
I stopped responding to similar texts and voicemails from him), and
for all I know, you won't reply to this one, either, but I had to try.

I'm not going to give you the same old guilt trip bullshit Dad tried.
You were always a straight shooter, so I will be, too. With Dad
gone and you in Colorado, I feel a responsibility for not just Nana
Nelle and Libby, but for Ashby House itself. Dad wasn't lying about
the repair work that's needed, but it's more than that. Maybe it was
everything with Ruby, all the husbands, the rumors. Maybe it was
because Dad was admittedly a dick to a lot of the locals. Maybe
we've all just been up on this mountain for too damn long. I don't
know, man. But I do know that the McTavish name used to mean
something—used to make shit happen—and I want it to again.

And none of that can happen until we untangle the mess Ruby left us with that damn will.

I'll understand if you don't answer this, but like I said, I had to try. I know we haven't ever been close, and I hate that Nana Nelle and Ruby spent so much time pitting us against each other, but we're not teenagers anymore, Cam. Come home, back to Ashby, and let's get this shit squared away once and for all.

Sincerely,
Ben

TO: CAMcTavish@goldenboysprep.edu
FROM: FightBlueDevils1969@AshbyLTD.org
SUBJECT: Ruby's will/house issues

Camden,

I hope this email finds you well, and that contacting you via your workplace is not out of line. Unfortunately, you've made yourself hard to get in contact with any other way (although I assume that is on purpose).

As you know, it's in my nature to be blunt, so I will put this as plainly as possible: while I understand your reasons for putting time and distance between us, and I regret the words spoken in anger that caused you to make that decision, I feel that now, after ten years, it is time to attempt some kind of family reconciliation.

I could tell you that my mother has not been well (which is true), or that it's occurred to me that thanks to the acrimonious nature of my divorce from the mother of my children, you are the only family they have besides me or their grandmother (also true).

I suspect that neither of these facts will sway you. However, despite our differences, I know that you loved Ruby and shared her deep affection for Ashby House. If family cannot bring you home, maybe the house can. There is flood damage to the east wing, plus I'm told that several of the windows will need to be replaced, along with sections of the roof, the steps to the back veranda, and Lord only knows what else.

Thanks to Ruby's will, accessing the funds to do these vital repairs involves a jungle of red tape and more phone calls to that dipshit lawyer of yours than I'd prefer to make.

You may have washed your hands of us, but you still have responsibilities here, Camden. Responsibilities that Ruby left for you and would expect you to fulfill. And if you can't do that, you can at least come down here and sort out a better fucking solution than making my almost eighty-year-old mother call Nathan fucking Collins twelve times a day just to get money that *her* father made.

So come home. Oversee the work yourself so that you know we're not scamming you out of money you've never even fucking *touched*. And let's fix this. Not just the house, but all of it. Because it's been ten years of bullshit at this point, Cam. I told you when you left it wasn't that simple, and now here we are.

Ruby is probably laughing at us down there in hell. Mother thinks she killed herself just to fuck us all over, to leave everything this goddamn mess, but I wonder, sometimes, Cam, I really do. Maybe we were too quick to cremate her and find out if she really took those pills herself. Thinking about it a lot here lately for some reason.

Do you ever think about it, Camden?

You may hate us but you always said you loved this house. You always said you loved Ruby. Now prove it.

H.

CHAPTER TWO

Camden

There's a moment, right before I close the trunk of the car, when I think about calling this whole fucking thing off.

I could. It's my home, my family. My decision, as Jules has reminded me a thousand times since that night in the kitchen, the night when I read Ben's email and realized that you can put miles and mountains between you and home, but eventually, home will call you back.

I'd actually forgotten about the other email, the one from Howell. It had come in about six months ago, and I'd read it sitting at my desk, the only sound my students' pencils scraping across the paper as they'd worked on their persuasive essays.

Clearly a lesson Howell had missed because nothing about that drunken rant had made me even think about coming home. I hadn't spoken to Howell since the afternoon of Ruby's funeral, but reading that email, I could hear his voice in my head as clearly as if he'd been standing right in front of me, ten years swept away clean.

I could smell the whiskey, too.

The email was classic Howell, starting out formal and mannered, the benevolent King of Tavistock, North Carolina, calling for the return of a wayward noble. Then by the end, devolving into a typo-riddled, expletive-filled mess dripping with guilt trips and vitriol.

And a threat.

A poorly worded one, but a threat nonetheless.

Ruby's death had been officially listed as "heart failure," but the empty pill bottles in her nightstand had told a different story.

That was the first—and maybe the only—time in my life I'd ever wielded the McTavish money and name like the rest of them did. I insisted that there would be no autopsy, no questions, just a simple cremation and a subdued memorial service with only the family in attendance. I hadn't wanted the circus, hadn't wanted all those old stories about Ruby dug up and splashed on the pages of magazines again.

If I hadn't been so young and desperate, I might've thought more about how it all looked—how, to minds as poisoned and suspicious as Howell's and Nelle's, covering up Ruby's suicide would make *me* look like I had something to hide. So it hadn't been a surprise, that sly, ugly sentence there at the end of his email—*Do you ever think about it, Camden?*—but it had landed like a weight in my chest all the same.

When I'd gotten my lawyer's voicemail last month, telling me Howell had driven drunk straight into a tree not far from Ashby House, I hadn't been surprised. There had been dozens of smaller accidents like that with him, god knows how many cars crumpled, but Howell had always walked away.

Until he didn't.

I hadn't told Jules about the call, Howell's death, any of it. I'd planned on just ignoring it like I did all things Ashby House, but Ben's message . . . I don't know. It got to me.

He was right—he and I had never gotten along as kids. He was a couple of years older than me, and knowing that his family fortune was being left to some skinny kid he wasn't even related to had not exactly endeared me to him. The Ben I remembered was a preening jock, an asshole who drove a truck that could've doubled as a tank and always wore whatever the year's most expensive sneakers were.

But he'd sounded different in that email. More . . . I don't know. Human. Like someone who wasn't necessarily the Enemy.

Howell's email from all those months ago had been easy to ignore, but something about Ben's gave me pause.

We'd talked late into the night, me and Jules, weighing out the pros (Jules had never seen Ashby House, or North Carolina for that matter; it would be the first trip we'd taken together since that camping trip in Estes Park two summers ago; Ben was right, something needed to be done about the tangled bullshit that was Ruby's will—all that money, all that house) and the cons (literally, every fucking thing else).

In the end, it had been Jules who'd made the decision for us. Sitting there at our kitchen table, our fingers intertwined, exhausted in that way you get when you've been talking in circles for hours, she'd finally said, "I think we should go."

I'd watched her, not saying anything, my heart a steady drumbeat in my chest, and then she'd added, almost sheepish, "It might be nice to know you a little better."

Married ten years, and my own wife feels like she needs to know me better.

I could understand it, though. When I'd left North Carolina for California, I was so closed off, so determined to keep to myself.

It had seemed safest that way. Ashby House had been a crucible and a fishbowl all at once, the sort of place where despite all the rooms and the endless square footage, it was like you were never alone. There was always someone watching, always someone listening, and all I had wanted was to feel invisible. Unseen.

Unknown.

Until Jules. I'd let her in, but I knew—and apparently, she did, too—that there was still some part of me holding back.

Ashby House was the reason for that.

So maybe it could be the solution, too.

After that, things moved fast. Jules quit her job at Homestead Park and pulled out of the local theater production of *Chicago,* where she'd been cast as Velma. I put in for extended leave at the school. "Shouldn't be more than a few weeks," I'd said to the head of the English department, hoping it was true, but knowing it probably wasn't.

My ninth graders were reading *The Odyssey,* and just a few weeks ago, we'd gotten to the part about the lotus-eaters, a tribe of people living on an island, gorging themselves with the lotus flowers that make them forget home, forget anything that's not the island and their fellow lotus-eaters, all of them settling into peaceful, blank apathy.

Ashby House was like that.

Stay there long enough, and you forget there's a world outside its tall doors, its oversize windows, and shadowed lawns. It swallows everyone eventually. Look at Ben and Libby, for fuck's sake. Look at Howell.

I barely remembered his ex-wife, Ben and Libby's mom, Rebecca. She'd taken off early on, when Libby was about five or six, and after that, it was like she had never even existed. Like anyone who left Ashby House had to be erased from the collective memory or something.

But Howell had stayed, and while they'd briefly left for college, both Ben and Libby had drifted back to Ashby eventually. Nelle, of course, had never left. Never would.

Four people rattling around a fifteen-bedroom mansion because the idea of life outside its walls, of buying a smaller place—or, god forbid, renting an apartment like a normal person—was completely unthinkable.

It had been unthinkable to me once, too.

Until the idea of staying had seemed even worse.

I stand there, cold in the chilly morning air, the light jacket I threw on over my long-sleeved T-shirt not doing much against the bite of Colorado in mid-September. I haven't worn this jacket in years. It's been buried in my closet alongside the other clothes I brought from North Carolina that I never touched once I got out west. A pair of camouflage cargo shorts, a seersucker suit Ruby had insisted I buy, khakis, Docksiders, and a fucking bow tie of all things, all remnants of a past life—not so much of the Cam I'd been, but the Cam that Ruby had wanted me to be.

Does he still exist, that Cam? Is he tucked somewhere inside my soul, or is he a ghost, wandering the halls of Ashby?

I guess I'm about to find out.

There's a rattle of keys at the front door as Jules steps out onto the porch, locking up behind her. Her hair is pulled into a messy bun, sunglasses sliding down her nose as she turns to face me, an oversize duffel bag on one shoulder, and something seizes in my chest as I look at my wife.

Again, there's that overwhelming urge to say, Fuck it—to email Ben that I'm not coming; to instead call my lawyer, Nathan, and tell him to release any funds any of them ask for.

To do whatever it takes to sever that tie for good and keep the thousands of miles, rivers, and a whole goddamn mountain range between me and what I left behind in North Carolina.

But then Jules smiles, practically bouncing down the steps, and says, "I'm so glad we're doing this."

I smile back, reaching to pull her close, her chin tilting up so that I can kiss the tip of her nose.

"You're doing that face," she tells me, and I don't have to ask what she means. Any time I'm overthinking things—brooding, Jules would say—I apparently make a face. Jules mimics it for me now, her jaw tight, her brows drawing slightly together, and I huff out a laugh like I always do.

"It's going to be fine," she continues, reaching up to rub her thumb over that trio of wrinkles on my forehead. "You'll see."

She thinks it's all the money shit that has made things tense. She gets that Nelle and Howell were never the most welcoming of family members, even though Ruby adopted me when I was only three—still a baby in most regards, and who the hell cold-shoulders a baby? She knows that Ben and Libby are spoiled and more than a little vapid and that I don't have much in common with them. She understands that I chose to leave the money Ruby left me mostly untouched because I knew that that kind of wealth came with strings attached.

Everything about my estrangement from my family makes perfect sense to Jules because I've made it make perfect sense. I've told her the truth, or at least the most basic version of it, and she's accepted it.

And if I call this trip off right this second, she'd probably accept that, too. But she'd be disappointed. Confused, probably. A little sad.

Worst of all, she might be curious.

We've already left our jobs and shut down the house. The car is packed. I've got Tavistock, North Carolina, plugged into the GPS and hotel rooms booked for nights in Kansas, Missouri, and Kentucky. Sure, we could get there in three days instead of four, but Jules liked the idea of taking the scenic route, and besides, I'm in no hurry to face my family. And if I back out now, how long before my wife starts wondering what was so bad about going home that I'd rather undo all of that planning, all of that effort?

How long before Ben sends another email, one a little sharper, a little colder?

No, I made my choice when Jules slipped her hand into mine that night and said those words.

It might be nice to know you a little better.

She deserves that. *I* deserve that.

I give her one last squeeze then, lightly swatting at her hip, gesture her toward the passenger seat of the car. "I'll take first shift," I tell her. "Seven hours until Wichita."

"Okay, but I'm picking the music," she replies as she tosses her bag in the back.

"Shotgun rights, sacred rules of the road," I say, solemn, and she laughs like I knew she would.

I hold tight to that laugh as I slide into the driver's seat, my fingers flexing on the wheel. The sun is bright, making me squint and reach for my sunglasses, and as I do, the light catches on the clasp of my watch.

An eighteenth birthday present from Ruby. There's an inscription on the back, one I haven't looked at in years, but remember all the same.

For Camden. Time Brings All Things to Pass.

And as I drive away from the new life that I'd built for myself, heading back toward my past, I wonder if those words were supposed to be an encouragement or a warning.

Or a threat.

From the Desk of

Ruby A. McTavish

March 12, 2013

Well, darling, here we are.

You asked for me to tell you the truth, all of it, the glorious and golden, the ugly and unvarnished. I think you wanted me to tell it to you all at once, the last time we spoke. I could see how disappointed you were when I told you that it would take time. I'm seventy-three, for goodness' sake, and I've lived an eventful life. Too eventful, honestly. And anyway, this isn't the kind of thing you chat about over coffee. Something like this, it needs an old-fashioned touch, a bit of formality (I can see you rolling your eyes already, and if you were in front of me, I'd slap your hand for it).

After you read these letters, you'll probably think I'm a mad old fool for putting any of this in writing, but I've found that writing things down makes them real. Firms up details. Allows less room for . . . eliding, let us say. (If you don't know what that word means, then I'm clearly overpaying for your education.)

And to be honest—that's what you're after, yes?—I don't care anymore. If people find these and read them and finally know the truth of everything, it no longer matters to me. I know my end is coming—soon for some, I suppose, but right on time for me. And if you can't tell the truth at the end of it all, then what, I ask, is the fucking point?

I've never written that word before. I've hardly ever said it.
I know I got on you about crass language, but now I see why
people use it. How satisfying! This experiment is already going
so well!

You wanted to know mostly about the men, I think. The
pile of dead husbands, "Mrs. Kill-more," all of that. And we'll
get there, I promise.

I also promise to skip the non-interesting bits. My school
years, the business, most anything to do with Nelle (although
she will make an appearance in this letter, I'm afraid, but sadly
for Nelle, the only times in her life when she has ever been
interesting are the times she was being a nasty little bitch, and
the story I'm going to tell involves one of those times).

But before I can get to all of that, we have to talk about my
tragic disappearance and miraculous rescue.

You can read the newspaper articles about the whole saga.
They're all saved in the top right-hand drawer of my desk.
Or you can go on the internet. Libby tells me there's an entire
entry about it on some online encyclopedia.

And yes, yes, I know we've already covered some of this,
but only the facts. How I vanished on a family picnic when
I was just three, how I was found months and months later
living with the Darnells in Alabama. How Mrs. Darnell
insisted that I was not Ruby McTavish at all, but her own child,
Dora, and how Mr. Darnell eventually confessed that while
in North Carolina on a construction job (for my own father,
as luck would have it), he had gotten drunk on a Sunday
afternoon and wandered into the woods. How he had seen
me alone, a miscommunication between my nanny and my
mother meaning that both women thought the other was
watching me. How he had thought of his wife, Helen, and the
child just my age who had died only a month or so before.

How easy it had been to scoop me up, carry me to his truck parked on some back logging road, and spirit me away to his family's shack in Alabama. A replacement for the child his wife so mourned.

Of course, I remember none of this.

Or rather, I remember fragments that I'm not sure are actually memories. I read the stories so many times, you see, and envisioned so much of it that I can't be sure if something is a memory or a conjured-up image.

A dream.

That's why I spent so much time in my father's office as a child.

He kept all the newspaper clippings there, in the very same drawer I mentioned earlier.

I learned that by accident one afternoon in 1950, when I was just ten years old. I'd had a doll, one of those fancy ones with the eyes that opened and closed and silky blond hair, her lips strawberry pink, and her cheeks dotted with painted-on freckles.

I'd gotten her when I was seven or eight, for Christmas or a birthday, I can't remember which. What I can remember is Nelle howling that her doll had *brown* hair and mine had *yellow* hair, and that was unfair since Nelle herself was a blonde and I was a brunette. I had been worried that my parents might make me trade dolls with Nelle, and I had sat there, only a little bitty thing, thinking, *If they do, I will throw this doll into the fire. I will burn it before I let Nelle have it.*

I meant it, too. The image of that beautiful doll melting and folding in on itself, the yellow hair sparking, the pink paint of the lips bubbling and cracking, was far less painful than picturing the doll, whole and complete and perfect, in Nelle's arms.

Do all children think like this? I've never spent much time with children other than the ones either born into or brought into this family, so I couldn't say. Maybe it's all perfectly normal, and not some quirk of either my DNA or the very essence that seems to emanate from the walls of Ashby House. But at the time—and hell, who am I kidding, even now—it seemed that there must be something uniquely wrong with *me*.

In any case, Mama didn't ask me to trade, and Nelle was eventually consoled with an extra piece of cake or some other sop, and the doll was mine. I had named her "Grace," but when I said the name, something had passed over Mama's face, an ugly look like someone had suddenly hit her.

"I don't like that name," she'd said sharply. "What about Kitty?"

I thought Kitty was a stupid name, but Mama so rarely paid any attention to me that I'd readily agreed even as I'd known that in my head, I would still call her Grace.

And it was Grace's fault I was in Daddy's office that hot summer afternoon.

One of her eyes had gotten stuck, half-opened, half-closed. There was something about that half-mast gaze that reminded me of Mama when she had her headaches. That's what we called them then, although of course now I know that Mama drank too much, which meant that she was perpetually either intoxicated or dealing with the aftermath.

Do you know, to this day, I cannot stand the smell of gin? It was her favorite, and any time I get a whiff of that herby, medicinal scent, I think of Mama, swaying in her bedroom door, her face puffy, eyes red.

The last time Grace's eye had gotten stuck like that, Daddy had fixed it with a paper clip, and the only place I could think to find one was his office, so I'd crept in there, the air stifling, smelling like cigar smoke, furniture polish, and the faint hint of my father's cologne.

We weren't forbidden from entering, exactly. It's just that Daddy was out of town for business (well, "business." Later we'd learn he was driving to Charleston to stay with his mistress and our future stepmother, Loretta), and I'd never been in there without him.

I can still remember how hard my heart was beating as I crept across that thick green carpet, the same carpet that is under my feet now as I write this. How the brass knob of the drawer felt hot in my hand, my fingers sweaty.

I didn't mean to snoop, but when I opened the drawer, the very first thing I saw was my name. It was emblazoned across the top of a newspaper, the letters inches high, bold and black:

BABY RUBY HOME AT LAST!

I remember wrinkling my nose at the "baby" part, already sophisticated enough at ten to reject anything that smacked of babyishness, but then I started to read.

And kept reading.

I'd known about the kidnapping. This is not that moment where a child learns some dark family secret by accident. Our town was too small, our family too well known for that kind of thing to stay hidden. But I only knew about it in the vaguest sense. A bad man had lost his child and saw me, taking me home to his wife so she wouldn't be so sad anymore, but that wasn't right, you could not take someone else's child, and Daddy had spent so much of our money to find me, to bring me home where I belonged.

But here, in this newspaper, I learned the name of the man who had taken me.

Jimmy Darnell.

His wife was Helen. They had called me Dora. They had another baby, too, born just after I was returned to my family. Her name was Claire, a pretty name that I immediately resolved to give to the next doll I got.

And then I'd seen another name.

Grace.

There in black and white, a sentence: *The child's former nanny, Grace Bennett, left North Carolina after questioning, and her current whereabouts are unknown.*

Paper clip and doll forgotten, I'd sat in Daddy's big leather chair and pulled out all the papers in that drawer.

It took me awhile to find it, but eventually there had been a picture splashed across the front page of *The Atlanta Constitution*. I recognized Mama and Daddy, their expressions serious, Mama's hat tilted so that the brim covered most of her face. And behind her, another woman, younger, her hair dark, her face a rictus of anguish, tears streaming, one gloved hand clapped over her mouth.

The parents of Baby Ruby leave the Tavistock, North Carolina, police station accompanied by the child's nanny—and the last person to see Baby Ruby—Grace Bennett.

I looked at that face for what felt like hours.

The grief on it. The pain. The horror. How she must have loved me. How tormented she must have felt, letting me slip away on her watch.

Guilt crept into me, too, a sick, slippery feeling.

How could I not remember someone who loved me this much? How was the only thing left of this person the faint memory of a name, a name I gave to a *doll*?

But mixed in with the guilt was that strange sort of elation you feel when reading about yourself. Pages and pages of newsprint, all about something scandalous that had happened to *me*.

What child can resist that?

So, naturally, I wasn't listening as closely as I should have been, which is why, when Nelle pushed her way in and pointed at me, I actually jumped in my seat.

"You're in Daddy's office!" she cried, triumphant. "I'm gonna tell him!"

"I'll say you're lying," I fired back. "You're just a baby. He won't believe you."

Her narrow face creased into a frown. Christ, I've just realized it's the same expression she wears ninety percent of the time now. How tragic for her.

"He will, too!" she replied, her voice shrill. "He'll believe me over *you*. You're not even my real sister."

Every argument with Nelle reached this point eventually. It was her favorite weapon, even though the one time Mama heard her say it, Nelle had gotten a whooping with a belt, a punishment neither of us had ever received before or since.

But, apparently, even that wasn't a deterrent.

"I'm gonna tell Daddy you said that."

Her little face flushed, and she crossed her arms over her chest, lower lip wobbling. If she started crying, she might wake Mama up from her nap, and then we'd both be in trouble.

"Or-r-r," I said, drawing the word out, "I won't tell, and you won't tell anyone I was in here."

It was always like this with Nelle. Attack, counterattack, and then, eventually, a reminder of mutually assured destruction, and we headed back to our corners until the battle began anew over something else.

It was exhausting, frankly.

It's *still* exhausting. How are two women our age still

locked into such silliness? I sometimes think about asking her. Was there ever a time when we could've broken this pattern? Been something more than wary enemies? There must have been. Obviously, there was no chance of it after everything with Duke, but maybe before that.

Maybe that moment in Daddy's office was our chance, and I'd missed it.

Ah, well. No use in trying to undo what's long been done. And besides, I can admit that I could never forgive Nelle for voicing my greatest fear so often.

That I wasn't Ruby McTavish. That I was Dora Darnell, a cuckoo in the nest, and that's why Nelle hated me, had always hated me, wailing her head off when she was just a baby anytime I came near her. Because she knew, even then, that I wasn't her sister.

What chance did we ever have, with something like that between us?

In any case, she slunk out of the office, and I carefully replaced the papers, picking up my doll as I went, forgetting the paper clip altogether. Although now that I think about it, I never played with that doll again after that day.

It sat there with my other toys, one eye forever half-open until I was old enough not to have toys anymore.

I wonder where it ended up.

But you didn't ask for childhood memories, you asked for the truth! That's what you're saying to yourself right now, aren't you?

Darling, I've given it to you.

The fear that I was not Ruby McTavish was an open wound, one Nelle knew to pour salt in and one that I, with my newspapers and my dreams I called memories, was forever trying to heal. It was a fear that I could never speak aloud myself because even as a child, I knew it would shatter something inside my family for good.

Because what would that mean?

Too many horrors to contemplate.

Even for me, even now.

Especially when there are still so many horrors to come.

-R

HOPE DIM, BUT NOT YET
EXTINGUISHED FOR
FAMILY OF BABY RUBY

Tavistock, North Carolina

When Anna Ashby McTavish was a young girl, she tells us, the only thing she ever wanted for Christmas was "ribbon candy and a sack of oranges."

A modest wish for a girl born to one of the finest families in Wichita, Kansas, but in keeping with Mrs. McTavish's character. This is a woman who offers reporters tea poured by her own hand rather than relying on the maids that surely people the halls of Ashby House, and whose anguish is only visible in the slight redness of her eyes, the elegant fingers reaching up to touch a delicate diamond cross around her neck as she tells us of the one wish she has for Christmas 1943.

"I want my baby to come home to us," she says, her voice cracking slightly. "There's nothing I wouldn't do to have Ruby back."

Ruby McTavish has been missing for over three months now after disappearing on a family picnic. Even now, Mrs. McTavish tells us, she can hardly bear to think that such a lovely day ended in tragedy.

"It was such a pretty afternoon, and Ruby was so sweet in her little sailor dress. She'd fallen down at one point and scraped her knee, but she didn't even cry. I think she was as happy as her daddy was to be out in these mountains."

The Blue Ridge Mountains surrounding the McTavish mansion are indeed stunning, but they are also full of hidden dangers—steep cliffs, boggy areas, and, of course, wild animals.

Faced with such perils, it's no wonder the Tavistock County Sheriff's Department says that, while the search is ongoing, they do not hold much hope of finding the child alive.

"With children this young, if we don't find them within the first few hours, we don't anticipate a happy ending," Sheriff Nicholas Lewis told this reporter.

But Christmas is the season of hope, and Mrs. Mc-Tavish clings to it with all the tenacity of her pioneer ancestors.

"Ruby is out there," she says, her aquamarine eyes shimmering with tears, but her words firm. "This is her home. She belongs here. And we will do whatever it takes—*anything* it takes—to bring her home."

This reporter has covered enough tragedies to know how unlikely that is, but walking the graceful halls of Ashby House, looking out as light pierces a cloud over those same mountains that seem to have swallowed Baby Ruby, one feels that surely, this family must have angels on their side.

The Atlanta Constitution,
Thursday Morning, December 23, 1943

CHAPTER THREE

Jules

You probably know this already, but this country?

It is fucking *big*.

I thought I knew that, too. I'd grown up in Florida, ended up at college in California, then landed in Colorado. That last move, Cam and I had driven, and it had taken us over thirteen hours. I'd watched the dreaded Inland Empire of San Bernardino turn into the bright lights of Vegas, the high desert of Utah, and eventually, the jagged peaks of the Rockies, but there's something different about driving farther east.

How all the land flattens out, the sky arching overhead, a big blue bowl turned upside down. The ugliness of nondescript interstates giving way to rolling hills and massive rivers, and then, finally, mountains again.

But not like the mountains out west.

We're in Tennessee when they first appear, rising gently in the distance, dark and covered in trees, and it makes my stomach drop with nerves and excitement, knowing that we're close now. Just a few more hours, and we're at Ashby House.

Cam's house.

My house.

It's a very weird thing, living in a just-okay rental when you know that your husband technically owns an *estate*. But Cam had made it very clear, very early on that he wanted nothing to do with the house, the money, all of it, and I'd done my best to respect that.

But a girl can google.

The first time I saw pictures of the house online, I'd damn near swooned. The gray stone made the house look elemental somehow, like it had carved itself out of the rock of the mountains around it. There was a wide green lawn, and dozens of windows sparkling in afternoon sunlight. A wide veranda in the back had views down the mountain, the treetops covered in mist, and I figured if you sat out there with your coffee for enough mornings in a row, you'd probably be physically incapable of ever being unhappy again.

Camden would, I know, disagree. He'd been plenty unhappy in that house, but that's because of the people that were in it. If it were just the two of us, just him and me and all that space, all that beauty . . .

"Okay, now *you* are doing a face."

I shake myself out of my real estate fantasies.

"I just can't believe we're almost there," I say, pointing out the windshield. "I mean, those are the mountains of your homeland! Where your family is from! You actually came from this place and did not spring to life directly from my hot wing–induced fantasies."

Cam grins at that, lifting one hand off the steering wheel to rest on my knee. "Yup, a real live boy, Appalachian born and bred."

"I always thought that was why you chose Colorado," I say. "After we got married."

Neither of us had had roots in California (or anything resembling a career), so a few years after we got married, we started talking about where we might like to settle on a more permanent basis. Even then, I think, I'd been hoping Cam might decide to head back to North Carolina, but instead, he'd started looking for teaching jobs in Colorado.

Now he glances over at me, eyebrows raised in question.

"Mountains," I elaborate, waving one hand. "That they reminded you of home."

He scoffs, taking his hand off my knee. "The Rockies are beautiful, but they don't have shit on the Appalachians," he says, and now it's my turn to raise some eyebrows.

"Are you honestly going to tell me the 'purple mountains majesty' we left behind only rates a 'meh' from Camden McTavish?"

He laughs, leaning back a little. It's nice, seeing him relaxed. I've felt like the farther east we've come, the tighter his shoulders have gotten, the longer his silences have grown. Last night, at our hotel in Kentucky, when I'd gotten into bed after my shower, my hand moving toward the waistband of his boxers, he'd stopped me with a murmured, "I'm half asleep already, sweetheart, not much use to you tonight."

But he hadn't gone to sleep for hours. I knew, because I'd lain awake next to him, feeling the tension in his body, practically hearing the whirring of his brain.

What was he thinking about? Normally, I would have asked, but there was something that prevented me, instead making my own breathing slow and steady so he'd think I had already drifted off.

Now, though, he seems more like himself. He must have been worn out from the drive, worrying over the logistics that awaited him once we arrived.

"No," he tells me, his hand coming back to my knee. "I love the Rockies. I love Colorado. I just mean that the Rockies are . . . they're babies, right? Young mountains, all jagged and rough. The Appalachians, though, they're older. *Much* older."

I turn back to look out the windshield at those dark shapes in the distance, drawing closer. "All mountains seem pretty old to me."

"They are," Camden says with a nod, his hand squeezing my leg. "But the Appalachians are older than just about anything else. They were here before mammals, before dinosaurs. Those mountains"—he points to them—"are older than *bones*."

He's smiling as he says it, fully in Teacher Mode, but the words still make me shiver. Now those looming shadows against the blue sky don't seem quite as welcoming.

"And your family has lived there for *almost* as long, I take it?" I ask, hoping the joke will make me feel a little less spooked, but it's clearly the wrong thing to say.

Camden's smile fades and his hand returns to the steering wheel. "My birth family, who the fuck knows," he says, signaling as he changes lanes. "But the McTavishes showed up sometime in the 1700s. Or at least that's what Nelle says. I'm sure she's done all the genealogy for the Daughters of the American Revolution or Highland Heritage or whatever rich old white lady organization she's terrorizing."

"And Nelle was Ruby's older sister?" I ask. I know that she wasn't, but I'm trying to find some way of getting Cam to talk about his family. For the past few days, we've talked about everything under the sun—a lot of time to kill when you're crossing a continent—and I've been waiting for him to bring up something related to where we're going, what we're doing. I'd thought once we started getting closer, he might start revealing more, memories unlocking and all of that.

But no. Ask him about what he's reading (the Roman history book I gave him for Christmas), ask him his thoughts on the hierarchy of fast-food chains (Burger King is overrated, Arby's deserves more love, he can't fuck with Taco Bell after some drunken incident in college), ask him about politics (a conversation that lasted for nearly all of Missouri), and he has plenty to say.

When it comes to his family?

Nothing.

Now, however, he sighs, tipping his head back against the seat. "Younger," he says. "Nelle is about four years younger. She was born right after they got Ruby back in the forties. Literally just a few months later."

I assume that's all I'm going to get, but then he shocks me by adding, "I sometimes wondered if that's why she was always so pissed off. She knows she was conceived to replace Ruby, but then Ruby showed up and no one really needed her anymore. An understudy with no role to play."

"She sounds fun," I say, aiming for a playful tone.

Camden makes a noise that might be a laugh if it weren't so bitter. It's a side of him I've never seen before, and it's kind of intriguing. What a weird thing to learn ten years into a marriage, that your person can still surprise you.

"She's a piece of work," he replies. "But at least she left me alone for the most part. Didn't make hating me at least eighty-nine percent of her personality like the others did."

"It is impossible for anyone to hate you."

"You only think that because I go down on you so often," he jokes, but his shoulders are tight again, his knuckles white around the steering wheel. Overhead, the sky is starting to darken, thunderheads forming on the horizon. It's still summer here in the South, no matter what the calendar says, the heat and humidity thick outside. Camden says it will be cooler in Tavistock, but nothing like Colorado this time of year.

"I am not the most unbiased of women, no," I reply, trying to keep things light, but we were so close to actually getting somewhere that I can't help but add, "So out of the two who are left, Ben and Libby, which one hates you the most? I need to know so that I can adjust my fighting strategy accordingly."

That gets me a genuine smile, and he glances over again. "God, I would pay a *lot* of money to see you take on either one of them. Both of them. But you'd have unfair advantages."

Lifting his thumb off the steering wheel, he wiggles it. "One, Ben thinks he's hot shit because he played football, but he played for a small private school that played against *other* small private schools, which means they all sucked."

"Ah, so he'll overestimate his skills, and then I'll *strike*," I say, nodding.

"Exactly. And two"—another finger—"Libby is a fuckup. Fucked up school, fucked up the two or three different careers she's attempted, fucked up two marriages, and she's not even thirty yet. I have no doubt she'll also fuck up fighting. So." He shrugs. "You should be set."

"Thanksgiving just got extremely fucking real," I say, and now Cam laughs, reaching over to take my hand, his fingers lacing with mine.

"It's stupid, but it's like I keep forgetting that I'm going back there with someone," he says, and then he squeezes my hand. "With *you*. Whenever I think about being back there, I picture it like it was before. All of them as this . . . united front. And me. Alone."

He lifts our joined hands, kissing my knuckles. "But now, I'm not alone."

"Never will be again," I tell him, meaning it.

With my free hand, I reach over to tuck his hair behind his ear. It's longer than he usually wears it, more like it was when we first met, and I feel a sudden rush of affection.

He's doing this for me. Walking back into the lion's den because I asked him to. Because he loves me.

Guilt is oily and hot in my stomach.

Tell him, an insistent voice whispers. *Tell him now, while there's still time. Because if he finds out after you arrive . . .*

But we're almost there. We're so close now, and soon, everything I've done will be worth it. And I *will* tell him. All of it, the whole story, no lies between us, just like it's always been.

But not now. Not yet.

North Carolina has its share of beautiful homes. This is, after all, where you can find the world-famous Biltmore Estate, palatial home of the Vanderbilts.

Ashby House, just a few miles away in Tavistock, is not as grand and certainly a good deal more private—no tours here, I'm afraid!—but should you find yourself in the area, it's worth the time to drive as far as the gates. In spring and summer, you'll be lucky to see a chimney, but once the leaves fall, glimpses of the magnificent McTavish family home can be seen.

Built in 1904 by lumber magnate Alexander McTavish, the house is as eccentric as the family who owns it. Part Victorian, part Palladian, it features smooth gray stone and peaked roofs, marble patios and leaded windows. It should not work and yet, miraculously—almost mystically—it does. Guests of the home have commented that there's something about Ashby House that makes you feel as if the rest of the world does not exist. As if you could stay safely tucked behind its walls forever and want for nothing else.

Originally called, rather fancifully, The Highlands, it was renamed in 1938 by Mason McTavish in honor of his (much younger) bride, Anna Ashby. Tragedy struck the home in 1943 when Mason and Anna's young daughter, Ruby, was kidnapped from the forest surrounding Ashby House, but, as is befitting such a magical home, the story had a fairy-tale ending when Ruby was safely returned to her parents nearly a year later.

Ruby McTavish would eventually marry several times, and inherited the home when her father passed away in 1968. Widowed for a final time in 1985, Ms. McTavish resided in the home with her younger sister, Nelle, and several other family members before passing away in 2013.

The current owner is her adopted son, Camden.

—"Hidden Gems: Houses off the Beaten Path"
Southern Manors Magazine, June 2021

March 14, 2013

I have to admit, I almost wasn't going to write this today.

I know, I know, I promised you, but what is that saying? "Promises are like piecrusts, made to be broken."

I've never made a piecrust, actually. Maybe I should learn? Probably too late now. Shocking how soon the "too late now" part of your life arrives. When you're young, there's nothing but possibility, just an endless line of tomorrows, and then you wake up one day and realize that no, you cannot move to Paris on a whim because so many of those old buildings don't have elevators and stairs are hell on your knees now. And besides, you never learned to speak French, and now your brain, once so fresh and spongy and ready to soak up knowledge, feels about as pliable as a peach pit.

I could tell you to learn from an old lady, to not let the "too late now" moments surprise you, too, but it won't do any good. No one listens to old ladies.

I certainly didn't.

In fact, if I'd listened to one particular old lady, this next part of the story might never have happened. Which, I think most people would agree, would've been for the best.

But even now, even *knowing* what came after, I can't bring myself to regret rejecting Mrs. Sidney's advice when it came to Duke Callahan.

Oh, yes, my dear. We're finally at the first of my husbands.

(*Finally.* That's the word you'd use, isn't it? Please bear in mind that I have made you read exactly *one* fucking letter thus far and that it was only around ten pages. You come by your impatience naturally, but that doesn't mean I have to like it.)

(Also, please note that I wrote that word again. I think I'm going to try to write it once per letter. And now I worry I've wasted it here when I could probably put it to better use later. Ah, well.)

I knew *of* Duke Callahan long before I met him. Everyone did. His father was even richer than mine, a tobacco millionaire with an estate in Asheville, a horse breeding operation in Kentucky, a penthouse in Manhattan, a pied-à-terre in Paris, and, rumor had it, a beautiful mistress installed in each location.

Duke was his eldest son and heir, the crown prince of Edward Callahan's kingdom, his father's pride and joy—and also the thorn in his side. The story was that Edward had named his son Duke because that's how certain he was that the boy would follow his lead and play football for Duke University, but Duke was nothing if not his own man. He went to Yale instead, and his father had, briefly, disowned him.

That had not fazed Duke.

This doesn't surprise me, by the way. One thing I quickly learned about Duke Callahan during our very brief marriage was that the man was completely unflappable—at least when he was sober. During an argument on our honeymoon, I threw a pair of earrings he'd given me into the Atlantic Ocean (emeralds, once belonging to Marie Antoinette, worth a not-so-small fortune, and yes, I do still regret this fit of pique).

Thousands of dollars sailing over the side of a ship, a brand-new bride in furious tears, what felt like half of first class gawking at us, and Duke had merely sighed, lit a cigarette, and said, "Suppose I should've given you rubies," before ambling back inside.

In fact, the only time I think I ever saw him look surprised was when I shot him.

But we're not there yet, are we?

No, now it is the night of Nelle's sixteenth birthday. Summer, 1960.

Nelle had, as you might imagine, been a huge pill about the whole thing. First, she wanted to wear red, then pink. Then finally it was silver, and I was told—*told,* mind you—that I could wear green, so I had chosen a mint-green chiffon draped over a gold taffeta lining.

Nelle had not seen the dress before the party, too consumed with making sure she had the right amount of flowers, the perfect band—no, not the one Loretta wanted, the one that had played at Nancy Baylor's Sweet Sixteen last year— and the cake had the lemon filling, yes? Not strawberry—Linda Hanson had had a strawberry cake—and the thing looked like it was *bleeding* when they cut into it, no one wanted to eat a *bleeding cake.*

I'd thought about pointing out that the lemon might look like pus simply because I'd wanted the pleasure of watching Nelle's head explode, but in the end, I'd kept my mouth shut, determined to get through the night with as little conflict as possible.

It had been a hard year for all of us. Mama had died in August of 1959, her liver shot to hell, her face sallow and lined and so much older than her thirty-nine years. Daddy had managed to wait until January of 1960 to make an honest woman out of Loretta, and while I wasn't exactly close to my stepmother, I didn't dislike her, either. She was sweet and a little simple, desperate to fulfill her role as An Important Man's Wife, and she and I mostly stayed out of each other's way.

I was home that summer from Agnes Scott, the ladies' college Daddy had sent me to in Atlanta. I liked it for the most part, but there was a sense that all of us there were simply killing time, waiting for a man to marry us. We read Chaucer and discussed Shakespeare and learned conversational French and filled our brains with knowledge that no one would care about the second a man went down on one knee.

I wasn't sure how I felt about that.

I liked Atlanta, liked living with other girls, but I missed the mountains of home. I missed Ashby House and its familiar hallways, the hidden corners where I'd sit and read or simply stare out the windows at the trees below.

But now that I *was* home, I missed the independence I'd had in Atlanta, missed going for malts with Becky and Susan and Trina after Western Civilization. Staying up as late as I wanted to read with no one calling, "Is your light still on? It's past eleven, Ruby!"

It was a strange feeling, being caught between two lives.

I think that's something you might understand.

So, there I was that summer night in 1960, twenty years old, growing out of being someone's daughter, not sure I was ready to be someone's wife, and searching for a place to hide in my own home because my sixteen-year-old sister was absolutely *livid* about my dress.

I told you, she'd "allowed" me to wear green. And so I had. But apparently it was meant to be *only* green, not green over *gold*. She was wearing *silver*, which somehow made her look "less special." (I still don't fully follow this logic, I should add. Maybe I'll go up to Nelle's room once I've finished this letter and ask her. I might get the pleasure of seeing her head explode all these years later!)

Normally, I would have given her hell right back, but as I said, it was a strange summer, and I had no real desire to engage in another sisterly skirmish, so I'd retreated, heading for the one room I knew would be deserted during a party—my father's office.

I opened the door, the only light a banker's lamp on Daddy's desk, the familiar smell of furniture polish and cigar smoke hanging in the air.

But as I closed the door behind me, I realized it was not cigar smoke I was smelling at all. It was a cigarette, freshly lit, and the cologne in the air wasn't the lingering hint of Daddy's Acqua di Parma. It was something sharper, warmer. Something that made my toes curl in their mint-green pumps.

"If my mother sent you to drag me back to the party, you should know that I'm not going without a fight."

Startled, I stepped back, my heel hitting the brass plate at the bottom of the door, the sound unnaturally loud in the quiet room.

I had known Duke Callahan would be at Nelle's party. Nelle had practically danced around the room when his RSVP had been delivered. I later learned that he had been something of her "white whale" for the past year, and long after Duke was dead, I found an old diary of Nelle's stashed behind those fancy copies of Charles Dickens that no one ever read. *Mrs. Eleanor Callahan* was scribbled on several pages, and I suddenly understood that Nelle's tears at Duke's and my wedding had had nothing to do with hay fever as she'd claimed.

I'd caught only the briefest glimpse of him earlier, as he'd made his way across the foyer to say hello to Daddy. That was

when Mrs. Sidney had issued her warning, lifting the little
skewer from her martini and gesturing at Duke's retreating
back with it, the pickled pearl onion on the tip nearly
slipping off.

"Trouble," she pronounced, puckering her lips. Her pale
pink lipstick had bled into the fine lines there, and I suspected
the empty martini glass in her hand was not her first cocktail
of the evening. "And, from what I hear, on the hunt for a wife.
Pretty and rich as you are, sweetheart? I'd steer clear."

And I had, until I walked into my father's study to find
Duke Callahan leaning against the bookshelves lining the far
wall.

He straightened up, walking closer to me, his eyes slightly
narrowed. The end of the cigarette tucked between his lips
glowed a bright, hot red as he took a drag, smoke curling
around his head when he exhaled.

"On second thought," he said slowly, "I think I'd go
anywhere you wanted me to."

Then he grinned.

It was a good grin, one he'd probably flashed a million
times in his twenty-four years, and never once thought
anything about it.

The people who'd seen it, though?

They thought about it.

The girl at the café who'd brought him his coffee, the boy
who'd shined his shoes at the train station in New Haven. The
mothers of his friends who'd welcomed him into their homes,
then spent the rest of the night conjuring up that smile and
wondering why it made their stomachs flutter, their blood feel
hot.

And me.

I still think about it now, more than fifty years later.

And I think, sometimes, how if he hadn't given me that grin, if I hadn't fallen so instantly and powerfully in what I thought was love, he might still be alive.

Duke Callahan, an old man. I can't even picture it.

Or maybe I just don't want to.

There's a picture of him in my nightstand if you want to see him. Oh, I know, you can look him up on the internet, but honestly, I think Duke would prefer to be admired in that silver frame. He's smiling, but you should know that's not *the* smile. It's close, but not quite the same.

Actually, don't look. The picture doesn't do him justice. To understand Duke, you had to see him in person, and I'm afraid that, thanks to me, no one can ever do that again.

He wasn't just handsome, you see. Handsome, I could've resisted. So many young men in my circle had those same good cheekbones, the chiseled jaw and straight nose, hair the same burnished gold as an old coin. All of them could wear a suit well and hold a cocktail just so and knew exactly how to light a woman's cigarette in a way that felt both chivalrous and the *tiniest* bit predatory.

I always found them boring, if I'm honest. There was a sameness to them that made me think they must all take the same class in that sort of thing at their various boarding schools. They all played at being some kind of debonair man-about-town, but they each ended up back in their hometowns, doing whatever it is their fathers did, marrying the girls their mothers wanted them to marry.

But Duke? No, underneath all those familiar traits and manners, I knew he was something different.

I remember being so glad for the dim light in Daddy's office because maybe he couldn't see me blushing. (He absolutely could, he told me later, and used that observation to launch into a soliloquy of things he noticed about me that gradually grew more and more explicit until I was blushing everywhere a person *could* blush, but I suppose that's not the kind of story you want from me. Fair enough.)

"The only place I want you to go," I said, making myself stand up as tall as I could, "is out of my father's office."

"Ah," he said, pleased. "So, you *are* the infamous Ruby. I thought as much."

I probably should've pressed him on that "infamous" bit, but at the time, there was a chorus in my brain shouting, *He said my name, he said my name, why does my name sound so different when he says it?*

"I can't believe I've never met you before now," he went on, stepping closer. "How come you didn't have one of these big parties when you turned sixteen?"

Hands clasped behind my back, I watched him from beneath my lashes. Later, I'd perfect this particular look, coy and careless all at once, but that night, there was no artifice in it. I just couldn't look directly at him without stammering.

"I did," I told him. "Four summers ago. You just didn't come."

I dared a glance then. He had moved even closer, standing just beside Daddy's desk. "Well, that was fucking stupid of me."

(Knew I was going to use it again later! Damn.)

He wanted to shock me, maybe. Watch my mouth drop into a horrified O, my eyes widen.

Instead, I met his gaze evenly while my heart threatened to pound right out of my chest.

"Yes," I said, as though ice water flowed in my veins. "It was."

That made him laugh, and if the smile was an arrow to the heart—and other, lower portions of one's anatomy—then the laugh was Fourth of July fireworks, wonderful, thrilling, the kind of thing that made you want to hug yourself with the sheer delight of it.

"Your father said you were at college in Atlanta," Duke went on. "Are you home for the summer or home for good?"

He propped one hip there on the corner of Daddy's desk as he reached into his evening jacket for a sterling silver case. It popped open with a loud *snick*, and he plucked out a cigarette from a neat little row of them. His family's brand, of course, Callahans, but a special blend made only for the Callahans themselves.

"For the summer," I told him. "I think."

"You think?" he echoed as he pressed the tip of the unlit cigarette to the smoldering end of the one still in his mouth. His cheeks hollowed slightly as he sucked at the filter, the ember glowing a hotter red, and then, newly lit cigarette between those long, elegant fingers, he offered it to me.

I never much cared for smoking, something that was probably more offensive to my fellow North Carolina blue bloods than all the dead husbands would end up being, so maybe it's a good thing I was only the tobacco heir's wife for those few months. But I took the cigarette from him all the same, and had you been alone in that room with him, you would have, too.

"Atlanta is fine and all, but . . . I've missed it here," I replied, and he snorted slightly at that, smoke puffing from his nostrils.

"You need to see more of the world if you think this mountain is worth missing, sweetheart."

I should've been offended by that, but I was twenty and the most attractive man I'd ever met had just called me *sweetheart*, so please cut me some slack, darling.

I moved a little closer to him, taking a drag on the cigarette, the flavor rich and bitter. "I'd like to," I told him. "See more of the world, that is. London. Rome. Paris. Paris, especially, actually."

"I'll book the honeymoon now," he said, teasing, and oh, how that thrilled me. Not just the word "honeymoon," and all the secret, wonderful things that implied, but the idea that there might be a third door besides Dutiful Daughter and Dutiful Wife. A wife still, yes, but the kind that didn't throw boring parties or pretend to be excited about Jell-O salads. Wife to a man like *this*, a man who would take her with him when he went out in the world, who wanted her to experience the same things he did.

A partner.

As I said, darling, I was twenty. Truly my only excuse. Not for believing that such men exist, because they do—I married one eventually—but believing that *this* man was one of them.

"Maybe you should take me out to dinner first," I told him, and he ground out his cigarette in the heavy glass ashtray just behind him on the desk.

"Maybe I will," he answered, and then threw me a sly glance from the corner of his eye. "Or we could have a picnic. Unless that brings back bad memories."

It was the first time anyone other than Nelle had ever referenced my kidnapping, and it was yet another thing that, in retrospect, should have offended, but instead just made Duke all the more intriguing, all the more *different* from anyone else I'd known.

"No bad memories," I confirmed. "No memories of it at all."

That was the truth. Other than that odd moment of naming my doll Grace, nothing from that time of my life ever resurfaced, the story continuing to feel like something that might have happened to someone else.

"I remember it," Duke said, rising to his feet. "Or remember people talking about it, I guess. You were quite the little celebrity for a while."

"Isn't it odd how that happens?" I asked, and, seeing his confusion, added, "Celebrity—or notoriety, really—all because of something that happened *to* you, not something you actually did. Like that poor girl back in the spring, the one whose fiancé fell at the falls. Daddy said her picture was in the paper for weeks."

I'd been in Atlanta at the time, but news from Tavistock still made its way to me through phone calls and letters from home, and there had been no bigger story than the death of Peter Whalen, a UNC student who'd taken his fiancée, Jill, up to the waterfall deep in the woods a few miles from Ashby House. He'd been leaning down to tie his shoe when he'd slipped on some wet rocks, plunging down to the rocks and water below.

"Never knew why that was such a story," Duke said with a shrug. "My grandfather had a cousin who took a tumble from those falls back around the turn of the century. It's a dangerous place, people should be more careful."

"It wasn't just that he died," I said, lowering my voice and stepping a little closer. "They didn't put it in the papers out of respect for his family, but Daddy heard it from the sheriff himself. Peter Whalen wasn't dead when he hit the rocks."

Duke lifted his eyebrows at that, and the clear interest in his gaze made me a little bolder. "He was hurt, very badly from what I understand, and Jill tried to get down to him, but couldn't. So she left him to go get help. But when she came back with the sheriff and his officers, Peter wasn't there."

Now Duke leaned forward, his fingers loosely clasped on one thigh. "Go on."

I could see myself in my room in Atlanta, the pale green phone cord twisting around one finger as Daddy relayed the gruesome story to me, my mind conjuring up the falls, those sharp rocks at the bottom. The sound of rushing water not loud enough to drown out Peter Whalen's screams or Jill's cries of horror as he lay broken and bloody.

It had felt like a scary story, the sort of thing you tell around campfires. Not a thing that had happened to real people, people in the same woods that had once taken me.

I suppose I should now say that I feel guilty for how much I relished the darkness of the account, how vividly I could picture those horrific details, but surely there's no point in lying to you.

"They found him—most of him, at least—a few hours later," I told Duke, my voice barely above a whisper, the air hushed and heavy around us. "He'd tried to crawl away, they thought, get out of the water. But something found him."

"Something?" Duke's voice was as low as mine now, his pupils wide and surrounded by the narrowest band of blue.

"A bear, probably. Maybe a mountain lion."

"Jesus Christ."

"No, I don't think it was him," I answered without thinking, the quip entirely inappropriate, one of those dark jokes that always sat on the tip of my tongue, but very rarely slipped out in front of someone.

And Duke laughed.

I found myself smiling back, secret, conspiratorial, and his eyes dropped to my mouth. "I have no idea what to make of you, Ruby McTavish," he said, and until that moment I had never realized that you could feel someone's voice like a touch.

"No one does," I said.

I didn't say it to be cute. It was just the truth.

No one knew what to make of me. I was a rich man's daughter who hid at parties rather than flirt with available bachelors. I was pretty enough, but there were other more beautiful girls. I did well enough in school, but wasn't a brain.

And there was this darkness that seemed to cling to me, a past that people only ever spoke about in whispers. A suspicion, even inside my own heart, that I had been placed in the wrong life, living out a role written for someone else.

Maybe it was the darkness that Duke liked.

He had his own streak of it, I'd learn, hidden beneath that smooth, implacable sheen.

But let's leave that for the next letter. For now, let me leave us here in the dim light of my father's office, the low murmur of voices and muffled music from the band downstairs the soundtrack to a kiss that would change my life and end his.

You'll let me do that, won't you?

-R

BABY RUBY A BRIDE!

She stole hearts around the nation as the famous "Baby Ruby" during the 1940s, but now, Ruby McTavish has captured one heart in particular--that of tobacco heir and man-about-town Duke Edward Callahan.

The bride, daughter of Mr. Mason McTavish and the late Anna McTavish of Tavistock, North Carolina, walked down the aisle this past Saturday, April 22, on the grounds of her family home, Ashby House. Wearing her mother's wedding gown from 1937 (altered and updated by Mme. Durand of Paris, a personal friend of the groom's father, Edward Alton Callahan), Miss McTavish carried a bouquet of white roses, pink camellias, and the crested iris native to her home state. Her maid of honor was her younger sister, Miss Eleanor McTavish, and the rest of her bridal party consisted of friends from childhood and her school chums from Agnes Scott College in Atlanta where, up until her engagement, Miss McTavish had been studying literature.

The couple plan on settling in the groom's hometown of Asheville, North Carolina, after a lengthy European honeymoon that will see them sail to Paris before moving on to Nice, the Loire Valley, Rome, Milan, and finally London.

Congratulations, and bon voyage to Mr. and Mrs. Duke Callahan!

—*Society Chatter Newsletter* (Southeastern Region),
Spring 1961

CHAPTER FOUR

Camden

I feel the house before I see it.

That probably sounds stupid to you, and if I had grown up in anything resembling a normal family, I'm pretty sure it would have seemed stupid to me, too.

But as our car winds its way up the mountain, my fingers tighten around the steering wheel, and cold sweat breaks out on my upper lip, my lower back. The trees here are still green, leafy and huge, their roots burrowing into the dirt and the rocks, and the blacktop cuts a dark ribbon in front of me as we go up, up, up.

It's impossible not to think about the last time I was on this road.

Back then, I was headed down, down, down, away from Ashby House, away from the McTavishes, away from memories that I couldn't bear to recall. I remember turning up the radio so loud that it made my back teeth ache, the drums and the bass crashing through my brain, the kind of noise that would have made Ruby say, "Turn that down, for goodness' sake, Camden! I can't hear myself think!"

That's what I was going for, a sound so loud that thoughts were impossible.

But it turns out there are some thoughts that no amount of noise can silence, and I'd made that drive down the mountain with nausea coiled in my stomach and my face wet with tears.

I swore I'd never go back.

So it feels slightly unreal to make that last turn, that place where the asphalt becomes dirt for just a few yards, pitted with holes, thick tree roots bumping us along hard enough that Jules grabs what she calls the "Oh Shit Handle" above her head.

Nelle wanted to pave this part of the road, but Ruby said that would make it too easy for people to come and gawk at the gates of the house. I always thought she overestimated just how much people wanted to see a random chimney or the hint of a window, but there had been several times I'd driven out of those gates as a teenager to see a family in a rented Subaru pulled over on the side of the road near the gate, phones in hand, standing up on their tiptoes in bright white sneakers as they strained to catch a glimpse.

Personally, I couldn't give a shit if tourists came to look—isn't that why people build places like this, anyway?—but I agreed with Ruby that we shouldn't make the road smooth. Let all these bumps and jostles and the fear of a blown tire serve as a warning of what they'd find at the top of this mountain.

A haunted house where the ghosts hadn't had the courtesy to die yet.

I clench my teeth.

This is why I didn't want to come back here. I don't think shit like that in Colorado. There, I'm mostly focused on work, on things I need to do around the house, on Jules. I like that version of myself—a normal guy, with a normal life—and I had started to believe that, maybe, that's who I was now.

But apparently not. Put me on the road to Ashby, and I'm *that* Cam again. Ruby's project, heir to the McTavish estate, the "Luckiest Boy in North Carolina."

That was a real thing someone wrote about me. It was for some magazine profile Ruby did when I was twelve. I remember the photographers coming to the house, the scratchy suit Ruby made me wear. The photographer took a picture of me in my bedroom, a massive suite on the west side of the house that had gorgeous sunset views, but was decorated like it belonged to one of the Golden Girls. All chintz and florals, a big canopy bed (every twelve-year-old boy's dream, a canopy bed).

They had me sit in the middle of that massive bed, wearing my suit and bow tie, holding a basketball in my lap. I didn't even play, but North Carolina is basketball country, and I guess they thought it would make me look more like a regular kid.

I looked like a fucking ventriloquist's dummy who'd come to life in an assisted-living facility. No basketball was going to undo that.

But I smiled and let them take the picture because that's what Ruby wanted and later, when the magazine arrived at the house, I flipped through it, mostly to see how bad the picture was. I needed to brace myself for the merciless mocking I was no doubt about to endure in school once the issue hit Tavistock mailboxes.

The picture was as terrible as I thought it would be, but what I hadn't been prepared for was the caption.

Camden Andrew McTavish: The Luckiest Boy in North Carolina.

Even then, I'd known what bullshit that was. But I also got it, I guess. I'd been an orphan, in and out of the foster system since birth. A multimillionaire plucking me out of poverty, installing me in her palatial home, making *me* heir to her fortune?

Yeah, I see where that sounds pretty fucking lucky.

If you didn't know Ruby.

The dirt track turns into gravel, and my heart beats faster. This is it, the last approach to the gates. The trees on each side nearly block out the sun now, their limbs arching and meeting overhead. It always made me feel like I was being slowly swallowed by something as I drove up this road. Everything gets darker, tighter, funneling you in.

I glance over at Jules, wondering if she senses the same claustrophobic air settling in, but she's sitting up in her seat, her sunglasses shoved up on her head, her eyes taking everything in.

She's smiling a little, hands clasped on her lap, and I try to see this place through her gaze.

It's pretty, of course: the trees are thick and lush, and a few glimpses of the sky and the valley below peep out between the leaves. The mist that tends to linger in the treetops can make you feel like you're up in the clouds, and I can see that for some people—for Jules—that might feel magical. That you'd feel tucked in and safe up here, not trapped.

I want to feel that way, too. More than anything. I want the past to stay buried, and to find a way to at least tolerate this place, because I think that Jules is going to love it. I think she *wants* to love it.

So for her sake, I'm going to try.

Making myself smile, I reach over and take one of her hands. "We're almost to the gates. Once we're through, the road turns a little, and you'll want to look out your window to get the best view. There's a sunflower garden on that side, and they should still be blooming. It's nice."

She smiles back at me, wiggling a little in her seat. "A *sunflower garden*? I was not aware that you grew up like a pretty, pretty princess, Cam."

The smile is frozen on my face, and I wonder if she can tell how hard I'm forcing it. "Ruby's idea," I tell her. "Planted at some point in the eighties. Nelle hated it, thought it was tacky, but I always liked it. Or I did, until the time I was hiding in there and found a corn snake. Slithered right over my foot."

Jules wrinkles her nose. "Okay, hard pass on that," she says. "Definitely going to admire the sunflower garden from *afar*."

I wish she could admire the whole damn house from afar.

I wish snakes were the worst things that lived on this property.

We're almost at the gate now, and my fingers drum on the steering wheel, my gaze technically in front of me, but my thoughts far away.

The passcode for the gate is still there, in my head.

13–6–61

It's the day Ruby's first husband, Duke, died. She switched the month and day because, as she'd told me when she first gave me the code, "He died in Europe, after all."

She said it with a light shrug, like it was obvious, just a completely normal thing to say. A completely normal thing to *do*, making the passcode to your house the date of your husband's murder. But then she always did that. She'd say the craziest shit in the most cheerful voice, and it was stunning how quickly you found yourself agreeing with her.

Right, yeah, day then month! Like in Europe, since that's where someone shot him in the chest with a rifle twice. Makes perfect sense, Ruby!

I asked her only once why that date. Why not his birthday or their wedding day? Or any other date that wasn't associated with blood and a dead body?

Well, no one will ever guess that date, will they, my darling? It's too morbid, so it's the last thing anyone would think I'd use.

Sitting at her dressing table in her room, slathering her hands with some fancy cream that arrived by courier every six weeks from France. I've never smelled it before or since, but I bet it still lingers in the rooms of Ashby House. Sharp lavender, so astringent it almost made your eyes water, and some other scent underneath, woodsy and rich.

I'd been ten, maybe? Something like that. Too young to point out the obvious alternatives.

No one would guess random numbers, either. Or digits from a phone number you barely use. Or my real birthday since you just told everyone it was the same day as yours so we could celebrate at the same time. So why the fuck *is it this day? Why do you want to remember that date every time you go in and out of those gates? Why—*

"Cam?"

I blink, and realize Jules is looking at me, her hand on my arm. I've stopped the car without realizing it, and the gates to Ashby House rise up before us.

There's a wrought iron fence running out in either direction from the granite columns, but—family secret here—it doesn't enclose the whole property. A section fell down about twenty years ago, and Ruby never bothered to get it fixed.

If I got out of the car right now, I could walk along this fence with my eyes closed, and I'd know exactly where that hole was, and I fucking hate that.

I hate that this place still lives inside of me.

"Sorry," I tell Jules now. "Zoned out trying to remember the code."

Her eyebrows draw together, concern puckering her lips. "The code?"

"To open the gate."

Now she's openly frowning. "Camden," she says slowly. "It's . . . it's already open, babe. See?"

In my mind, the gate loomed up to the sky, bars thick and black, locking McTavishes inside, locking anyone else out.

But now I see that if you were in decent shape and had stretched first, you could probably climb the gate with no problem. And the bars are thinner than I remembered, flecked with rust now, some of the filigree details almost eaten through with it.

And Jules is right—one side of the gate hangs half open.

Stepping out of the car, I get my first deep breath of that North Carolina mountain air, feeling my chest expand with it. Pine, the loamy smell of damp earth, the slight chemical tang of a thunderstorm not too far away.

It smells like home.

Because, like it or not, that's what this place is.

I push the gate all the way open and get back into the car.

Next to me, Jules is still looking a little worried, so I throw her a quick smile and make my voice as cheerful as I can. "You ready for this?"

"Are you?" she counters, and I laugh, but it's a weak sound, more like a huff of air than an actual chuckle.

"Ready as I'll ever be."

And then I put the car in drive, and let Ashby House pull me back in.

CHAPTER FIVE

Jules

Before Cam, I'd never been in love before. And before you're like, "Well, that's sad," let me remind you that we met when I was all of twenty-one years old, so pump the brakes on throwing me a Sad Spinster Shower, okay?

And naturally, given that I'd married the love of my life, I assumed I'd never fall in love again. One and done.

That was *before* I saw Ashby House.

I could tell as we drove up the mountain that Cam was tense, his jaw clenched, his fingers doing that nervous drumming thing. It made me feel shitty, sitting there with champagne bubbles in my veins while he seemed to sink further and further into misery, but I couldn't help it. We were so close, and I knew that once we were there, once Cam had *me* in Ashby House, he'd understand that it wasn't the place. It was the people.

The place could be amazing. The place could be *ours*.

It already felt like ours as we climbed into the clouds, the trees forming a protective arch overhead, shutting out the light and the rest of the world.

Even the gate, sagging open like a mouth, covered in red spots of rust, was beautiful to me, that's how much I was prepared to love everything about Ashby House.

But I still wasn't ready for the way my heart lifts and my stomach swoops when the house itself finally comes into view.

I don't see the sunflowers Cam had mentioned, but maybe that's for the best because it means there's nothing else vying for my gaze as I drink in the home in front of us.

The pictures I've seen on the internet don't do it justice. It looked gorgeous in 2D, and I could tell it was impressive in scale, but those Google images can't capture how perfectly the house seems to nestle into its surroundings. The way it looks eternal, immovable. A fortress on a mountain made of thick gray stone and tall windows, surrounded by trees on three sides and behind the house, nothing but treetops and clouds and sky.

The gravel we'd been driving on turns to stone, too, a smooth gray ribbon that makes a graceful arc at the front of the house. Wide steps lead up to a wraparound porch. I see a swing in one corner, rocking chairs lining the wall on the other side of the front door.

Big planters sit on either side of the steps, overflowing with dark purple mums, and I spot several hanging ferns in the shadows under the porch roof.

In the driver's seat, Cam gives a sigh that seems to come from the very bottom of his soul, and I turn to look at him, hoping that maybe he's realized he was wrong about this place after all. That he can see the beauty that is so plainly in front of him.

But he just seems tired. Wary.

He does smile, though, a little bit, when he meets my eyes. "Home sweet home," he says, his voice flat, and I lean over to press a kiss on his cheek.

"Thank you," I say. "For bringing me here. I know you didn't want to, but—"

"I want what you want," he replies, and if the words sound a little rote, I'm okay with that. We're here, aren't we?

I turn back to the house. The front door is actually two doors, big slabs of dark wood that look like they could withstand a battering ram.

Tall, narrow windows frame the entry, and I think I catch a flicker of movement on the left, the briefest flash of a face, too quick for me to see if it was a woman or a man.

As I open the car door and step out onto the drive, I keep my gaze on those doors, waiting for them to open. Someone's there, clearly, and has seen us, and I move around to the trunk to get my bag, expecting to hear the clicking of a lock, a greeting.

Cam comes up next to me, reaching for his bag as well, and I nod toward the house. "No welcoming committee?"

He snorts, throwing a quick glance at the firmly closed doors. "I'd be less surprised to walk into a firing squad."

"It just seems like they should be nicer to you," I say, slamming the trunk shut, "given that you own the place."

But Cam is already shaking his head. "First of all, you need to know that the word 'should' does not exist to these people. There are lots of things they 'should' do, but if they don't want to do something, they don't do it."

"Like be nice to the guy who pays the bills."

"Or tip," he adds, and I bump my hip against his.

"Or pay taxes?" I guess, and he makes one of those amused sounds that isn't quite a laugh.

"They do that now, but only because I hired a new accountant. And they also clearly don't take care of sunflower gardens."

He points, and now I see the brown, crunchy stalks that must have once been bright yellow flowers, tall enough to hide in.

Moving closer to him, I thread my arm through his. "We'll plant new ones," I promise, and he looks down at me, one blue eye, one brown, neither giving away what he's thinking.

"We won't be here that long," he finally says, and starts to move toward the front door, my arm slipping through his and falling back to my side.

We've just reached the steps when there's a rattling noise from behind us. A white Audi is tearing up the gravel drive, tiny pebbles spitting out from underneath the tires, and as it moves onto the pavement, I'm afraid it's going to crash right into the back of our SUV.

But there's a screech of brakes, the smell of rubber, and the Audi comes to a stop, a kiss away from dinging the heck out of our rear bumper.

Camden exhales noisily. "Well, here's a welcoming committee for you," he mutters.

The driver's side door opens, and a woman gets out, chestnut hair shiny even under the cloudy sky. She's wearing white jeans, and a floaty off-the-shoulder blouse, black with big multicolored polka dots on it, the kind of thing I wouldn't look at twice in a shop because I'd think, *Who can pull off Bozo Chic?*

Apparently, the answer is Camden's cousin, Libby.

This is the part where I really want to tell you that I simply guessed who she was. And you'd believe that, right? Who else could this twentysomething in designer jeans be? Context clues, a safe assumption, et cetera.

But actually, I recognize her from her Instagram.

@LaLaLibby.

I've followed her for . . . ten years now? Right after Cam and I started dating. From her senior year of high school (the duck-face era) to college number one (Duke, lots of navy blue in the photos) to college number two (UNC, also blue, but cornflower) to, finally, number three, Western Carolina (purple, sadly the *one* color Libby did not look great in).

I saw a photo of her wedding to Clayton Jefferson Davis, taken right here on the back veranda of this house, and then, two years later, I saw another of her "Divorcemoon" in Cabo. Then one of the second marriage to some guy who called himself "Bodhi," but whose Facebook friends kept calling "Kyle."

That one hadn't warranted many pictures, and had apparently been over within about six months. I also saw the rise and fall of her cupcake empire (RIP, Lil Lib Cakes), and the tentative push into interior design that mostly seemed geared toward selling three-hundred-dollar lamps with feathers on them.

And I know that right now, she's probably coming back from the little boutique she just opened in downtown Tavistock, Lil Bit Libby! (She put the exclamation point there, not me, and maybe if I'm here long enough, I can talk to her about her overuse of "lil" as a marketing gimmick.)

Cam, of course, has no idea about any of this. Well, he probably knows about the failed businesses since he's the one who had to sign off on her withdrawing money for them, but me following her? The throwaway account I made just for that purpose?

No, I haven't told him about that.

I've thought about it. I mean, is it such a big deal? Lightly internet stalking your husband's estranged family? I don't think it is.

But I also don't know if Cam would see it that way, and if I told him, he might ask other questions. Questions that have answers I *know* he wouldn't understand, and I've promised never to lie to him.

And I haven't. Not ever.

Not *really*.

Libby turns in a half circle to face us, cell phone in one hand, sunglasses covering half her face. "Did you close the fucking gate?" she asks Cam.

Like he's been here this whole time. Like she sees him every day and the last dozen years haven't gone by.

He had closed the gate, stopping once we were through and swinging it back into place despite its squealing protest, but he doesn't tell her that. Instead, he lets his bag drop beside his feet, and he slides both hands into his back pockets, elbows sharp angles at his sides.

"Yes, Elizabeth, thank you, it *was* a long drive, but we're happy to finally be here. Good to see you, too!" he calls, and she scowls at him, whipping her sunglasses off.

"Oh, I'm sorry," she says, her Southern accent turning the words sweet even as her eyes glare holes into him. "I assumed you were going to be a grouchy asshole about being here, so we could maybe skip the part where we all pretend this is fun for any of us. But hey!"

She shrugs, her tanned shoulders moving up and down in an exaggerated motion. "*So* glad you got here safely, darling cousin Cam, and I look forward to catching up and talking about old times with you."

Coming around the car, she leans against the back door,

crossing one ankle in front of the other, her face screwed up like she's thinking hard about something. "Actually, that reminds me, I had a question about one of those old times. Let's see, when was it?"

She taps her finger against her chin, head tilted to one side, and next to me, Cam holds himself very still, his expression blank.

"I guess it would've been, hmm . . . about ten minutes ago? Maybe five? If you can remember back that far, maybe you can tell me: Did you close the fucking gate?"

Cam's mouth curls into a sardonic smile, lips pressed together so hard that a dimple I've never noticed dents one cheek. "I did, Libby, yeah," he replies.

"Why?"

"Well, you see, the *purpose* of gates—"

"Forget it," she says, cutting him off and pushing herself away from the car. "I texted Ben to send me the code, but in the future, just leave it open. No one comes up here but us anyway."

"Or you could take the five seconds to punch in a five-digit code and *not* run the risk of randoms showing up in the front yard."

She marches up the steps, her boots loud on the stone, and stops just below where we stand, chin lifted. This close, I can see she's not quite as put together and polished as her Instagram makes her look. The concealer under her eyes is maybe a shade too light, her mascara flaking. Bright pink lipstick covers her mouth, but some of it has bled into fine lines around her lips, and there's the faintest brown splash on those white jeans, right on her thigh. Coffee, probably, and yes, now I can see the pink plastic lid of a reusable cup sticking out of her bag.

"The only *random* who ever showed up here was you," she tells him, and then her eyes flick to me.

"I guess you're the wife?"

"I go by 'Jules,' but that is my government title, yes."

A corner of her mouth kicks up, and it startles me how much that expression, just for a second, makes me think of Cam. He does that same thing, and it's weird, seeing his expression on another face. They're not blood related, so I can't chalk it up to a fluke of DNA.

"Cute," Libby replies, but I don't know if she's referring to my joke or to me in general. "Well. Good luck."

With that, she pushes past us and into the house, closing the door behind her.

In the silence, I can hear the wind through the trees, the faint twitter of birdcalls, and, somewhere far in the distance, the low hoot of a train whistle.

"Good to be home," Cam mutters to himself, leaning down to pick up his bag. "Can't imagine why I left."

"I'm sorry," I say, laying a hand on his arm. "Have you two always been . . . like that?"

"Not always," he says as he hefts the bag onto his shoulder. "When we were little, it wasn't so bad. But then . . ." He trails off, a grimace on his face. "Anyway, Libby is more bark than bite, though the bark is more annoying than I'd remembered."

I'm intrigued by that "but then," sensing there's a story there, but knowing now isn't the time to push it. Not when Cam is pushing open the front door, and Ashby House is finally opening up to me.

"Last chance," Cam says, pausing in the doorway. "Only Libby has seen us. We could get back in the car and be in Colorado by, oh . . . Thursday? Wednesday if we gunned it."

He's smiling, his elbow brushing mine, but I can see in his eyes that if I said, "Sure, let's go," there would be a streak of gray smoke on this porch in the shape of Cam and our Denali would be halfway down the mountain in two seconds.

I shake my head, once again linking my arm with his.

"I grew up in Florida," I remind him. "I eat overly tanned bitches who drive Audis for breakfast."

His gaze warms, and he leans in, kissing my forehead. "I love you," he murmurs against my skin, and I close my eyes briefly, curling my fingers into the fabric of his T-shirt, making myself stay here in this moment, with him, because I know that once we're inside that house, things will change. We've been happy, so happy, for the last ten years, but we were also playing parts.

Cam, the regular guy who taught high school English, and rented a nice but small house, and didn't have a bank account with nearly a hundred million dollars in his name and a mansion on the other side of the country.

Jules, the sweet wife who churned butter for tourists and did community theater and didn't care about said money or said mansion.

I let myself mourn that version of us for just a second, and then I turn to the open door and step inside.

CHAPTER SIX

Camden

I forgot about the portrait.

The moment I step into Ashby House, I feel almost disoriented, thrown back in time so violently that I half expect to look down and see soccer cleats on my feet, dirt and grass on my knees.

It's the smell, for one thing. That beeswax polish Ruby liked the cleaners to use, the sick, funereal scent of fresh flowers that have been left in their vases a day or two too long, the faint tang of woodsmoke that never went away, even in the summers, like every fire ever lit in every fireplace soaked into the pores of the place.

The Tiffany lamp on the table just inside the front door, a replacement for the one I broke when I was fourteen, casting little squares of colored light onto the black marble top of the table it sits on. The carpet runner on the stairs, held in place by brass rods, the navy-and-maroon pattern worn away in the middle of each step by more than a century of feet going up and down.

The way the front hallway widens, opening up into empty space, the better to display the massive windows that look out onto the back lawn before it drops steeply down into rocks and trees. I kicked a soccer ball off the edge of that lawn once, wanting to watch it roll down the mountain, but it was immediately swallowed by the trees, tangled in branches before it got more than three feet down.

All of that comes rushing at me, thick and dizzying, and I wonder if this is what having a heart attack feels like. Chest tight, mind reeling, air suddenly hard to come by.

And then I lift my eyes and see Ruby staring down at me.

The portrait hangs at the top of the stairs, massive in its gilt frame. It was painted by Ruby's third husband, Andrew. She was married to him the longest, ten years, and maybe she loved him the most because Andrew was the middle name she gave me. He painted her picture right after they met, around 1969, so she wasn't even thirty at the time.

Younger than I am now.

Her dark hair is loose around her shoulders, no bouffant for Ruby McTavish, even in the sixties, and she's wearing an emerald-green evening gown as she perches on the arm of some antique chair, her legs crossed demurely at the ankles, her hands clasped in her lap. Her smile is faint, but genuine, I think. I remember that expression. And it's a good portrait, objectively. True to life, and the contrast of the opulent dress and décor with her casual pose works well.

I focus on the other details of the painting because I don't want to look into those eyes.

But I have to, don't I? I owe her that, at least.

I'm back, I think, looking up, and even though I haven't heard her voice in more than ten years, I imagine her reply.

You certainly took your time, my dear.

"That's her," I hear Jules say—it's not a question—and I swallow hard, putting an arm around her shoulders.

I never called her anything else. By law, she was my mother, but the word never suited her or me for that matter. She was always Ruby.

"Cam, this place . . ." Jules starts, looking around. She doesn't finish her sentence, but she doesn't have to.

"It's something," I agree, and she turns to me with wide eyes.

"Okay, King of Understatement. God. How did you ever . . . I don't know. Do math homework here? Eat Oreos? Look up tits on the internet?"

My shoulders relax a little.

Jules is here. Funny, quick Jules who loves me and understands me—as much as I've let her.

I can do this with her here. I can get through this.

"I actually did my math homework right through there," I tell her, taking her shoulders and turning her to face another hallway, one that leads to the kitchen. "And I didn't eat Oreos at all because Ruby had a thing about junk food. As for tits on the internet . . ."

Keeping my hands on her shoulders, I turn her to face me, bending my knees slightly so that we're eye to eye. "These eyes never saw any tits at all until you took pity on me in the backseat of my car behind Senor Pollo's."

Her sputtering laughter chases away some of the shadows, just like I'd hoped it would, and that tightness in my chest fades as I pull her close, her body a soft, familiar shape against mine.

I'd always thought there was something about this house that poisoned everyone in it eventually. Turned the good to rot. But there's too much sunshine in Jules for that to happen to her, and I need to remember that.

"Hope I'm not interrupting something!" a voice calls out, and that slight lift of happiness I'd been feeling slides away as quickly as it came.

I drop my arms from around Jules and turn around.

"Ben," I say, and, sure enough, there he stands on the stairs.

It had been a shock to see that Libby was no longer a teenager, but Ben, strangely, looks almost exactly the same.

His hair is sandy blond, a few shades lighter than mine, and he's just as tan as his sister, his teeth blindingly white as he smiles down at us. Ben's dad, Howell, always wore polo shirts and khakis, his feet forever shoved into Docksiders, but Ben is in jeans and a fitted gray T-shirt, and as he makes his way down the stairs, I see he's wearing a spotless pair of those expensive sneakers he's always been addicted to.

I've got on a beat-up pair of leather ankle boots, but other than that, we're dressed almost exactly the same, and there's that dizzying sense of vertigo again because, as I sense Jules look back and forth between us, I know what she must be thinking.

Ben is two years older, and I'm maybe an inch taller than he is. He's a little less lanky than I am, chest and arms thicker, and his hair is shorter. North Carolina still drips from his voice in a way that it doesn't from mine, but, yeah, we look enough alike to be brothers. People used to assume we were, actually, an idea that horrified both of us.

Me in another life, I think now, looking at him as he offers his hand to shake. *Me if I stayed here.*

"Glad you made it," Ben says, his glance brushing off of

me, but fixing on Jules in a way that has my hands clenched into fists before I even realize it.

"The Prodigal Son returns," he continues even though he's staring at Jules. She's smiling back at him, polite, but her toe nudges mine just the littlest bit.

A reminder, probably, that I owe her five dollars. Somewhere around Nashville, she had bet me someone in my family would say those exact words and I, stupidly, had thought that even Ben wasn't that much of a cliché.

"And even better, he brings a new Mrs. McTavish," Ben goes on, gesturing at one of the photographs on the table with the Tiffany lamp. "This house is named after the last McTavish bride, you know. Anna. My great-grandmother. Her maiden name was Ashby."

He swings back to Jules. "What's yours?"

I should've warned her about this, the family's obsession with genealogy and who birthed who, like a dead relative you never met can tell someone everything they need to know about you.

Jules waves one hand. "Technically, I don't have one. I mean, I kept my last name when I married Cam, so it's actually *Ms.* Brewster. Jules Brewster."

She offers her hand for him to shake, and Ben stares at it for a beat, thrown off his game. "*Ms.* Brewster," he says, and, finally, he shakes her hand. "Okay, cool. I mean, it's the twenty-first century, why not?"

His free hand forms a fist, snakes out, and I brace myself out of old habit. The thump on my arm doesn't land as hard as it once did, though, and I wonder if he got weaker or if I got stronger. Maybe he has the same thought, because I see the way his eyes widen for a second, how he clenches and un-clenches his fingers at his sides.

I'm not some skinny seventh grader anymore, Ben, I think, remembering the purple bruises I'd study as I lay in the massive bathtub upstairs. Violet splotches on my biceps, my thighs. Never out of anger, no, Ben would *never*. Always just "messing around," just "guy shit," just "Cam gets it, dontcha, Cam?"

Always the brightest smile and the hardest eyes.

The smile has faded, but the eyes are still like granite as he says, "Well done, man, well done," like Jules is a twelve-point buck I've just brought home, not my wife. "Although, hey, some advice. You may wanna rethink that when you two have kids. Confusing for them, having parents with different last names. If Dad were still alive, he would've told you himself. *His* father was actually a Franklin, but of course Great-Grandad insisted Nana Nelle and my dad stay McTavishes."

He shakes his head with a rueful chuckle. "So, yeah, trust me, you wanna have the same last name as your child. Otherwise people might think you two weren't married at all. Or divorced. You wouldn't want *that,* would you?"

"I would rather die," Jules replies with big eyes, and I choke back a laugh as I take her hand, our fingers interlacing.

Confused again, Ben looks at her, a half smile playing around his mouth like he can't tell if he's being made fun of or not.

Men like him aren't used to being mocked, which is probably why men like him exist in the first place.

"I'm sorry about your dad," I tell him, taking his focus off of Jules, and those hard eyes meet mine, one corner of his mouth lifting.

"No, you're not."

"No, I'm not," I agree. "But it's the kind of thing you have to say, isn't it?"

Ben's smirk melts into a grin, and that fist hits my upper arm again. "Missed you, Cam," he tells me. "Mean it."

"I doubt that."

"No, I'm serious," he assures me, and then crosses his arms over his chest, his biceps bulging. "There was never any bullshit with you."

He looks back at Jules, and gives her another one of those killer smiles. "Pardon my French."

"No fucking worries," she replies, and he barks out a laugh, throwing his head back.

"All ri-i-ight, Miss Jules," he drawls. "But try not to say that in front of Nana Nelle. One funeral this month is enough for me, thanks."

"Where is Nelle?" I ask. I don't actually want to see her, but I'd like to get this over with. The sooner we've gone through the motions of the whole homecoming thing, the sooner I can leave.

"Not feeling up to company today, she says," Ben replies, rolling his eyes. "One of her headaches. She's had a tough time, since Dad died. She'll meet you both at breakfast in the morning. Libby is headed out with friends tonight, I'm pretty sure. As for me, I have work to catch up on."

It shouldn't surprise me that Ben has a job. He's thirty-four, for fuck's sake, he *should* work, but I still find myself blurting out, "What is it that you do? For a living, I mean."

Ben raises his eyebrows at me. "Umm. I'm a lawyer?" he says, implying that I absolutely should have known that. "Estate stuff, wills and trusts. I mean." He spread his arms wide. "I figured the family could use someone who actually knew his shit in that regard, right?"

He's smiling, his teeth still so damn white, but his eyes have gone hard. I make myself smile back even as I feel my throat go a little tight. "Right."

Ben keeps grinning. "Anyway, I trust the two of you can entertain yourselves for the evening? Cecilia left a casserole in the fridge that you're welcome to and, Camden, I assumed you'd want your old room back, so it's ready for you."

"Fine," I say. "Sounds good."

It doesn't, actually. I'd hoped to stay in some other room. Any other room. The idea of taking Jules back to my child-hood bedroom, even if it *had* been a bedroom prepared for a septuagenarian, is unsettling for some reason. Like I'm sliding right back into place here.

"Awesome," Ben says and jerks his head toward the stairs. "I'll get back to it then. I've got a shitload of paperwork for you tomorrow."

"Can't wait."

He gives another one of those smiles that doesn't come close to reaching his eyes. "Now that? *That* is clearly bullshit, Cam."

Chuckling, he turns back to Jules. "Nice to meet you, *Ms.* Brewster. Welcome to Ashby House."

His eyes linger on her for another one of those uncom-fortable beats, and then he's headed back to the stairs, taking them two at a time like he's still fifteen and not in his thirties.

He stumbles just at the top, barely noticeable, and he quickly recovers, but for a moment, I let myself picture another out-come.

The sneaker sliding on that worn carpet. The hand reaching out to catch himself, but finding nothing to grab. The racket nearly two hundred pounds of muscle makes as it crashes into the wall, the mahogany banister.

Head hitting the parquet of the hallway, the sound wet,

heavy. A pool of deep red spreading from beneath that blond hair.

I let myself hold that image as Ben rounds the newel post at the top, following his progress until he's at the landing, and then my gaze slides up to meet Ruby's.

It's just a portrait, I remind myself. Canvas and oil paint, brushstrokes from a man who died before I was even born.

But as I look into Ruby's smiling face, I suddenly feel her here.

Real. Alive. Watching me.

Knowing what's inside my head right now.

And the thing is? I think she'd be proud of me.

March 14, 2013

I suppose you want to know about the murder now.

Well, the first one.

It's only fair. I spent all that time telling you about my
parents and Nelle, Nelle's birthday and meeting Duke, and
maybe you wondered why I started there instead of getting
right to the meat of it.

As it were.

I can almost see you frowning at the pages of these letters,
unconsciously worrying at your cuticles as you read. (You
should stop that, by the way. Picking your cuticles. Not only
is it a bad habit, but it's a tell, darling. A few moments in your
company and anyone would pick up on it.)

But as any good writer—or hostess—would tell you, setting
a scene is important. If you don't understand what it was like
growing up in Ashby House, the way silences and secrets clung
to the drapery, littered the hardwood floors, spun webs just as
deadly as those black widow spiders my mother was always so
worried about, then you might not understand why I was so
desperate to leave. How Duke wasn't just a man I fell in love
with and wanted to marry, but an escape into a whole new life.

You have to know all of that for this next part to make
sense.

If a thing like this ever can make sense.

I've thought about this moment so much, you see. It's a scene I've replayed countless times in my mind, because it was the beginning of it all, the moment that unlocked something inside me. Something that, until then, I had only suspected might exist.

For a long time, I believed that if I analyzed my memories enough, some answer would come to me, or I might see a way in which it could have been avoided and never happened at all. Where Duke and I each made different decisions that night that led to . . . what, exactly?

This is the part I always get stuck on. What happened that night in Paris feels so inevitable that, much like trying to imagine Duke as an old man, imagining a world in which we came home from our honeymoon, settled into a life together, had children . . . it's impossible. Ludicrous, even.

It's as though we were always meant to end up there, on that Aubusson rug on the landing of Duke's father's Paris flat in a lake of blood.

I abhor blood, I should add, and I remember kneeling in it in my nightgown, the white silk slowly turning red. I was looking at Duke's shirtfront—what remained of it—and saw that it was no longer white either, and my muddled brain was thinking, *I've never seen Duke in red before*, like he'd simply changed into a new shirt.

Funny what the mind will do in trying times.

All right. I've gone to the kitchen and poured myself a glass of wine, and I've let myself remember the worst of it, that quiet aftermath, before the police—well, before anyone but me knew that Duke Callahan no longer existed.

Let's go back to the beginning.

The honeymoon started out well. Magically, even. We'd spent our wedding night here at Ashby House, not in the bedroom I'd slept in all my life (save, of course, those eight months I was with the Darnells and my year at Agnes Scott), but one of the other suites, near the back of the house. The Ruby Suite, my mother called it. Not after me, but because it was done all in red. Heavy red velvet drapes around the window, a deep red carpet underfoot, red bed hangings, red coverlet.

Looking back, perhaps all that red was a sign.

In any case, that's where I spent my first night as Mrs. Duke Callahan and became a wife in all senses of the word.

Are you cringing now, darling? Are you bracing yourself for an old woman to delve into purple prose as she details her sexual awakening? Are your eyes already darting ahead, praying to god you don't see words like "petals" or "engorged"?

Never fear. A lady does not kiss and tell.

All I will say is that, much like the night of his death, this is a night I've replayed over and over, both looking for some hint of what was to come and because . . . well, to be frank, because I've often wished that this night was not as good as I remembered.

It's much easier to recast Duke as a villain if I tell myself that everything I felt on our wedding night was due to being young and sheltered. I'd only kissed two boys before Duke, so naturally sex would be something of a revelation. It wasn't him, it was me, et cetera.

But these letters are the place for truth, are they not? So now I can admit that yes, Duke was wonderful. That night was wonderful, and I'm not sure I've ever been happier in my life than I was that next morning, waking up next to him. I remember our legs touching underneath the sheets, and how that thrilled me, a man's bare leg warm against my own, the hair there so different from my own smooth skin. I was fascinated by the contrast of us, of the sunlight playing on the golden stubble that had sprung up on his cheeks overnight, of how delicate and feminine my hand looked against the muscles of his chest.

I lay there in the early morning sun, my body pleasantly sore, my mind a soft muddle of happiness and sleepiness and pleasure, and looked at that gorgeous profile, softer as he slept, and thought, *I am the luckiest woman in the world.*

I believe they call this "ironic foreshadowing."

I held that thought in my head for the first few days of our honeymoon. On the train to New York, boarding the ship to Paris.

Lucky, I thought, watching the way women watched Duke.

Lucky, I thought every night as he slid down my body, his lips marking places I'd never thought lips would touch.

Lucky, I was thinking just seconds before his fist met my cheek for the first time.

We'd been married for five days.

I said I was sheltered, and I had been. I knew what alcohol could do to people, had watched it slowly eat my mother from the inside out, but that was my only real experience with drunkenness. I thought if you drank too much, you might cry, as Mama did, or sleep too much, as Mama also did. I didn't know that for some people, alcohol is the key to a cage inside of them, and inside that cage is a monster.

Duke had been gambling in the ship's casino that night, and I'd been irritated with how late he returned to our cabin. He kissed my cheek after dinner and said he'd only be an hour or two, then with a wink, whispered, "Don't you dare go to sleep before I get back."

The promise in those words had fizzed in my blood like champagne, so I'd had a bath, reapplied my makeup, put on one of the nightgowns from my trousseau that he hadn't seen yet. It was the same white silk I was wearing the night he died, though that was still a few weeks away.

And then I waited.

And waited.

And the longer I waited, the more irritated I became. My eyelids felt heavy with sleep, but I couldn't lie down because then I'd muss my makeup, and be a mess when he finally returned. And why was a smoky ship's casino, filled with boring men and their even more insufferable wives, more enjoyable than my bed?

Oh, the snit I worked myself into.

So by the time he did return, sometime past two in the morning, I was mad as a hornet.

And he was drunk as a skunk.

I could smell it when he walked in, that familiar and awful medicinal smell of gin, bringing me right back to dark hallways, to *shh, Mama's sleeping,* to muffled retching behind closed doors.

He'd lost his dinner jacket somewhere, his bow tie hanging around his neck, undone, and for the first time, jealousy raised its ugly head. I thought of my fumbling fingers undoing that tie on our wedding night, how I'd laughed to cover my self-consciousness, and how he'd kissed the tip of my nose and told me I was adorable.

Had some other woman undone that tie for him tonight? My head was full of images of elegant red fingernails, diamonds winking in the low light of the casino, and it made my words sharper than I'd intended.

"You said an hour, Duke," I reminded him. "It's been nearly four."

Holding up one hand, he swayed slightly. "Forgive me, Mrs.

Callahan," he said, and tried to give me that grin, but it was lopsided, and honestly, I was too mad for it to work anyway.

"Ran into an old friend from Yale, Darcy Butler. Did you ever meet Darcy? No, you wouldn't have. They never let you past the Mason-Dixon Line. Important to keep the princess safe in her kingdom."

I blinked at him, confused. He was still smiling, but there was poison in the words, hidden darts. I could sense it, but I didn't understand it. I didn't know the dangers that followed that tone of voice.

"Anyway, Darce and I did some catching up, and then I lost abysmally at blackjack, so I had to keep playing until I'd dug myself out of the hole."

Alarm bells began to ring faintly in my head. I didn't like the sound of any of that, but then he pulled out a wad of cash, tossing it to the dressing table where most of it slid to the floor.

"And so I did," he finished up, giving a bow. He was trying to charm me, I think, but I was in no mood, and I turned away, my robe fluttering.

"Well, thank god for that," I told him, leaning down to pick up the bills that had fallen. "I would've been furious if you'd given all of Daddy's money to some cruise ship gambler."

My father had given us a honeymoon gift, you see. Fifty thousand dollars to spend as we saw fit, and it had been a joke between us since the morning after the wedding, *what would we spend Daddy's money on?*

A camel, I had suggested, and then we'd wondered how much camels even cost and if you could buy one in Europe at all.

The crown jewels of England, Duke had decided, and I reminded him that, while fifty thousand dollars was a lot of money, I wasn't sure it could buy that treasure.

So you see, I wasn't trying to anger him or shame him. I wasn't pleased with Duke, of course, and maybe that made the words sound more waspish than they were, but I thought I was pulling him into a familiar joke.

I straightened up, the money in my hand, quite a lot of it, and as I went to set it back on the dressing table, I thought to myself, *Maybe Duke is the lucky one, not me.*

And then he punched me.

Not a slap, but a closed-fist *punch* to my left cheek that made stars explode in my vision and sent me half slumping against the table. My bare feet tangled in my nightgown and robe, and I fell then, landing hard on my backside with my mind so dazed I hardly knew which way was up.

It didn't hurt, not then. Or perhaps my brain was so busy trying to process the fact that my husband had just hit me that there was no room for anything else.

I felt like some kind of stunned animal lying there, looking up at him, blinking stupidly into that handsome face that, just hours before, I'd held in my hands as I'd kissed him on the deck, the night wind ruffling his hair.

It was the disorientation I remember the most. The feeling that I had just been violently hurled from a life I understood into one that made no sense at all.

"I don't need your father's fucking money," Duke said, sniffing as he pulled the tie out from under his collar and tossed it on the bed. "Besides, that's my money now, do you understand? And I'll do what I want with it."

He stepped over me to make his way to the en suite, and when I heard the door shut and the sink begin running, I made myself stand up, my legs shaking.

My cheek had finally begun to throb, but the rest of me was numb as I made my way to the dressing table, picking up a tissue to wipe away my lipstick. I didn't meet my eyes in the mirror, didn't want to see the bruise I knew was forming because then it would be real. This would all be real.

I have no idea how I slept that night, but somehow, I did, and when I woke in the morning, Duke was leaning over me, his hand—the same hand that had hit me so hard the night before—gently cradling my face.

"Christ, I'm a beast," he murmured softly, his voice so tender. "I know better than to drink gin, and now look what I've done."

"It's all right," I told him.

I know. I still can't believe I said that. I can't believe that in that moment, I genuinely felt sorry for him. He looked so sad. So remorseful.

And how benevolent I felt, laying my palm against his cheek and looking into his eyes and telling him I knew he hadn't meant it, that this wasn't who he was, that of course it was the gin, and I knew it would never happen again.

But I think even then I knew I was lying to myself.

My cheek turned a light purple, then a sort of sickly yellow green, and I covered it with makeup, and laughed at dinner about how too much champagne and the rolling of the ship had sent me into the side of my dressing table, whoopsie-daisy! And the other couples we ate dinner with at night laughed, and teased me when the waiter opened a fresh bottle of bubbly, and I pretended not to see the understanding—the pity—in some of the wives' eyes.

He didn't raise a hand to me for the next two days of that voyage, though. There was the fight with the earrings I told you about, but he was sober then, and I was the one who'd indulged in too many martinis before dinner, crying with rage because I found out he had canceled the Italian portion of our trip without telling me, preferring to linger in France once he'd heard from Darcy Butler that "several of the old gang" would be staying there.

Isn't that funny? The man punched me in the face and my eyes stayed dry, but rob me of my chance to see the Colosseum and I was a mess of tears. Confusing time, one's twenties.

And then, there was Paris.

The city I'd dreamed of my whole life, a place I'd imbued with magic and romance and every fanciful thing you can think of, and yet it was somehow still even better than I'd hoped. Even lovelier.

I've never been back, of course, and sometimes I think I resent Duke for that more than anything.

We stayed at his father's pied-à-terre in the eighth arrondissement, just off the Champs-Élysées, a beautiful building made of white stone where bright pink flowers spilled out of window boxes and the most famous names in French fashion—Dior, Chanel—were just steps away. I still have one of the gowns I had made at Dior. The green one I'm wearing in Andrew's portrait of me.

The days were glorious. I set off on my own in the mornings, drinking in the beauty of Paris in the spring, enjoying the solitude, the feeling of being a grown woman out in the world alone, buying what she wanted to buy, stopping into any little shop or museum or gallery that caught her interest.

Duke sometimes joined me in the afternoons, once he'd woken up, and that could be lovely, too. We'd walk arm in arm along the Seine, and I would pretend that everything was going to be fine, that we could be these people forever.

And then the nights would come.

Every night, we dressed and went out, trying new

restaurants, new nightclubs, and it would feel thrilling and fun, and I'd smoke Gauloises in a long ivory holder, and Duke would light each one for me with a practiced flick of his platinum lighter, and I thought how people must look at us and think how young and bright and beautiful we were.

How lucky.

But then the champagne would lead to whiskey sours, the whiskey sours to straight whiskey, and I would learn that it wasn't just gin that turned Duke into a beast.

A shove on the stairs when we got home because I'd been "flirting" with a waiter.

His fingers, clamped around my jaw, tilting my head back so far that I thought my neck might snap, the awful wormwood scent of absinthe in my nose as he demanded to know what I was implying when I asked who he'd been with that night.

The back of my skull, bouncing off the marble floor of the bathroom because I'd been crying in there, and didn't I know this house had servants? They could hear me, and what were they going to think of Mr. Callahan's new bride sobbing her eyes out in the downstairs toilet?

He got rid of the servants at night after that, sending them all home by seven. Another one of those choices that doomed him, although he couldn't have known it at the time.

Every day, I put my makeup on, dressed well, and set out on the streets of Paris, thinking how lovely it was—and how nothing lovely would ever really matter again. This would be my life now, until Duke pushed too hard, or my head hit something at just the wrong angle, and I would never know when that moment was coming, only that it was.

That was the part I hated the most. Not the hits and the shoves, although those hurt. It was the uncertainty.

And the hope of it! God, I hated the hope. Because it was always there. This belief that maybe, today it would all somehow be different. Duke wouldn't drink so much, or I wouldn't say the wrong thing to set him off, and it would, miraculously, set us back on the right track.

I still loved him, sadly. Or I thought I did. I know now that what I felt for Duke was mostly lust, but that's a powerful emotion in its own right, especially when you're only twenty-one. I dreaded his hands even as I craved his touch, and it nearly tore me apart, those wildly disparate feelings. A terrible thing, wanting someone and hating them all at the same time. Is it any wonder, pulled taut as I was, that I finally snapped?

June 13, 1961

No sign that anything would be different that night. We'd been in Paris for well over a month by then, our other accommodations and travel plans canceled because Duke was having such a lovely time with all his old friends, a pack of men he'd known at Yale who were all pale imitations of him and therefore made him look even more golden in contrast. We'd stay until August, he'd decided, and I didn't even try to protest.

I hadn't been feeling well for days by then, nauseous, my head aching. I was terrified that I might be pregnant, but also, I'd fallen down the stairs the week before in an attempt to avoid one of Duke's swinging fists and hit my head hard on the banister, so it was equally likely to be that.

I'd managed to make it through dinner, but begged off when Duke wanted to move on to a club. He hadn't had much to drink at that point in the night, so I was sent on my way with a kiss and a fond farewell instead of glares and ugly words.

I'd returned to the flat, let myself in, and gone to bed.

I awoke hitting the floor, my head bouncing against the wooden frame of the bed.

For a moment, I thought I'd fallen, but then I felt the warm band of fingers around my ankle and looked up to see Duke crouching over me.

He was smiling, his bow tie once again undone, his shirt very white in the near darkness of the bedroom.

In his other hand, he held a rifle.

The sight of that blue-black barrel in the moonlight made my breath stop, my lungs tight, and a distant buzzing started up in my ears.

"Look what I won tonight," he said, letting go of my ankle to caress the gun, his long fingers elegant and deadly against the metal. "Belonged to Darcy's dad. Shot three elephants—no, four—in Rhodesia, and a tiger in India. Kept it over the mantel in his place here, and Darce fucking bet it on a pair. A *pair.*"

He laughed, and rose to his feet while I lay on the carpet, a rabbit in a predator's sights.

Shifting the gun against his shoulder, he pointed it at me, one eye closed as he looked down the barrel.

"What do you think is more impressive? Shooting a tiger or shooting a person?"

I couldn't breathe now, my skin numb even as every nerve in my body lit up in panic.

That laugh again. "Tigers are bigger," he said, adjusting the angle of the gun slightly. "Deadlier, maybe. But people are smarter. Still, you don't brag about that kind of thing, do you? Don't hang the gun on the wall and say, 'You know, boy, I shot my first wife with that gun.'"

My mouth was so dry that it was an effort to lick my lips, to make myself say something, and when I did, it was just his name.

"Duke."

"When people kill tigers, they make them into rugs. And when they kill deer, their heads go on the wall. What would you even make out of a dead wife, I wonder?"

He was still smiling, and I realized, lying there on the floor, that this was fun to him. That he was thoroughly enjoying watching me tremble at his feet.

But the question you must be asking, the question I've asked myself: Did I think he would shoot me, right then and there?

Darling, I want so badly to say yes. I want to say that what happened next was true self-defense, because I feared for my life in that very moment.

But it's the truth you asked for, and the truth you'll get.

I was afraid for my life, yes. But no, I don't think he would have shot me. There was no fun in that, after all. Just like there was no fun in beating me over and over, breaking skin, knocking out teeth. It was the fear he enjoyed, the threat. My terror made him feel in control, and all these years later, I wonder who taught him that. His father? His mother? A sadistic teacher at that all-boys school he went to in the mountains of north Georgia?

Or was he born like that? Was that desire for power, the satisfaction that came from having someone at his mercy, simply a quirk of his biology, just like his green eyes or his height?

I have no way of knowing.

What I do know is that he heaved a sigh and lowered the gun, setting it upright on its butt against the little bench at the foot of my bed.

"Head's killing me," he muttered, turning away.

Terrible last words.

I watched him walk out the door, heading for his own bedroom at the other end of the hall, and all the terror that had raced through me just seconds before ignited into something hot and wild, and I was moving almost before I knew it.

The metal of the gun was still warm from Duke's hand, the weight familiar to me as I carried it out of the bedroom. I'd been hunting in the woods around Ashby House with Daddy since I was five, and I knew my way around firearms.

The flat was dim, moonlight spilling through windows high up on the wall above the landing, and the sconces on the stairs providing the only light. The carpet was soft underneath my bare feet, the silk of my nightgown cool, and Duke was just in front of me, almost to his bedroom door.

"Duke."

I didn't shout it, and my voice sounded surprisingly flat in my ears.

The butt of the gun nestled in the hollow of my shoulder like it had been meant to sit there.

He turned.

He was frowning, I remember that. He wasn't scared, just irritated that I had decided to keep playing a scene he had already grown tired of.

I pulled the trigger.

I only wanted to scare him. I didn't even think the gun was loaded.

Ah. And there I go. Giving you lies when I promised truth.

Let me try again.

I didn't know whether the gun was loaded, that's true. In retrospect, it's insane that Darcy Butler's father was displaying a loaded gun in his Parisian flat, and that Darcy and then Duke toted it all over the city.

But honestly, I wasn't even thinking about that. Only later did it occur to me that the gun might have harmlessly clicked, and Duke would've flinched and then made me pay for my empty threat.

The shot was loud, so loud it seemed like it would blot out any other noise forever. I'd cried the first time I'd fired a gun, aiming for a rabbit I hadn't wanted to hit, and my father had told me I was going to need to toughen up if I expected to run Ashby House one day.

I didn't cry this time. I watched, feeling outside my own body, as the bullet tore through that clean white shirt of Duke's, just along his ribs, as his face bloomed with surprise, eyes wide as they looked at me.

Remember, this was a gun meant for killing elephants and tigers.

You can imagine what it did to a person.

I fired again.

It's that second shot that makes me a murderer to my mind. The first? I'd been terrorized for weeks at that point, scared past the point of endurance that night, and I can forgive myself for reacting. Maybe anyone could.

I think you can.

But the second bullet . . . that's when I adjusted my aim. That's when I knew exactly what I was doing.

That's when I sent a bullet straight into the heart I thought would be mine forever.

It was so quiet after. My ears wouldn't stop ringing, and Duke was slumped on the carpet, his eyes staring. His chest moved up and down in a jerky movement, once, maybe twice. There was a sound in his throat I never wanted to hear again, and I was glad when it was over, when he was still.

I knelt beside him for a while there in the darkness, like I told you. His blood soaking into my nightgown while I waited to feel something. Horror, remorse, fear. Anything at all.

Relief came first. It was over now. I'd never again wake up wondering if this was the day he went too far. And then, a flicker of sadness followed. Not for the Duke he'd actually been, but the Duke I'd thought he was.

But that was it. No shame. No grief. No worry or frantic thoughts of police and punishments, and good god, did they still have the guillotine in France?

It was more like I'd just solved a math problem that had been vexing me, and I wondered if this was what it was to be in shock. That was it, surely.

All those feelings—those natural, human feelings, like grief and regret—would come in time.

Or so I thought.

For now, however, there was one last thing to do.

I went to where I'd left the gun, and moved it to the top of the stairs, taking care to wipe it down with the unbloodied hem of my robe. Then I went back to Duke's body, wrapping my arms around him, letting more of his blood cover me, pressing my cheek to his so that his blood soaked into my loose hair.

And then I began to scream.

You know the rest, darling. Or you can look it up. That part is less important to the story I'm trying to tell you. There were police (my "Conversational French" from Agnes Scott was sadly inadequate when it came to discussing something like this, it turned out) and of course it was a bit of a scandal, but the official story was that someone had seen Duke flashing his cash at a seedier casino he'd been in that night in Montmartre, and followed him all the way home with the intention of robbing him.

Duke himself assisted with this version of events by conveniently leaving the front door wide open when he came home, so eager was he to show me his new prize.

A scuffle, a loaded rifle, two panicked shots, the cash Duke's friends swore he'd had in his jacket pocket that night all missing (tucked inside a hideous china dog I'd bought for Nelle, buried deep in one of my trunks), and there you had it.

Tragic, made more so by our youth and beauty, our clear love for each other. And on our honeymoon, too! Married less than two months.

Did people believe this story, or did Daddy's money make it go away? I've never really known. It doesn't matter.

I got away with it. That was all I cared about.

It feels good to write that down, I must say. The clear, pure truth of it, no excuses, no explanations.

I had gotten away with murder, and I was glad for it.

Is that enough truth for you, my dear?

-R

AVAILABLE SCHOLARSHIPS

The Duke Edward Callahan Memorial Scholarship was established in 1963 by Mrs. Ruby McTavish Callahan, Duke Callahan's widow and a generous benefactor to the Preston Boys Academy, her late husband's alma mater.

The scholarship, totaling $25,000, is presented to a graduating senior who best exemplifies the qualities Mrs. Callahan says were most present in her husband: a love of knowledge, a curiosity about the world, a skilled analytical mind, and, most important of all, kindness to his fellow man.

"While my time with Duke was sadly too short, it brings comfort to know that I can keep him alive with this scholarship to the school that shaped and molded him into the man he became. It is my dearest wish that every recipient of the Duke Edward Callahan Memorial Scholarship will use this opportunity to make the world a better, gentler place."

—*Mrs. Ruby Callahan*

CHAPTER SEVEN

Jules

I was right, just so you know.

About drinking coffee on that back veranda and never being capable of unhappiness again.

As I sit in an Adirondack chair on my first morning at Ashby House, hands curled around a steaming mug, the mountain sloping down into treetops in front of me, I feel a kind of contentment I hadn't known existed.

The quiet wraps itself around me like a cozy quilt, the soft gray of the sky giving way to a hazy blue as the sun begins to burn off the mist, and I want to start every day of my life like this, serenely gazing out at this view, knowing it belongs to me.

I'm not going to lie: last night, I was a little worried. The house was everything I dreamed, and while Libby was a bitch, she wasn't all that bad. Neither was Ben, honestly, but Cam had seemed distant all evening. We'd eaten maybe the most delicious casserole I'd ever had, something with chicken, cheese, buttery crackers . . . comforting, homemade food that I couldn't imagine anyone else in this house eating, let alone cooking. Cam had said it was the work of Cecilia, the housekeeper, and that the dish had been one of his favorites growing up.

It was a thoughtful gesture, and it should've made him happy, but he'd barely touched his plate, and we'd ended up going to bed before nine o'clock, like we were grandparents or something.

I'd been surprised by Cam's room, which felt more like a very pretty guest room at a stuffy bed-and-breakfast than a place where a teenage boy had once slept. It was filled with heavy oak furniture, a big canopy bed dominating the space. But it felt like it had its own center of gravity—like if you moved a piece of art or a throw pillow out of place, the room would right itself, put everything back where it belonged.

Given that we'd gone to bed so early, I had joked about us finding *some* way to pass the time until we were sleepy, walking my fingers along Cam's chest just in case he wasn't getting the message. But once again, he'd kissed me and told me he was beat, and then lay awake next to me for hours.

It bothered me, and the hurt lingered this morning. I woke with the sunrise and went into the massive bathroom to take a shower. But after a few minutes, I heard the shower door open, felt a rush of cool air on my back, and then Cam was there, his hands smoothing down my sides, his lips finding the place where my neck met my shoulder, and we fell back together just like we always do.

So yes, life was good this morning. Comfy chair, gorgeous views, excellent coffee, and two orgasms before 8:00 A.M. What more did a girl need?

From behind me, I hear the door to the veranda open, and I turn, hoping it's Cam. He'd promised to join me for coffee once he'd finished getting dressed and checking email. Instead, I'm greeted by an older woman, her red hair faded to a sort of apricot color, a pair of glasses hanging around her neck from a sparkly chain.

I wonder if this is Nelle—if so, she looks *amazing* for seventy-nine—but then she smiles and gives me a little wave. "You must be Jules. I'm Cecilia, the housekeeper."

Rising to my feet, I cross the veranda, offering her my free hand. She waves it away and opens one arm, so I let myself be pulled into a hug as she pats my back hard enough to almost spill my coffee.

"I am so happy to meet you!" Cecilia says, and I actually believe it. "And I'm so happy Camden has finally come home where he belongs."

Ah. An ally, then.

"It's a beautiful house," I tell her, and she beams at me as she pulls back.

"You'll have to get Cam to give you the full tour," she says. "That boy knew every nook and cranny of this place. I swear, sometimes I'd go looking for him, and find him in a room even *I* didn't know existed."

I picture Cam, a serious little boy finding hiding places and secret alcoves, sneakers scuffing the hardwood, and I can see it so clearly that I know we've done the right thing coming back here. He loved this place once, and I can make him love it again.

"I see you've found coffee, but let me get you something to eat," Cecilia says, turning back into the house, and I find myself following her even though I hadn't planned on leaving this perfect spot.

"You don't have to feed me," I say as we step back into the den, ceilings soaring high overhead, a stone fireplace big enough to roast an ox along one wall, sofas deep enough to sink into for days angled to get the best views out the windows.

"That's her job," a voice says from the doorway.

Ah. So *this* is Nelle.

Her hair is white, a puff of snowy curls that I bet she gets "done" in town once a week and never touches otherwise. She's wearing a tartan skirt that hangs to mid-shin and sensible shoes, a beige cardigan over a white blouse, and if a prune could talk, it would probably look like her.

There's just something . . . pinched about her entire being. Her lips, puckered in distaste, her eyes narrow, her knobby fingers clenched together. As she moves closer, her shoes squeak on the parquet.

"You must be Camden's wife. Julia?"

"Jules," I correct, and her mouth somehow, impossibly, gets even tighter.

"Is that not short for Julia?"

"It's short for Julianne, actually, but only my mom called me that."

Nelle sniffs. "Well, I'm Eleanor, Nelle for short, but you may call me Mrs. McTavish."

Oh-kay, then.

"I was just telling Cecilia what a lovely home you have, Mrs. McTavish," I say, sugar and sunshine, but that only makes the old bitch glare even harder.

"I suppose I should be saying that to you," she says. "Given that this is Camden's house. Built by *my* grandfather in 1904, named after *my* mother, but since I had the misfortune of being born second and my sister loved nothing more than hurting me, all of it now belongs to some boy from the streets who might as well be a stranger."

"Morning to you, too, Nelle."

Cam appears behind her, his hair still damp, wearing a dark gray T-shirt and jeans, hands in his pockets. It's an outfit I've seen him wear a thousand times, it's practically his uniform, but he looks different this morning, standing in the halls of Ashby House.

It's a weird sensation, looking at your own husband and not quite recognizing him.

Nelle turns around, not even a little embarrassed. "You know my feelings on all this. Why bother to pretend?"

"Why indeed," he murmurs, moving past her. He gives me a quick, warm look, then smiles at Cecilia, hugging her tightly.

"Thank you for the casserole last night. Can't believe you remembered."

"Can't believe you think I'd forget," she says, and there's a sheen of tears in her eyes as she pulls back and looks at him.

"How long are you staying?" she asks, and he shrugs.

"Depends how long it takes to see all that needs to be done. A few weeks, maybe?"

Longer, I think. *Forever.*

"Well, it's good to have you back," Cecilia says, and I hear Nelle give another one of those sniffs.

"Speaking of, where's Ben?" Cam asks, looking around. "I figured he'd want to show me where to spend my money."

He throws a look at Nelle as he says that, and I see the satisfaction in his eyes when the barb lands.

Another side of Camden I don't fully recognize.

But then Ben comes in, all bright smile and too-white teeth, and there's talk about flooding damage and wainscoting and contractors, and I tune it out, already feeling the pull of the veranda, the desire to sink back into that chair and dream of the day when it's just me and Cam here.

We have a good life in Colorado, I know that. Cam likes

his job, and while I don't love being Mrs. Burch over at Homestead Park five days a week, I could probably find something else. I may not have finished college, but I'm a quick learner. We have friends there, other teachers from Cam's school, a few of the other women who work out at Homestead, some neighbors. We go for margaritas on Fridays at this cute Mexican place downtown, and we know that that one Safeway is always packed on Saturday, so it's better to drive a few miles out of town to hit that *other* Safeway, and one of the baristas at the coffee shop closest to our house has figured out what we always order (me, hazelnut latte with oat milk; Cam, a plain black coffee that always smells, and I assume tastes, like burnt sadness).

All those little things that make up a life.

We have them, but at the same time we don't.

Because we're still renting a tiny little house that neither of us even likes that much. Because those friends of ours? I think we've only had them over to said house twice in the last few years. Because when my job wanted me to list a second emergency contact after my husband, I just left it blank. When I mentioned it to Cam, I learned that he had done the same thing on *his* forms at work.

We have been floating in Colorado, bobbing happily enough on the surface, but never going any deeper, and I've believed—or at least, I've told myself—that it's because we always knew we'd end up here eventually.

And so we have. *Finally.*

Now I just have to convince Cam to stay. Because I haven't come this far—I haven't done the things I've done—to pack it up after a week or two. But I also know that until Nelle, Ben, and Libby are out of this house, there is no chance of making that dream a reality.

So, what's my grand plan? To be honest, I can't say I have one yet. But don't worry.

I've always been good on my feet.

I DON'T SEE much of Cam for the rest of the day. I spend the morning on the veranda, then help Cecilia in the kitchen with lunch. Cam and Ben come back in to grab a bite, but then they're gone again, and I decide to go up to our room for a nap.

But when I get there, the bed is made up, and there's no trace of our things anywhere. Frowning, I look in the closets, in the bathroom, even under the bed, but our bags are gone, our toothbrushes aren't by the sink. Even my shampoo is gone from the shower.

Confused, I start to head downstairs to ask Cecilia if she just got a little overenthusiastic with the cleaning this morning, but as I do, I see an open door at the end of the hall, and there, sitting on a blood-red bedspread, is my bag.

I walk down the hall, pushing the door open, and it's a fucking *sea* of red. Red curtains, red carpet, red fabric hanging from the bedposts. Cam's bag sits on an armchair, and my toiletries are arranged in the bathroom.

When Camden finally comes in for dinner, looking sweaty and more than a little worn out, I ask him about it.

"I decided we should change rooms," he says, shrugging like it's no big deal.

And it isn't—one opulent bedroom is as good as the other— but it's still weird. Why doesn't he want to sleep in his old bedroom? And why would he prefer *that* room?

Dinner is another scattered affair, with Nelle taking a tray upstairs, Ben retreating to his office, and Libby god knows where. We eat roast chicken that Cecilia left, drink a few glasses of a gorgeous sauvignon blanc, then head up to our new room, once again much earlier than we usually turn in.

"Well," Cam says with a sigh as he reaches for one of the throw pillows on the bed, catching it by its lacy trim and tossing it aside. "First full day at Ashby House. Impressions?"

I grab a pillow as well—there appear to be roughly eight thousand of them, arranged from the headboard all the way to the middle of the paisley bedspread—and throw it onto an armchair.

"The house is incredible," I say. "And Cecilia is the best."

Cam nods as another pillow hits the hardwood. "She is."

He lifts his mismatched gaze to mine. "And my family?"

I pause, fingers still curled around the edge of a throw pillow, and study Cam. "You know, the whole time we've been together, I kind of thought it was an act."

Now it's Cam's turn to pause, his arms folded across his chest, his expression a little closed off. "What was?"

I shrug and continue to pull pillows from the bed. Behind Cam, a giant bay window reflects my movements, the lawn and forest beyond completely dark now.

"It's just kind of a cliché, you know? The rich kid who turned his back on his shitty family. I thought . . . well, I *believed* you, but man, Nelle is indeed a real piece of work. Libby, too. And Ben seems decent enough, but I don't trust a man whose teeth glow in the dark."

Cam's face relaxes a little, one corner of his mouth lifting in that smile that's not quite a smirk. He smiled like that the first night we met, and I was a goner.

"I don't know whether I should be smug or apologize to you," he says now, the bed finally clear of pillows, and I move onto the mattress on my knees, holding out my hands to Cam.

He takes them, both of us kneeling as we face each other.

"I'm still glad we came," I tell him, and his fingers flex against mine. "Are you?"

"Hard to say," he replies. "I needed to come. The sheer amount of shit they all let slide . . ."

He trails off, thinking. "She would've hated it," he finally says, his voice soft, and I don't have to ask who he means.

I lean in and kiss him, gently, almost chastely, and assume that's as far as it'll go, especially after this morning, but he surprises me by pulling me in closer, his mouth hungry on mine, and I let him pull me down onto that red, red bed.

Afterward, he sleeps peacefully, none of that tension I've sensed the past few nights vibrating through his body. Instead, it's my turn to lie awake in the darkness, thoughts churning.

One full day in Ashby House down.

A lifetime to go.

CHAPTER EIGHT

Camden

So you're a teacher, huh?"

Ben and I are in his truck, heading down the mountain into Tavistock. We'd spent yesterday taking stock of what needed to be done, fixing what we could with the few tools Ben had around, but today, we were pulling off the damaged paneling in the upstairs bathroom, and that took more supplies. I should've just hired some guys to do it—Lord knew I had the fucking money—but I'd wanted to do it myself. Maybe it was guilt, maybe it was some attempt at atoning for all the years I'd been gone, or maybe I'd just wanted to lose myself in grueling but mind-numbing manual labor.

I'm actually on my phone, trying to price new paneling despite the shitty signal, when Ben asks his question, and I briefly glance over at him.

He's got one arm resting on the door, his elbow jutting out the open window, and the scent of earth and trees is thick in the truck. I always forget just how long it takes to get into town, and now it looks like Ben has decided to fill the time with small talk.

"Yeah," I reply. "Boys' school in Colorado."

"I knew that part," he says. "What do you teach?"

I look back at my phone, and even though several people, including Ben's dad, have died on this twisty road, I wish he'd step on the gas.

"English."

Ben nods at that, thumping his hand on the side of the truck. "You always were reading."

"And you were always smacking books out of my hands and wondering if I was the first person in my family who ever learned to read," I can't help but remind him.

He loved that shit. Not just the mocking—although I'm sure that was very fun—but making sure I knew I came from, as he liked to put it, "fucking hillbilly trash, probably."

Not One of Us. Could've been the McTavish family motto.

Now, though, Ben sighs and reaches up, adjusting his baseball cap. "You know I was just a dick to you because I was jealous, right?"

I can't help but snort, turning my attention back to my phone. "Sure."

"I mean it," he says just as we reach the base of the mountain. I spot a huge oak tree, its bark splintered and raw, but Ben keeps his eyes on the road ahead of us. "Dad was always in my head, man. Nana Nelle, too. 'All this should be yours, you're the real heir, maybe Ruby will come to her senses one day.' Used to drive me nuts."

"Wasn't exactly a great situation for me, either," I say, and he looks over at me then, one corner of his mouth lifting.

"No, I guess it wasn't."

A pause.

And then, "But knowing you had all that money coming probably helped."

It always comes back to the money with them. Even now, even when Ben is, in his own way, trying to make amends, he just can't help himself. It would almost be funny if it weren't so fucking tragic.

He doesn't get that the money means fuck all when everything else around you is so toxic. If Ruby had genuinely loved me, if growing up in Ashby House hadn't felt like I was starring in my own personal version of *The Hunger Games* every day . . .

"Whatever," I say now, like I'm a surly teenager again, and he reaches over to thump my arm.

"You really haven't touched it?" he asks. "Everything Ruby left you?"

"I told you, I never wanted it," I say as we pass the big sign welcoming us into Tavistock. It's a small town, sleepy and quaint, and I'm surprised at how quickly my brain starts racing, reminding me that the K–12 school I went to is just down Main Street and to the left. The bookstore whose aisles I haunted is three doors down from the coffee shop we're passing now, and up ahead I spot the bright blue door of the Jay, a cozy restaurant with gingham tablecloths and leather booths. It was my favorite place to eat when I was a kid, and when we drive past, there's a part of me that expects to look through the plate glass window and see Ruby sitting at our usual table.

She liked the booth looking out onto Main Street so she could "people-watch," she said. I can conjure her up so clearly, red nails clicking on the white mug of coffee the waiter always brought her as soon as we sat down, dark gaze scanning the town outside, a queen secure in her kingdom.

But the restaurant is dark, the painted letters on the glass flaking off, and I look over at Ben. "The Jay closed?"

He shrugs. "We had to raise the rents downtown, and the owner decided it was time to retire."

My gaze moves over the street, and now I see that the Jay isn't the only shuttered building. The tearoom is dark, as is the tiny bookstore. So, too, the jewelry shop, where Ruby had an account.

I shouldn't care about any of it. Tavistock isn't my home anymore. Hell, I'm not sure it ever really was, but there's still an oily sensation in my stomach that I'm pretty sure is guilt.

"Did you actually need to raise the rents?" I ask Ben now, and he shoots me another one of those sideways glances.

"If we didn't want to ask you for more money, then yeah."

Tavistock itself is another one of those complications in Ruby's will. Big chunks of the town still technically belong to me, but back in the early 2000s, Ruby sold a couple of blocks of downtown to Nelle. Howell wanted to open a brewery or something, and Nelle had a bunch of money after her husband died. I hadn't paid much attention to the details because I'd been only about twelve or so, but Ruby had still made me go down to the lawyer's office with her, dressed in a fucking suit and tie like I was the world's youngest Realtor.

I can still feel the cool weight of her hand slipping into the crook of my elbow as we left that office, smell her perfume as she leaned in and muttered, *Sometimes it's fun to give people enough rope with which to hang themselves, my Camden.*

I hadn't understood what she meant, but the words had made something twist in my gut. By then, I knew about all the "Mrs. Kill-more" stuff, the string of dead husbands. I'd found out accidentally the summer before, an offhand comment sending me to the internet, and when I'd asked Ruby about it, she'd taken me to the Jay, to our favorite booth, and calmly told me the story of each of them.

Duke, killed in a robbery.

Hugh, electrocuted in the barn.

Andrew, sick with some mystery ailment.

Roddy, partying too hard and going over the side of a boat.

It all made sense when she laid it out, a series of unrelated incidents, bizarre, sure, but nowhere near as sinister as it had been made out.

I believed her.

Then, at least.

Ben pulls his truck into a parking place just in front of one of the few stores still open along this stretch, a sign reading HENDERSON'S HARDWARE AND SUNDRY GOODES swinging faintly in the breeze.

There are two men at the counter when we step in, one behind, one in front, and they're smiling as they chat, the familiar accents sliding over my ears and into my heart in a way that makes me feel homesick even as I stand in my hometown.

They stop talking as we come in, and I watch something in both their faces change when they see Ben standing there.

He smiles brightly at them, lifting a hand. "Steve, Hank. How's it going?"

The guy behind the counter—Steve Henderson, I recognize him now despite the paunch and the gray hair—nods at us. "Mr. McTavish," he says, and then his eyes slide over to me.

The tightness fades from his expression and his eyes widen slightly. "Holy shit, Camden," he says, and then he's coming around the counter, pumping my hand and slapping my back. "How the hell are you, boy? Hank, you remember Ruby's son, don't you? Camden? Lord, what's it been? Ten years now?"

"Something close to that," I reply, smiling back at him as

Hank leans on the counter and takes off his cap, running a hand over his thinning hair.

"Tell you what, son, we still miss your mama something fierce around here," he says, and I can tell he means it. Ruby was a celebrity in this town, their magnanimous benefactor. If people in Tavistock ever whispered about all those husbands, they did it behind firmly closed doors.

No wonder she never wanted to leave.

"I miss her, too," I tell him, and I am surprised to realize that's true. I've spent the past ten years trying not to think about Ruby, and when I have, I've remembered only the bad things.

There was a lot of bad to remember, after all.

But there had also been good. The meals at the Jay. The standing account at the local bookstore, how Ruby encouraged my love of reading and always let me buy any book I wanted. The way she would ruffle my hair and say, *You and me against the world,* whenever Nelle or Howell or Ben was being a dick.

Ben emerges from the shelves with an armload of supplies. A crowbar, tarp, some respirators, and a putty knife. He's still smiling at Hank and Steve, but there are those hard eyes again, and once again, the other men's smiles fade as they study him warily.

"What are you working on today?" Hank asks, nodding toward the supplies Ben's holding, and Ben gives him a broad wink.

"Found those hikers, decided to take care of the cleanup ourselves."

Hank blanches, and, at my side, I feel Steve stiffen slightly even as Ben laughs, loud and long, shaking his head.

"Fucking with you," he says, then turns to me, gesturing behind the counter where, for the first time, I notice a faded flyer bearing the word MISSING. Underneath, there are two blurry, photocopied pictures of a couple of young men in hiking gear, forested mountains rising up behind them.

"It's been a whole thing," Ben explains. "Over the summer, these two dumbasses decided to hike the trail on the east side of Ashby House."

The mountain the house sits on actually has a name—Mount Trossach, after some place in Scotland—but no one in the family ever uses it. Everything up there is discussed in terms of the house, like it's the only landmark that matters.

I know the trail Ben is talking about. It's steep and tough, narrow enough in places that you can barely keep both feet on the mountain, and I have a sudden memory of me and Ben on that trail, years ago, his hands gripping my shoulders, his braying laugh in my ear as pebbles skittered from underneath my boots, and the sky and trees swung dizzily around me, my stomach lurching.

Fucking with you.

He'd said that then, too.

"They found one of their packs, but nothing else, and man, we had people crawling all over the mountain for *weeks*. Nana Nelle nearly had a fit because she could see them from her bedroom window. You were up there, weren't you, Steve? Were you one of the ones Nana called the cops on?"

Steve's face is granite now, and I see him clench and release a fist against his thigh. "Nope, can't say I was. Think they talked to my cousin, though. It was his son that went missing. Tyler."

I wait for something like shame or even embarrassment to color Ben's face, but he just shrugs. "Not the first people to go missing up there, won't be the last," he says. "My dad used to say that it was like the mountain needed a sacrifice every once in a while. Sucks for Tyler, though."

He gives the men another nod. "Anyway, thanks, man. Just put it on my tab. You ready, Cam?"

Ben doesn't wait for an answer, pushing the door open with his hip, the bell overhead ringing.

"Be right there," I call after him, and once the door slams shut behind him, I turn back to Steve.

"How much does he owe?"

Five minutes later, I'm back in Ben's truck, over a thousand dollars put on my Visa, and Steve's last words echoing in my brain.

It's good to have you back in town, he'd said, his voice low and serious. *But if I were you, I'd sleep with one eye open in that goddamn house.*

6/28/2004

Dear Ruby,

Camp is okay, I guess. I like the horseback riding, and tomorrow we start archery. Ben won some kind of award in that last year, so I'm probably going to have to listen to him brag about that all day, but that's nothing new.

I wish you had told me about how much of this place your family owns or bought or whatever? It's kind of embarrassing seeing my last name on so much stuff, and for the first few days, kids kept asking me if we owned this place. I said no, but do we?

There's also a picture of you and your dad in the lodge. I guess you came up here when they opened the swimming pavilion? It says you're "Ruby Woodward," so I thought maybe it was a mistake or something, but then I looked it up on the computers in the library (those are the only good things in there, by the way. All the books are old Hardy Boys mysteries that I've already read, or weird Westerns from the fifties, so if you could send some books, that would be good).

You've been married four times? I only knew about Andrew. I guess it's none of my business, but it was still weird. I asked Ben about it, but he laughed at me and called me a dumbass. (I'm not swearing, I'm repeating a swear someone else said. You can't get mad at me for that.)

I have to go now or I'm going to be late for canoeing. Thank you for the money you sent to the canteen, but please don't send any more because they write your balance on this little sheet behind the counter and everyone can see it. The other guys have like twenty bucks in theirs, and now I have five hundred. Even Ben only has fifty, and one of his friends asked if that meant our family liked me more or something. It sucked (that's not a swear no matter what you say).

I really want to talk when we get home. There was some other stuff about your husbands I saw online, and it kind of freaked me out. You always say we can't have secrets from each other, but I think maybe you just meant *I* can't have secrets from *you*.

Your Son, Camden

From the Desk of
Ruby A. McTavish

March 20, 2013

Isn't it enough that I wasted three years of my life with Hugh
Woodward? Do I *really* have to waste another few hours on
him now, in my twilight years?

Well, I won't do it. Or rather, I'll tell you the important bits,
namely what I learned about myself through Hugh—or, more
specifically, Hugh's death.

I returned from Paris to North Carolina somewhere
between a celebrity and a pariah. Honestly, I hardly remember
anything of the rest of 1961 or the first half of 1962; I spent
most of it in my room at Ashby in a haze of pills. Pills the
doctors gave me, pills Loretta gave me from her own stash,
pills that friends offered when they dropped by, ostensibly
to talk to me, but mostly so they'd have a story for their next
bridge night.

"I saw Ruby, and oh, she just looks *dreadful,* poor thing, I
don't know how she *bears* it."

When something as cataclysmically horrible as your
husband being shot to death on your honeymoon happens,
people are both fascinated and repulsed by you. Fascinated
because, my oh my, *what* a tale, what a juicy bit of gossip
to spend in every dining room and nightclub you enter.
Repulsed because . . . well, what if tragedy is catching? And
such a thing would *never* happen to them, of course. No, they

would've done this or that differently, because in the end, this is probably somehow all your fault anyway.

To be fair, it *was* my fault, but they didn't know that.

So there I was, a widow at twenty-one, a daughter who became a wife, who was back to being a daughter again, ensconced in my childhood bedroom, no one quite sure what to do with me, least of all myself.

I'd envisioned a whole life for myself with Duke, you see. Before the honeymoon, obviously, before I knew just who I had married. But those months of planning the wedding had been some of the happiest of my life up until that point. It's always exciting, living in hope.

Oh, darling, the hopes I had had. My own lovely house in Asheville or maybe Raleigh. New friends, new society, an identity separate from "Baby Ruby," or Mason McTavish's odd daughter. Yes, my family was rich, yes, we basically owned Tavistock, but I wanted something bigger for myself, something that felt uniquely my own.

And that dream, it seemed, had died with Duke.

I managed to go out in society again in August of 1962, when Nelle married that dreadful Alan Franklin, but other than that, I stayed at Ashby, turning down dinner invitations because I knew I was not a guest, but the main attraction.

Once I emerged from my haze, it was nearly 1963, and every time I went into Tavistock, or drove Daddy's Plymouth over to Asheville to shop, I had the strangest feeling that I had somehow aged twenty years in two. Everyone seemed so much younger than me, so much freer.

I wondered if it was my penance, this malaise, for killing Duke.

That was what consumed most of my thoughts those days, Duke's murder. I waited for nightmares to come, for a sudden rush of guilt to prompt me into some drastic action, like throwing myself off one of the bluffs—or, even worse, becoming a nun—but there was nothing of the sort.

Well, not *nothing*. Mostly, I felt empty, a bit numb, and if I'm honest, rather bored. But sometimes when I lay in bed at night, reliving that moment, I felt a strange sort of elation. I'd *done* that. This dreadful, horrible thing, a thing they hanged or electrocuted or poisoned or shot you for doing—I had done it and not gotten caught.

At the time, I thought no one even suspected me, but now I know there were whispers and rumors, which is probably why Daddy turned faintly gray when I mentioned that I might be interested in going back to college, and learning about the law.

That must have been why he decided to bring me so firmly into the family business.

I'm going to tell you a little secret, darling. One you'll eventually find out for yourself, but let me go ahead and spill it now: once you're as rich as we are, you are not really actively doing things that make money. You're not, say, selling a product or providing a service. You had an ancestor who did those things once, and he made so much money that now that money *makes* money. I suppose this is why some countries eventually round up people like us and cut our heads off.

That said, we'd seen families like ours lose everything within a few generations. All it took was one reckless heir, one overindulged new bride, and suddenly you were selling art, selling furniture, off-loading surplus property, and— most offensively to Daddy—selling off parcels of the land you owned.

Would we have gone that way eventually had it not been for me? I really can't say. What I *can* say is that I was the one who'd invested in those three nightclubs, the two in New York and the one in Miami. Not with McTavish money, but with the settlement Duke's father gave me. (Not that he'd wanted to give me one red cent, I should add. But Daddy drove over to Asheville to have *a talk* with him, and next thing I knew, I was a wealthy woman in my own right. Daddy was always very persuasive.)

I took all that money and poured it into the clubs, and also into the stock market. I had an uncanny knack, it turns out, for investing in the right things. Never finished college, certainly didn't keep up with the market all that much, but I picked things I liked the name of. Xerox, for one, which sounded like an alien planet to me. And Caterpillar because I'd always loved catching them and setting them up in little jars as a child, watching them make cocoons on the little branches and leaves I stuck into their habitats.

I hadn't expected either to make me rich, but oh, my darling, did they ever. And soon I was buying up an entire block of Tavistock that Daddy's father had sold years before, and opening the hotel and restaurant.

If I could not, as I'd once hoped, escape the McTavish name, I decided to simply be the best McTavish that had ever been. Within a year of Daddy bringing me into the fold, our bottom line was healthier than ever, and so was I.

It helped, all that business, all that math, all those numbers. They cooled the fevered thoughts in my brain until Duke's murder started to recede, a terrible thing that had happened to—and been committed by—someone else.

It also helped that others around me seemed to start to forget, too. I went to more parties, and no longer thought people were using me as some kind of macabre draw. I went to the cinema with one of my childhood friends, Betty-Ruth, and

drove to Raleigh to visit a cousin where I ended up going to
bed with a man I met at the bar of my hotel.

Slowly but surely, I began to come back to life. To become
Ruby McTavish again, not poor Duke Callahan's widow. (There
was a slight setback in November of 1963 when the president
was killed—since I was the only person most people knew
whose husband had *also* been shot, that made me the closest
thing to Jackie Kennedy that anyone in Tavistock, North
Carolina, had ever seen.)

Enter Hugh Woodward.

Lord. I've just gotten up from my desk and gone downstairs
to brood at the fireplace for an hour because I am *that* loath to
discuss Hugh.

He was Daddy's right-hand man back then, an accountant
who worked his way up until he oversaw all our financial
affairs, and once I went to work for Daddy, not a day went by
without hearing someone say, "Ask Hugh."

That's how it started, actually. I'd been in Daddy's office
in town—he was spending more and more time those days
back at the house, indulging in his twin passions of shooting
random animals and drinking bourbon—and needed to know
why McTavish Limited had spent more than thirty thousand
dollars for something obliquely labeled *L* in the ledger.

"Ask Hugh," said Daddy's secretary, Violet.

"Ask Hugh," said my cousin Shephard, one of roughly a
dozen men in suits who spent time at the office, but seemed to
have no actual job there.

"Ask Hugh," said Daddy himself when I called up at the
house.

And so that's how, on a January morning in 1964, I found
myself knocking on the door of Hugh's office on the second
floor.

I can still remember the way his face turned red when he
saw it was me standing in his doorway, the very tips of his
ears a bright scarlet. I'd seen Hugh before, of course, but never
really thought about him. He was twenty-five years my senior,
and handsome in a bland way—comforting, familiar, will do
in a pinch, but nothing to get all that excited about.

The saltines and tomato soup of men.

So it was a surprise to see those red ears and notice the way
his eyes—a light blue so colorless as to almost be gray, nothing
like Duke's deep green eyes—roamed over me as though he
couldn't believe I was actually there in front of him.

And yes, it was appealing to see myself through such
an admiring gaze. I always made sure I looked nice when I
was in the office, my dark hair held back from my face with
little ivory or tortoiseshell combs, my skirts and sweater sets
expensive, but not flashy, my jewelry tasteful. I had taken
off my wedding ring when I returned from Paris, but I still
had Duke's engagement ring on my right hand, a stunning
cabochon ruby on a simple platinum band, and that day, I was
also wearing elegant ruby studs in my ears.

Later, Hugh would shower me with rubies, including a
ring almost identical to the one Duke gave me, but somehow
nowhere near as impressive.

A fitting metaphor for Hugh himself, really.

"Loretta," he told me when I pointed to the *L* in the ledger,
and then he'd given a sheepish smile. There had been a spot of
mustard on his tie, and though his sandy blond hair was still
thick, I'd seen the slightest hint of pink scalp shining through
when he leaned down to tap his finger against the book.

"Your stepmother comes by every few months with her
bills, and we pay them all at once for her," Hugh had gone on,
and I'd felt my eyebrows creep somewhere near my hairline.

"What on earth has Loretta spent thirty thousand dollars on?"

Hugh shrugged, perching on the edge of his desk. "Horses this time. Some furs, I believe, as well as a new painting for her bedroom, and . . ." Trailing off, he'd studied the ceiling. "A necklace, I think."

I closed the ledger with a snap that made him flinch, but his eyes kept moving over my face, drinking me in, and he said, "I'd be happy to go over the accounts with you sometime. A lot of this stuff is in my own little code."

(His "own little code" was literally just the first letter of whoever was being paid. *L* for Loretta, *N* for Nelle, *AH* when something was purchased for Ashby House. In retrospect, this says more about Hugh than this missive ever could.)

I can't remember how I replied to that. I demurred, I'm sure, because it was weeks before I actually took him up on that offer, and then, it was only because of Nelle.

My sister had married, as I mentioned, and she and her husband, the limp dishrag known as Alan Franklin, had taken up residence at Ashby. Within a few months of their marriage, Nelle was pregnant, and that January in 1964, Howell was born.

He was an ugly baby, if you asked me, which no one did. But he was a boy.

Not just any boy, of course. The first McTavish male heir since Daddy, and oh, how Daddy doted on him, right down to making sure Howell's legal name was Howell Franklin McTavish. He'd take Howell into Tavistock, Howell in one of those ridiculous outfits Nelle always dressed him in that made him look like the tubercular heir to some tiny European country, all smocking and lace and his monogram emblazoned across his chest.

"My grandson!" Daddy would boom, Howell in his arms, little face red, and soon Nelle had a new car, a beautiful and sleek Chrysler that would "be safe enough for the baby." And then her husband, Alan, had a new office in the McTavish building, an office nearly as large as Daddy's. And soon Nelle and Alan had moved bedrooms to one of the larger suites, and one night at dinner, I realized that Alan was sitting at Daddy's left, Nelle at his right, and I was all the way at the other end of the table.

Alone.

That night, I lay in my childhood bed, staring at the ceiling, and those old fears, fears I thought I'd banished years before, began to creep along the walls, sliding in the shadows, slithering up the mattress and into my brain.

He has an heir now. An undoubted McTavish, and a boy at that. What does he want with the cuckoo in the nest?

Before I'd married Duke, I'd dreamed of being more than just Mason McTavish's daughter, but I'd spent the last few years wrapping the McTavish name and fortune around me, and I suddenly found that I was terrified of losing it.

And since we're being honest, I can also admit that a part of me wondered just how much my name and Daddy's money had counted in the aftermath of Duke's death. Had there been phone calls I hadn't known about? Money wired to police stations in Paris, whispered conversations and assurances that had kept me free?

I didn't know, but I was determined to hang on to my position in the McTavish family by any means necessary.

So.

Hugh. A man Daddy depended on above all others. A man who adored me with a kind of simple worshipfulness that was, after Duke, a balm of sorts. A man who, once we were engaged, slid into Alan's office, moving him back to the smaller space on the third floor where he belonged.

We married on an autumn afternoon in the front room at Ashby. No silk gown this time, no five-piece band and glass lanterns in the garden. A smart powder-blue suit, a dry kiss on the lips in front of a judge, and I was a wife yet again.

Mrs. Ruby Woodward.

I was miserable almost instantly.

Hugh wasn't a bad man. Certainly not a dangerous one like Duke.

But he asked me where I was going every time I left a room.

He never wanted me to drive myself anywhere, insisting on taking me himself.

He picked up the extension when I was on the phone to ask who I was talking to.

He blew on my coffee before he handed it to me. "It's too hot, my dove," he'd say, an endearment I loathed. "Let me get it *ju-ust* right."

Now see what you've done? I'd blocked that out until just now—can you blame me?—but here it is in my brain again, Hugh Woodward cooing, "*ju-ust* right."

You can see how it didn't take long for my mind to begin to drift to thoughts of ridding myself of him.

Divorce, you say. And yes, that was an option. But a costly one, because, like I said, Daddy adored Hugh—not to mention relied on him and trusted him implicitly. Which meant there had been no legal wrangling to protect my—and Daddy's—fortune from him. What was mine was his, so say we all.

Hugh wouldn't have wanted the money, exactly. It was me

he was after, but if I were to leave him? I wasn't sure what that devotion might turn into, were it thwarted.

Plus, I had married him to secure Daddy's favor. If I divorced him, I'd be right back where I started—only worse, because now, I would've *disappointed* Daddy.

I did bring it up, vaguely, to Daddy once. We were driving into town, rain pelting down on the car, so heavy we could barely see the road. Earlier that year, one of the handymen Daddy hired to keep up the house had driven down the mountain in just such a storm, and ended up running off the road, his car plunging down the side of the mountain. It took them three days to get to him, due to all the rain, and when Daddy took a curve just a little too fast, I had bitten my lip so hard I'd tasted blood.

It was still on my tongue when I started to talk about Hugh, about maybe marrying too soon, about how you don't really know someone before you start sharing a life together.

Daddy hadn't replied at first, the only sound the steady drumming on the roof, and then he had tapped his fingers against the steering wheel and said, "Hugh's a good man, Ruby. I'd reckon any woman who couldn't make a go of it with him couldn't make a go of it with anyone. Or anything. She wouldn't be the kind of woman I'd have much use for."

I didn't reply because he didn't expect me to, but that put a very neat end to any idea of divorce.

And yet I couldn't see myself pointing a rifle at Hugh's chest and pulling the trigger. He hadn't done anything to deserve that, although the coffee situation does come close.

But there were times when he was on top of me in our bed, my nightgown rucked up, his pajama top still on, when I watched his shadow on the ceiling, moving over me, inside of me, and thought, *Maybe his heart will give out one of these days. It's how he'd prefer to go, probably.*

(A side note: Duke was an amazing lover, and a shit human being. Hugh was a terrible lover, and a . . . well, not amazing, but decent enough person. It seems to me that it should not be that hard to be both good in bed *and* a good man, and yet the vast majority of men never cease to amaze me in their refusal to master this particular skill set. Something to make note of for yourself, perhaps.)

So this is where my head was in the autumn of 1967. Hoping for some accident to befall Hugh, or for some trick of biology to snuff him out, anything that meant I would no longer have to put up with him driving *my* car and singing all the wrong lyrics to songs he didn't actually know on the radio.

It was that car that set the whole thing in motion.

I'd gotten a flat tire on the road up to Ashby House, and managed to limp into the drive, planning on calling a mechanic in the morning.

Hugh, however, had decided to be my knight in shining armor as usual, and went to change it himself.

An absolute comedy of errors.

The jack was in the wrong place and dented the body, lug nuts were spilled not once but *three* times, the hubcap nearly went spinning off the mountain at one point, and then, even though he'd finally gotten the jack in the right position, it slipped just as he'd come out from under the car, one of those missing lug nuts in his hand.

"Oof!" he said cheerfully, looking at the car and the place where, only moments before, his head had been. "Almost found yourself a widow two times over, Roo!"

(I do not need to tell you how I felt about this nickname, or how I felt when I discovered he signed all our correspondence to friends and family, "Love from Hugh-Roo!")

Yes, almost a widow again. Seconds away from finally being free, but despite being the klutziest man alive, Hugh had gotten lucky.

Would that luck hold?

It took awhile, figuring it out. I ginned up and tossed out a million different schemes from a fall during a hike to a swimming mishap, all of them discarded because they required my presence. I could be present for one husband's terrible death, that was one thing. But there when the second one corks it?

Harder to explain.

And then I remembered the barn.

It wasn't really a barn, in that at no point had it ever held animals. It was more an outbuilding that my father had had grand plans for at one time, a place to entertain his hunting buddies and drink while trading war stories. He'd had it wired for electricity, no easy feat, back in 1949, but it was dodgy, and once, when I'd gone out there exploring, I'd found a dead raccoon on the barn's wood floor, its body stiff, tiny droplets of blood on its mouth and nose.

When I'd told Daddy later, he'd nodded and said, "Probably touched the wrong wire."

I hadn't thought about that barn in ages, and had rarely been into the woods surrounding Ashby House since I was a child. Daddy took me on walks and shooting expeditions when I was younger, but I'd never much enjoyed it. I'd always told myself it was the memory of being taken from those same woods that made the trees feel so close, the light seem so far away, but the truth was, being in the wilderness was not my idea of a good time. Honestly, it wasn't until I married Andrew that I started . . .

Well. We'll get to that later.

In any case, when I began to think of the issue of What to Do with Hugh, the barn—and that dead raccoon—came back to me in glorious Technicolor.

I could not ask Hugh to go string lights up in the barn. Obviously.

What I *could* do was start dreamily sighing to others when he was nearby about how I wish Daddy had fixed up the barn, remember how he was going to hang Christmas lights out there? Oh, that would be so pretty. Why, if we had those, it might be nice to hold my and Hugh's anniversary party out there! But no, it was too much work, and who had the time to fuss around with silly little lights in a barn when we could have the party in Ashby House?

I maintain that I did not really kill Hugh Woodward. I had no way of knowing if the plan would work, after all. He might have hung those lights up just fine, or hired someone else to do the job, and I would've had to dance with him under their twinkling glow while he sang "Let Me Call You Sweetheart" off-key in my ear.

I left it to fate.

And fate, once again, was on my side.

-R

Tavistock, North Carolina, doesn't have as much to offer as its nearby neighbor Asheville, but it is a charming slice of Appalachia with a walkable downtown, various shops selling everything from hiking gear to stationery, and a selection of surprisingly good restaurants.

And if it's an Instagram Moment you're after, be sure to head to the square where you'll find a classic gazebo lit up with fairy lights on all sides. The site of many a wedding, the gazebo is surrounded by green lawn, and if you time it just right, you'll get a gorgeous sunset background, complete with the Blue Ridge Mountains rising in the distance.

The gazebo was financed by local philanthropist Ruby McTavish in the 1960s, and a bronze plaque on the floor bears the inscription: *In Loving Memory of Hugh Woodward, Devoted Husband to the End of His Days.*

—*North Carolina Hiking Guide*, 2015 Edition

CHAPTER NINE

Jules

It's wrong that I find this so hot, isn't it?"

I'm standing in the doorway to one of the upstairs bathrooms, leaning against the wall as Cam looks over at me, safety
goggles on, a sledgehammer in his hands. What was once a
1960s-era avocado green toilet is in pieces at his booted feet.

He grins at me, pushing the goggles up. "If I knew smash-
ing outdated fixtures was your kink, I would've torn out that
sink back in Golden."

Ah, yes, the sink. The one in our master bathroom that had
clearly been installed sometime in the mid-eighties and featured
a truly bizarre red swirl in the marble, making it look like Lady
Macbeth had just been washing her hands.

"You couldn't have," I remind him, "because that was a
rental."

His smile fades just the tiniest bit, and I hate it even as something in me wants to cross the bathroom and grab his face and
say, That was never our home, and you knew it. We could've

bought a house, but we never did. You always knew we'd be back here. To claim what's yours.

What's ours.

But that's a little intense for a random Tuesday morning, so instead, I just step forward, kicking a stray piece of green porcelain. "Correct me if I'm wrong, but this wasn't actually one of the bathrooms that was fucked up, right? I mean"—I gesture to the aggressively floral wallpaper—"ugly as sin, but technically functional."

"The man's a machine."

I turn to see Ben just behind me in the hallway, smiling as usual. This morning, he's wearing a pair of dark gray pants made of some kind of waterproof material, hiking boots replacing his usual expensive sneakers. A long-sleeved T-shirt in navy blue brings out his eyes, and I guess there are women who would appreciate how well it clings to his gym-toned torso, but I am definitely not one of them.

"He's already replaced the floors in one of the third-floor bedrooms, and I hear we have a cement truck coming tomorrow?"

Ben has his hands in his pockets as he rocks back on his heels, and a muscle in Cam's jaw ticks as he turns back to his work. "The terrace steps" is all he says, but Ben gives a hooting laugh.

"Shit, Camden. If I'd known you'd go this gung ho, I would've emailed you years ago."

"I would've deleted it."

He would have, I know. For the past decade, any communication with his family has gone straight in the trash, both virtual and real.

Ben chuckles, shaking his head. "Yeah, you would've. Still. Glad you're here now, man."

Cam doesn't reply, but takes another swing at the half-destroyed toilet, and I feel it again, that tug of guilt low in my stomach.

"Mind if I steal your bride for the morning?" Ben asks, and Camden pauses, his knuckles white around the shaft of the sledgehammer.

I turn to Ben, surprised. "What for?"

He gives me a wink, one that I guess is meant to be charming, but just makes my skin crawl. "You've seen Ashby House, and it's impressive, no doubt, this bathroom being an exception. But Ashby's real worth is the land around it. Thought I'd give you a tour."

I bite back a grimace. The land around Ashby is beautiful, I can't argue that, but I like looking at it safely behind these walls. I'm not sure I actually want to go traipsing through the forest that once swallowed up "Baby Ruby."

And it's clear from Camden's expression that he's not too wild about that idea, either.

But I can't think of any reason to object, and besides, I wouldn't mind getting a better sense of what Camden, and therefore *I*, actually own.

"Works for me," I say with a shrug. "Am I dressed for it?"

I'm wearing an old pair of jeans with a lightweight sweater and a pair of Converse sneakers, nothing too fancy, but also nothing too rugged, and Ben takes a little longer than I like looking me over.

"Yeah, we're not gonna venture all that far," he says, and then, looking past me, adds to Camden, "No farther than the falls. Does that sound okay?"

I almost scoff at that. Camden is not in charge of me, doesn't get to say what I do or where I go, but when he doesn't answer Ben right away, I feel my pulse kick up a beat.

We're not in Colorado anymore. We're no longer just a simple English teacher and his wife who works at the local tourist attraction. Here, Camden is a McTavish, the de facto owner of Ashby House, and maybe that means he *could* say no, and Ben would have to accept it. *I* would have to accept it.

I don't know how to feel about that.

But in the end, Cam nods, swallowing hard as he meets my eyes. "Be careful," he tells me, then steps forward, cuffing a hand around the nape of my neck and kissing my forehead. "And stay away from the edge."

"Obviously," I tell him, giving him a light shove, but he's still watching Ben, his expression serious.

Something passes between them that I don't quite understand, but then Ben is turning away, waving at me. "Let's go, Mrs. McTavish!" he calls, and with one last lingering look at Cam, I follow.

THE AIR IS cool as we head out into the woods, autumn creeping up the mountain slowly but surely. It's just a little past nine in the morning, and the sky is overcast, darker clouds gathering over the mountains in the distance. Below us, I can see a few yellowed leaves among the mist, and I shiver, shoving my hands deep into my pockets. Ben is just ahead of me, his stride confident, his chin lifted.

"So—" I start to say, but he cuts me off.

"Do you know how many people have died in these woods?"

I nearly stumble over an exposed root, but manage to right myself just in time, so that when Ben glances back over his shoulder, I'm sure-footed and casual.

"No, but I feel like you are absolutely about to tell me."

A little of the glee bleeds out of his expression, which I appreciate.

"No one actually knows," he says ominously, and overhead something rustles in the trees.

I make myself look as calm and collected as I can, stepping over a muddy puddle in the middle of the trail. "You should probably make up a number, then," I say. "I mean, if you want this campfire scary story bullshit to be effective, concrete details are important. No Girl Scout ever wet her pants over, 'And then this guy had . . . something on his hand. Maybe a hook? Could've been a can opener though. Or maybe he had a hand, but was wearing a weird bracelet that *looked* like a hook.'"

He turns around and fixes me with a glare.

I stop, tucking my hair behind my ears. "I'm just saying, if you wanna be creepy in the woods, I have notes."

We're not that far from the house, close enough that if I glance behind me, I can still see one of the chimneys over the trees, but I'm aware of just how quiet it is, how primeval this forest feels.

Still, I'd die before letting *Benjamin Franklin McTavish* know I'm a little freaked out.

And I must be doing a good job at convincing him I'm unbothered because he stares at me for one more beat before shaking his head. "Camden doesn't deserve you," he says.

"Trust me, it's the other way around," I reply, and he smirks at that.

"Maybe you're right."

More leaves crunch underfoot, the last remnants of the trail slowly merging back into the forest floor, and when I glance to my right, I realize there's a pretty steep drop-off just a few feet away. If you weren't paying close attention, it would be easy to slip right off the side of the mountain, especially with everything so wild and overgrown, the trees so thick together.

"So this trail is only, like, a hundred feet long?" I call out to Ben, and he looks over his shoulder at me, his sunglasses dangling from a cord around his neck.

"Ruby had the trails made and maintained," he tells me. "Or one of her husbands did. Anyway, the money for that kind of thing is Cam's, so maybe take it up with him."

I don't reply, but tuck that information away for later.

We're quiet for the rest of the walk, the only sound our footsteps and the occasional birdcall. I pull out my phone to check how long we've been walking, and see that it's been only about ten minutes, but the three bars of signal I had at the house have dwindled down to one, and when we take a downward turn on the trail, that one bar turns into an X.

For the first time, I realize just how isolated Ashby House really is. Once you're just a few hundred feet away, there's no way to call for help. Even if you could, help would take its time getting up the mountain.

Ben must have seen me check my phone because from just up ahead, he calls out, "I never get why people want to hike up here knowing that if something goes wrong, they're dead. Even when the trail wasn't this fucked up. We timed it once, me and Cam. Back when we were in high school. Hiked down to the falls, then I ran back to the house and called 911, saying Cam had fallen."

I startle, almost tripping again, and Ben is suddenly there at my elbow, steadying me and smelling like expensive body wash and the detergent that clings to all the bedding at Ashby, a slightly sickly mix of sandalwood and vanilla.

"He hadn't, of course," Ben continues, his touch cold even

through my sweater. "But we wanted to test how long it would take before help came."

By now, I can hear the distant rumble of the falls. Hikers went missing up here not too long ago, I know. Camden mentioned it to me the other night, after he came back from town. And I know there have been others who have disappeared in these woods. A family from Kansas back in the eighties. A wannabe commune of hippies around 1970. Some college kid back in the fifties, his body never found after a fall from these cliffs.

Ruby herself, lost in these trees all those years ago.

"Forty-nine minutes," Ben says, his face so close to mine that I can smell the toothpaste still on his breath. "Forty-nine minutes before the ambulance even crested the driveway. Probably at least an hour before it could get all the way out here."

My breath sounds harsh in my ears, and Ben is still smiling, and Camden is only a short run away, but he might as well be on the moon.

"What are you doing?" I hear myself ask, taking a tentative step backward. But I'm not quick enough, because Ben jerks my arm, pulling me up tight against him.

"I did my part," he says, his voice low even though there's no chance of us being overheard. "I got him here. Now, *Mrs. McTavish*. When are you going to do yours?"

March 24, 2013

In my last letter, I said I didn't want to talk about Hugh
Woodward because he was so damn boring. And now we've
come to the least boring man I ever met, Andrew Miller.

I don't want to talk about him, either, but for different
reasons. Sadder ones.

I married Duke out of lust, and Hugh out of obligation, but
Andrew? Andrew, I married for love.

And he loved me, too. I think you can see it in the portrait
he painted of me, the one that hangs over the stairs at Ashby
House. It was a bit of a scandal at the time, that portrait. My
hair down and loose, the hint of bare feet underneath that
Dior gown, that smile on my face.

Of course, I myself was a bit of a scandal by then. While
I'd taken great care to ensure that Hugh's death was a true
accident, it seems you really cannot lose two husbands
prematurely without people beginning to whisper. And not
just strangers. I could have handled that.

No, it was the way I sometimes caught Daddy looking at
me, his eyes dark and sad—so sad—and the way Nelle's mouth
seemed to draw in tighter whenever I entered a room.

She and Alan were having a rough go of it by then. He'd
been sleeping with Violet, Daddy's secretary, and despite
Nelle's insistence that she'd fill the halls of Ashby House with

babies, there was only Howell, a little boy with her light hair, Alan's round face, and my father's temper.

So, as you can imagine, the time had seemed right to take myself abroad for a bit.

Paris was out, naturally, but I decided that I'd like to see the other great cities of Europe that Duke had deprived me of. So I spent a few weeks in Rome, then on to Milan. I'd thought about Madrid next, maybe Barcelona, but then I got an invitation to visit one of my old friends from Agnes Scott, Betty-Ruth. She'd done quite well for herself, marrying a Scottish laird and settling into some medieval fortress in the Highlands, so when she suggested I come stay with them while I was overseas, I leapt at the chance.

A thing about castles: they're actually terribly drafty and cold, and the hallways from the kitchens are so long that by the time food reaches the table, it's barely lukewarm.

My first night there, Betty-Ruth's husband, Hamish, had poured me a generous draft of whiskey and said, "How does it feel to be home?"

I'd been shivering in an uncomfortable armchair that smelled like horses, and I'd looked at him, puzzled. "Home?"

"Aye," he'd said, nodding toward the windows. "Yer a McTavish. They come from not far from here. Just the next glen over."

I had known that my ancestors came from Scotland. Daddy was very proud of that fact, and I'd felt a familiar tug of grief as I thought about how much he would have loved to be here. He had died not long after Hugh, and that was another reason I'd decided to travel, hoping to shake off some of the sadness that had begun to settle over Ashby House.

And so, for Daddy, every morning I put on the ugliest jacket and a pair of Wellingtons, and tried to summon up the appropriate amount of familial pride as I strode around the grounds of Hamish's castle. *I came from these hills,* I would tell myself, waiting to feel some sort of tug, some remembered past deep in my blood.

I must've walked for miles every day, looking for some sign that my ancestors had once called this place home.

All I felt was cold. And vaguely damp.

This is the part where I should tell you that even before I came to Scotland, sometime around Hugh's death, my thoughts had begun to turn, more and more frequently, to that old fear of mine.

That I was not Ruby McTavish at all, but Dora Darnell, stolen from her poor family and raised in the lap of luxury. That the real Ruby McTavish's bones were somewhere in the forests surrounding Ashby House, and that everything that was wrong with me—because once you've killed two men, you really must begin to suspect you're not *quite* right—was because I came from some other, cursed bloodline.

Sometimes, I thought it might be a relief to find out that was the case. Maybe it would explain why, when Hugh had begun to grate on me so, my mind had immediately gone to his death.

Now, I know that nature versus nurture is a subject that fascinates people these days, but I was a rich woman from North Carolina in the 1960s. Our kind didn't exactly stay current on the latest psychological research.

So I only had my own thoughts to consult, and those thoughts were growing increasingly loud when I met Andrew Miller.

He was already fairly well known as a painter then, popular for his relaxed, natural portraits of various aristocrats, and when Hamish mentioned he was coming to stay, I was curious to meet him. I'd never met an artist before, and yes, I was already thinking it might be nice to have him paint my picture.

Andrew arrived on a Saturday, harried because the train had been late, which meant the car sent to pick him up had had to wait, and by the time they made their way up to Hamish's, a torrential downpour had started.

When he and the driver entered, Andrew had mud up to his knees, a hole in his jacket pocket, and his dark hair, streaked with gray even though he was only in his midthirties, was plastered unflatteringly to his face.

What a shabby-looking fellow, I thought, *but that's artists for you.*

When he introduced himself to me, his hand was cold, and I remember thinking that he had the saddest eyes I'd ever seen, and not much past that.

As you can see, a very different first impression than the one I had of Duke, the man I *thought* was the love of my life.

I had no idea this tragic, sodden person in front of me was the real thing.

Darling, you'll have to forgive me, but I have to get through this part quickly or I won't be able to get through it at all.

I tumbled into love with Duke, a violent upheaval that left me breathless, dizzy in its wake.

It was nothing like that with Andrew. I sat next to him at dinner, and he joined me on my morning walks, and we talked about everything and nothing. I told him about North Carolina, and he talked about growing up in Yorkshire and the life he now led in London, surrounded by other artistic types. He mentioned a wife from years ago, when he was barely twenty, how she had gotten tired of the starving artist's life and left him, going back to her family in Glasgow, and oh, darling, how casual I thought I sounded when I asked if there was any woman in his life now.

How relieved I was when he said no.

He offered to paint my portrait, and I said I'd like that.

We talked as he painted, and one afternoon, sitting in the chilly library of Hamish's castle, me perched on that chair in my Dior gown, Andrew studying his canvas, his brush moving so quickly, flecks of green paint dotting his shirtfront, I said, "It must be hard painting my mouth when I'm chatting away like this."

Andrew didn't speak for a moment, focused on the canvas. And then: "I could paint your mouth from memory alone."

He looked up at me with those sad dark eyes, and I felt as though there were an audible *click* when our gazes met. "From my dreams."

What else could I do after that but marry him?

-R

Andrew Miller is the first to admit that he never saw himself "ending up in the wilds of America, married to an heiress. It's like something out of a novel, isn't it?"

He says those words with a slight twinkle in his eye as we walk around the grounds of his wife's family home, the magnificent Ashby House in Tavistock, North Carolina. There is no shortage of natural beauty to be found here, from the pines, oak, and chestnut trees that surround the home to the mist-shrouded views down to the valley floor, and Miller muses that if he were a landscape painter rather than a portraitist, he would never lack for inspiration.

"It changes all the time," he tells me, gesturing at our surroundings. "The light's always shifting, the colors changing. It's fascinating."

I mention his wife, then, Ruby McTavish, and he gives me that same twinkly look as he says, "Oh, she's fascinating, too."

That is one word for it.

Miller is her third husband, her first having been killed in a robbery in Paris on their honeymoon, the second falling victim to an electrical accident here on the grounds of Ashby House.

She and Miller were introduced by Sir Hamish Ogilvy in 1969, and married the next year in a small ceremony in Miller's native Yorkshire. When it came time to decide where to settle as a married couple, Miller says there was no question of living anywhere else but here, in the house Ruby's grandfather built, high above the town *his* father founded, Tavistock.

"I worried I might become bored up here," Miller tells me. "Or lazy. A fatted calf and all that, drowning in excess. But here we are, six years later, and I don't feel as though I'm seconds away from the slaughterhouse.

If anything, this place has been good for me and my work. New faces, new people."

Miller is endlessly interested in people. Who they are, what they think, *why* they think it. Several times in this interview, I feel he's asking me more questions about myself than I am about him, and he admits that his wife teases him about his insatiable curiosity all the time.

In Tavistock, Ruby McTavish is talked about the way some ancient people must have discussed deities— a distant figure, mysterious and unknowable, but benevolent, a magnanimous provider, and when I mention this to Miller, he laughs.

"I assure you, she's flesh and blood," he tells me, and later, when she joins us for tea on the spectacular back veranda of Ashby House, I find her to be surprisingly warm and clearly besotted with her husband.

They're an odd match, the heiress and the painter, but as they sit side by side in matching Adirondack chairs, hands loosely joined, I can see why Miller has said that Ruby "saved my life, really. I'm not sure I fully came alive until I took her hand in that dreary Scottish castle."

Mrs. Miller remembers that moment differently.

"He looked like a drowned rat, and I thought it was no wonder he was an artist. He had that sort of tragic air about him."

Miller laughs again at that, raising her hand to kiss the back of it. "And then the fair maiden rescued me and swept me away to her own castle," he says. "Tragedy averted."

And looking at them there, gazing fondly at one another as the sun sets over the mountain, Ashby House rising behind us, I do indeed feel as though I've stepped into a fairy tale.

A happy ending to believe in.

—"At Home with Andrew Miller," by Ethan Lorimer,
Painter's Quarterly, Autumn 1976

CHAPTER TEN

Camden

It's unreal how quickly I slide back into place here.

A decade of not thinking about Ashby House or the Mc-
Tavishes, a decade of building a whole new life for myself, and
within three days, it's like I've never left.

I'm eating Cecilia's cooking, avoiding Nelle, walking the
woods surrounding the house, driving into town for groceries . . .

It's like there was always a Camden-shaped hole here, just
waiting for me to slip back into.

Jules loves it.

I can see it in her face every day, the way she grins when she
gets out of bed, how eager she is to curl up in that one chair on
the veranda she likes so much and watch the world wake up
around her. She's content to do that for hours, to just take in
the views, or wander the rooms.

I'd been worried about letting her go off with Ben, remembering other hikes through the woods with him, my feet skidding on pebbles, his laugh in my ear.

But Jules had come back with rosy cheeks and a bright smile, proclaiming the hike "exactly what I needed."

If anything, Ben had been the one looking a little spooked, and I'd reminded myself yet again that I had an invaluable ally in my wife.

Today when I go looking for her, I find her in what used to be Ruby's office, sitting on the floor and going through an old photo album.

"I'm snooping," she says, unrepentant, not even looking up, and I laugh, crouching down next to her.

"Well, I hope you're enjoying a tour of Dead White People because I'm pretty sure that's all that's in these albums."

"Au contraire," she objects, flipping to a page near the back. "One very alive Camden McTavish, aged fifteen!"

And there I am, standing next to Ruby in the den. It's Christmas, clearly, the tree stretching up behind us, too tall to fit into the picture. Stockings and tinsel, a crystal glass of eggnog in Ruby's hand, and I look . . .

Happy.

No tight smile, no faking it for the camera. It's a real, goofy smile as I look lovingly at Ruby—I'd grown taller than her by then, and my arm is slung around her shoulders, her head just reaching my collarbone.

I don't remember that picture. Don't remember taking it— hell, I don't even remember being that kid. But there I am, and there's Ruby's neat handwriting on the little card next to the photo with my name and age, just like Jules said.

"I bet Christmas here is something else," she says, her voice gone slightly dreamy.

She's picturing it, no doubt. That same huge tree, the twinkling lights. The snow that falls gently outside, locking the house into its own winter wonderland.

And in that moment, I want so badly to give her the fairy tale. I want to take back every horrible thing that happened here, take back what I did, just so she can have that.

Which is why I almost tell her the truth.

If she knew—if she *understood*—the real reason why I left, then she would see that it was impossible for us to stay. That there was no Christmas at Ashby House in our future, and that was for the best.

The words are right there, so close I can almost hear myself saying them.

But in the end, I just cuff a hand around the back of her neck, pulling her in to kiss her temple before rising to my feet and saying, "I'll leave you to it. But hey. Any embarrassing pictures of me in there, it's your wifely duty to burn them."

"Gonna blow 'em up life-size and hang them all over our room," she singsongs, still flipping through albums, and I laugh as I close the door behind me.

And walk almost straight into Nelle.

She's dressed in green today, another tartan skirt and sweater set, and for the briefest second, I see her expression soften, the hint of a smile turning up her lips.

"Oh," she says, and that near-smile becomes a scowl. "It's you."

She must've thought I was Ben. That had happened when I was a kid, too, and I'd get a glimpse of the Nelle who was actually human. But once she realized I wasn't her own flesh and blood, the persona of the devoted grandmother would promptly disappear.

"It's me," I confirm, and go to step around her, but she plants herself in my path.

"We need to talk about your wife," she says, and I glance over my shoulder at the door I just closed.

"I don't think that we do," I reply, keeping my voice light, though I know she hears the warning underneath, that she sees it in my eyes.

But Nelle is a McTavish, and she doesn't back down. "She's been in every room of this house other than my bedroom, and honestly, I think she'd go in there if she thought she could get away with it. I'm not sure what it is she's looking for, but kindly remind her that she is a guest in this house."

Anger sparks, my pulse picking up, and I shove my hands into my pockets. "I own this house, Nelle," I remind her. "Which means that it's Jules's house, too. She's allowed in any room, in any closet, in any tiny corner of this place she wants."

I wait for Nelle to draw herself up so tightly she squeaks, but instead, she actually smiles a little. Not the warm, indulgent smile she'd let slip when she thought I was Ben, but an ugly, sardonic one. "You sound like my sister," she says, and my anger fades, replaced with a wariness that has me stepping back.

"When she died, I thought I'd never actually be rid of her because I'd always have to deal with you, her little . . . project. The child she molded into her own image. But then you left, too, and finally, I was free. Finally, this house was my own."

Nelle steps closer, her feet silent on the thick carpet. Howell's email may have said she wasn't doing well, health-wise, but there's no sign of that in this moment. Right now, Nelle looks like she's made of solid steel.

"I thought you might come back when Howell died, and I was so relieved when you didn't. Bad enough that I'd lost my only son. The last thing I needed was Ruby's ghost swanning around the place again." She pauses, her face hardening even further. "You should have stayed away, Camden. I think you'll be sorry that you didn't."

As she walks away, I give a long, shaky exhale. "Your threats are improving, Nelle, I'll give you that," I call after her. "Bonus points for being cryptic."

But Nelle continues shuffling down the hallway, ignoring me, and I try to shake off her words as I make my way to the stairs. She was always saying shit like that, glaring darkly across the dining-room table, catching me alone to remind me that I was nothing but trash, an "experiment" of Ruby's. I'd learned to tune it out over the years, but something about this most recent exchange slides between my ribs like a knife, lodging there.

I reach the landing, and without thinking, I lift my eyes to Ruby's portrait.

They're going to hate you. I won't sugarcoat that. Her voice sweet as syrup, that old-fashioned drawl that you'd think people have only in bad movies softening and rounding every vowel. I was sixteen, and we were sitting in the parlor upstairs, the one with the striped sofa, and she had a folder open on her lap, filled with printouts, so many numbers on the pages.

So many zeros.

I don't want it.

She thought I meant the money, and I did, but I also meant that hatred. The McTavishes hadn't tried to hide their belief that I wasn't one of them. But this would make it far worse. This made me a weapon Ruby had decided to wield against them, and there was nothing they could do about it.

Well, I want you to have it, Ruby had replied, picking an invisible piece of lint off my shirt. *And that's all that matters.*

And that's how it had been.

Ruby's sly smile follows me all the way to the kitchen.

Libby is mixing up some viscous green liquid in one of

those little blenders made for that kind of thing, and when she glances over her shoulder at me, I bite back a groan.

This house is something like twenty thousand square feet, how in the *fuck* does everyone in it always end up on top of each other? I should be able to go days without seeing anyone else, but no, just like it was all those years ago, it's as if the house keeps forcing us together, making us bump up against each other until we snap.

"Ben said to get started without him today," Libby calls out over the noise of the blender.

I swing my leg over a stool at the kitchen island, sitting down and pulling out my phone. "Where is he?"

Libby shakes her head, her long hair in loose curls halfway down her back. No polka dots today, but those same white jeans, this time with a white top and a navy sweater, rows of necklaces around her neck, rattling as she turns around.

"He had to drive into town to meet with some lawyer buddy of his. Don't ask me what for," she adds, holding up one hand even though I had not even started to ask. "I could not give a shit."

Again, a distant kind of alarm bell ringing, a queasy sensation that something isn't right. But is it real, or is this place just making me paranoid? It can do that to a person. Even Ruby thought so.

I look back at my phone, scrolling through emails, looking for anything I might have missed from Nathan, my lawyer.

Just in case.

Libby moves around the kitchen, pouring her noxious juice into a pink cup emblazoned with a cursive *L,* before leaning back against the counter, watching me.

I ignore her, my eyes on my phone, hoping she'll go away

now, refusing to cede the space, but Libby can't pass up the opportunity to catch me alone.

"So. Your wife."

I don't reply, my fingers tightening around my phone.

"She's pretty," Libby goes on. "Like, prettier than I thought you could land, if I'm honest."

"Can't disagree with that," I say, still refusing to meet her gaze. I'd been surprised myself at how Jules, with her blond hair and big eyes and gorgeous smile, had wanted me, a skinny, sullen kid pouring beers at a cheap wing place. I'm not as skinny now, and I finally figured out how to style my hair so that I don't look like I'm in the Vienna Boys' Choir, but there's no doubt I'm punching above my weight.

"I guess I thought maybe you didn't like girls or something. But maybe you just like blondes."

I look up sharply and our eyes meet. She's tapping the pink straw of her cup against her lower lip, studying me.

"Does she know—" she starts, and I cut her off.

"Don't."

Maybe it's my voice, low and dangerous even to my ears, or something in the way I'm glaring at her, because Libby shoots me a dirty look, dumping the blender, base and all, into the sink with a clatter, remnants of green juice splattering on Cecilia's clean counters.

"Don't act like it's some big shameful secret, Camden," she says, turning and bracing her hands on the sink behind her. "Because, honestly, if you hadn't been so *weird* about it, everything would've worked out a hell of a lot better than it has."

My gut twists even as I give a shocked laugh because, Jesus, she really *believes* that.

"What do you think would have happened?" I hear myself

say. "We would've gotten married? Lived happily ever after here at Ashby?"

It's such a perverse thought—me and Libby, married, shacked up together in this house—that I can hardly picture it, but Libby must not have that hang-up because she's suddenly crossing the kitchen, she's suddenly standing there in front of me.

"It would've solved *everything*," she replies, her voice almost cracking, and for the first time, I realize that that night—that fucked-up, deeply *wrong* night—might have meant something different to her than it did to me.

"We were kids," I tell her, trying to be gentle, even as my mind fights to push down every memory, every detail. The soft breeze coming through my window, the green-apple scent of her shampoo, the way her hands slid over my skin.

How long I'd let her kiss me, let her touch me, before shoving her away. Seconds, but they lasted an eternity.

"No one's ever said no to me, Camden," Libby says now, her hand resting lightly on my chest, and I can't help but laugh as I cover her fingers with mine.

"I don't doubt that," I tell her. "But . . . fuck's sake, Libby, you're my cousin."

"Not by blood," she says, too quickly, and there's a sudden sour taste in the back of my throat.

"Maybe not, but in every way that matters," I reply firmly. "And besides, you didn't want me anyway."

That part I remember maybe *too* clearly. Pushing her away, even as every cell in my stupid teenage body had wanted to pull her closer, my voice raspy as I'd said, *Your dad will kill me.*

And Libby, gorgeous and naked and all of seventeen, shooting me a look far too old, far too knowing, and saying, *Who do you think sent me in here?*

If Howell wasn't already dead, I'd kill him myself just for

that. For deciding that if he couldn't change Ruby's mind about her will, he'd do whatever it took to make sure his family wouldn't be cut out of it. Including sending his teenage daughter into my room to seduce me.

That was the night I knew I couldn't stay here. That I couldn't be a part of this so-called family any longer.

Libby is still standing in front of me, one shell-pink nail resting on the middle button of my shirt, and as I look in her green eyes, I see something there. Something real.

Something that turns my stomach and breaks my heart all at the same time.

"Who says I didn't want you?" she asks, her voice low. "I mean, you were weird, and you always looked at me like you were afraid I was going to bite you or something, but you were cute even back then. And smart."

She steps closer, so close that I can smell her perfume, feel her breath on my face.

"And you're still cute and smart now," Libby goes on. "And tall. I always forget that you're tall."

Reaching up, she rests her hands on my shoulders, squeezing slightly as I hold myself very still.

"It's just . . . Cam, think how much easier it would've been." Her voice breaks, her eyes searching mine. "You and me? It would've made Daddy happy, it would've made Nana Nelle happy . . ."

"Would it have made you happy?" I ask, and she smiles a little, giving that uniquely Libby shrug.

"It would've made me rich," she says. "And that would've made me happy."

I suck in a deep breath through my nose, and I see Libby's smile start to curve up at the corners as she leans in even closer, her lips almost touching mine.

Stepping back so fast that I nearly overturn one of the bar-stools, I jerk my chin up and away from her mouth. My heart is pounding and there's an acrid taste at the back of my throat as I picture Jules walking in, seeing us, seeing *me*. I've never looked at another woman since the night Jules walked into that shitty bar, and even though nothing about Libby in this moment is tempting, that familiar oily slick of guilt is slithering through me again.

"I'm not the answer, Libby," I say now. "I never was. Find something better."

My words take on a slightly desperate edge as I reach out to take her hands in mine. "You *deserve* better. Fuck this house, fuck this family, fuck the money. Just . . . be *you*. Whatever that is."

I squeeze her fingers, smiling a little, hoping she hears me, and for a minute, I think she might. Her beautiful face softens, her fingers press into mine.

And then a smirk twists those symmetrical features, her lips pinching together in a way that brings Nelle to mind. "Oh, Camden," she purrs. "That's beautiful! Maybe save it for someone who needs a fucking Hallmark card, hmm?"

She pivots away sharply, her sandals smacking on the tile.

"Libby," I call after her, but she just throws one hand up, dismissing me.

"You had your chance, Camden," she calls out as she heads through the massive arch leading into the hallway. "Remember that."

Her footsteps echo, then fade, and eventually, I hear the front door open and slam shut.

Sighing, I go over to the sink, picking up the base of the blender and setting it on the counter before turning on the hot water to wash the container.

There are other dishes in the sink, and I wash them methodically. My hands are moving, but my brain is far away.

I don't know how long I stand there, the water running, steam curling around me.

I should've left that night and never returned. I probably could've saved myself then. I wasn't a teenager anymore, old enough to live on my own. If only I hadn't let Ruby call me back that last time . . .

My cell phone rings, pulling me out of my daze, and I shut off the water, drying my hands on the back of my jeans before picking up the phone, glancing at the name on the display.

Nathan.

My lawyer.

I'd left a message with him earlier about making an appointment to go over some paperwork, so it's probably just that, I tell myself, answering the call.

But there's a heaviness in my gut that tells me it's something else.

And my gut, it turns out, was right.

OOH LA-LA LIBBY!

It's easy to forget Elizabeth Eleanor "Libby" McTavish is North Carolina royalty when you step into her boutique in Tavistock, North Carolina. The unassuming heiress is wearing jeans with a vintage T-shirt showcasing the cover of Lara Larchmont's *Aestas* album, and her feet are charmingly bare save a bright coral polish on her toenails and a silver ring winking from her pinkie toe.

But spend a few minutes in the magnetic twenty-seven-year-old's company, and you quickly realize she is breathing rarified air.

"I found this in Indonesia, isn't it *divine*?" she'll say, holding up a gorgeous batik blanket, and that will lead into a thirty-minute conversation about her second honeymoon in Bali.

While the marriage didn't last long, Libby is not one for dwelling on disappointments. "I really think you have to make your own way in the world, and that means you'll sometimes make mistakes. I'm just thankful my family gave me that grace."

Her family is, of course, the legendary McTavishes of Tavistock, her notorious great-aunt Ruby the much-married "Mrs. Kill-more" of tabloid legend, but Libby doesn't like to focus on scandal.

"Aunt Ruby was a Girl Boss before we knew what that was," she tells me. "People forget that it wasn't just her dad's money, or her husbands'. She was *super smart*. She made her own way. And I think, in my own little way, I'm trying to do the same. Honestly, if she were still alive, I think she'd be really proud of me."

No doubt she would, although unfortunately, no members of Ms. McTavish's family were available for comment by the time this interview went to press.

—*Southern Living,* February 2022

CHAPTER ELEVEN

Jules

So, I guess I have some explaining to do, huh?

I know, I know. It looks bad. Me on that trail, Ben revealing I was the reason he asked Camden to come home. The heavy implication that I'd promised something in return.

Second-act plot twist, your heroine is actually a potential villain.

But I'm not, I swear. Everything I've done, everything I'm *doing,* is for Cam.

Yes, I want this house. And yes, I'm not the kind of person who willingly turns their back on hundreds of millions of dollars. (Are you?)

I'm not as good a person as Cam is. He can reject all of that because he knows the strings that come with it are too tightly knotted, but what he doesn't understand is that we can cut those knots.

Together.

It's just . . . I couldn't ask him myself.

It would've broken something inside him, knowing I wanted him to walk back into this place. It had to be someone else, someone he already hated, who pulled him back in. Once we were at Ashby House, I could handle the rest.

But that first part? Getting one of the McTavishes to reach out?

I'm not going to lie, that was tricky.

Like I said, when we first got married and decided to leave California, I thought Cam might choose that moment to return home. And when he didn't, I thought, *Maybe that's for the best*, and I tried to put all thoughts of Ashby House out of my head.

I really did.

Yes, I kept up the Instagram stalking, and I might have set a few Google alerts for anything McTavish or Ashby House related, but I told myself to let it go. To let Cam live the life he wanted, a life where we were happy—if not Living in a Gorgeous Mountain Estate Happy.

And then, a few months ago, Howell died in a car accident.

I found that out thanks to one of those Google alerts, and I waited for Cam to mention it. Waited for some kind of summons from North Carolina. There would have to be a funeral, right? The whole family would gather to mourn the McTavish patriarch. It would be the kind of thing Camden couldn't refuse.

But he never said a word. Honestly, I wasn't even sure he knew Howell was dead.

This probably isn't much of a defense, but I want you to know, I *did* wait at least two weeks before I finally opened Cam's laptop when he was at work and searched his email for any communication from his family. Anything that might clue me in as to whether Camden had even been contacted about his uncle's death.

That's when I found the email Howell sent, just a few nights before he died. Yes, it was full of drunken assholery, but Cam hadn't deleted it, and I'd started to wonder: if the same request—to come home, to sort out the financial tangle they were all trapped in—came from someone more reasonable, someone who didn't write the first email I'd ever read that actually *smelled* like Johnnie Walker Black, would Cam heed it?

It was a risk. A big one.

But like I said, I'm a quick learner.

I knew reaching out to Nelle was out of the question—I was going to have to play this carefully, and enlisting the help of a septuagenarian whose only online presence was a listing in her church's directory and one blurry Facebook photo from something called "A Cake Bee" was not going to get this done.

I considered Libby for a long time. For one, she was very online and very easy to contact. For another, we're close in age—we even look a little bit alike—and I thought that might make it easier to build some kind of kinship with her. But there was always something about her, some slyness in her expression, something about all the jobs, the vacations, the flightiness, that made me think I couldn't trust her.

And of course, there were the exclamation points. Couldn't risk Camden seeing an email with the subject line, JULES AND LIBBY'S SUPER SECRET PLAN!!

So in the end, Ben was really the only choice. But he was also the right one.

Ben wasn't quite as hard-core as Libby when it came to social media, but he was on there, and it didn't take very much scrolling to see that almost everything he posted had a common theme.

A picture of him in the woods, hiking poles planted firmly on either side of him, his teeth glowing, and a caption reading,

*Nothing like hiking in your own backyard! #TavistockNC
#AshbyHouse #RootsWhereIStand #BothMetaphoricalAndLit
eral #lol*

A long Facebook post about some hardware store in Tavistock, reminding us to "shop local," and "when my great-great-
grandfather" this, and "being a steward, not an owner," and,
I shit you not, the word "ancestral" used three times in two
paragraphs.

Over and over again, from his handles—@McTav on Twitter, @McTav_2 on Instagram, @TavistockedAndLoaded on Tik-
Tok, where he exclusively posted videos of Tavistock and Ashby
House—to his online bio at the law firm where he worked (Benjamin McTavish resides in the iconic Ashby House), it was clear
that being a McTavish was maybe the most important thing in
Ben's entire life.

How it must sting, knowing that the name was the only
thing he could really lay claim to.

Once I knew the bait to use, dangling the hook was easy.

And that's why Ben thinks I'm on his side. That I'm going to talk Cam into taking some kind of reasonable settlement from the trust and turning over the rest of it—the house,
the bulk of the money, whatever else comes with this kind of
life—to the McTavishes. Ruby's *actual* family. Everyone gets
what they want, or so Ben believes. Camden gets his freedom,
I get some money, and they get to keep Ashby House, and preserve the McTavish legacy.

But as you and I both know, I'm playing for the whole
thing.

This is why I wanted you to understand that I really do
love Camden. This isn't *just* about the money. This is about us
taking back what belongs to him and living the life we deserve.

Yes, *we*. Because I deserve this shit, too.

I grew up in a trailer park in Panama City. I've dug in the seats of my car for spare change to pay for hamburgers at Mc-Donald's. I've gone without running water for a week so that we could keep the power on in the summer.

I've watched the Nelles and the Libbys and the Bens from the fancier suburbs drive by in nice cars, spending money like they'll always have it.

So, yeah, fucking sue me: when I found out the man I was married to had access to that kind of wealth, but wouldn't touch it because the family who adopted him was a bag of dicks?

I thought, *Fuck that,* and tried to figure out how to fix it.

That was a lot of swearing, but this topic always gets me heated. Camden is worth a thousand of them, a genuinely kind and decent person. Ruby McTavish saw that, and I'd wager she saw what her family was, too (though she probably wouldn't have called them a bag of dicks). That's why she left Camden everything. She saw what I see in those different-colored eyes every time I look at him—someone worthy. Someone with integrity.

That's not me. Like I said, I'm not that great of a person. Lying, scheming, sins of omission . . . I didn't major in theater for nothing. But that's why Cam and I are so perfect together.

He makes me feel like more than some Florida trailer park trash, like I'm every bit as shiny and good as he is. But he needs me to do the harder things, the shady things, the *necessary* things. Things that might tarnish his shine.

So, are we good? Do you get it?

Because right now, I have some shopping to do.

When Camden came back from town the other day, he told me it was looking "down in the mouth." I could tell that it bothered him, the idea of his hometown drying up, but to me? The girl from Shady Palms Trailer Park near Tallahassee?

Tavistock seems pretty goddamn idyllic. It's like every small town from a Hallmark movie, but on speed. Vaguely Bavarian buildings, a whole section of the main thoroughfare that's closed to traffic and is pedestrian-only, and more places to buy LIFE IS GOOD T-shirts than any town probably needs.

I love it immediately.

I wander for a while, stopping into a bookstore, a stationery place. I pick up a journal for Cam, and a pretty plaid scarf for me, the kind of thing I can see myself wearing on foggy mornings, driving down from the mountain in my brand-new Mercedes SUV, picking up coffee, tipping extravagantly, hearing people say when I leave, "That's Mrs. McTavish. She owns Ashby House."

Oh yeah. If this works out the way I want, I will *happily* change my name and become Mrs. McTavish.

I pass by Libby's shop, but there's a CLOSED sign hanging on the door. Not surprising since she was still at the house when I left, collecting an assortment of powders and freeze-dried vegetables to make a green juice.

However, after grabbing a quick lunch at a crepe place near the square (a crepe place! By the *square*! This town is officially a *Gilmore Girls* Wet Dream), I duck into another shop and am surprised to see Libby, leaning against the counter, talking to the guy at the register.

She straightens up when she sees me, and I give a little wave, unsure of the proper decorum for running into your husband's bitchy cousin in public.

But Libby gives me a bright smile and totters over in her nude platform heels. "Taking in the sights?" she asks, and I nod, holding up my bags.

"And supporting the local economy. It's a gorgeous place."

"Mmm," she hums. "There was basically nothing here until my great-great-grandfather built it."

She takes a long slurp of her iced coffee, and I nod even though I know that's not true. I've read up on the history of Tavistock, and there was a little village here before Angus McTavish showed up. It wasn't much, just a series of ramshackle cabins, but still. There were people who called this place home, and it was a place that mattered to them, that belonged to them.

That would obviously mean fuck all to Libby.

"Honestly, it's kind of weird when you think about it," she goes on. "Like, because my great-great-grandfather did something over a hundred years ago, I don't really have to do anything, you know?"

I look into her eyes, trying to figure out if she's fucking with me. Is she really *this* out of touch, or is she just being sar—

"Then again, I guess it's also weird to have a great-great-grandfather who did nothing, so your best bet is marrying some guy who was a charity case to a rich old lady, huh?"

Well, there's that question answered.

She winks at me, chewing on the end of her straw. "See you back at the house."

She glides out of the store, and I take a second to pull out my phone, open up Instagram, and unfollow LaLaLibby.

I don't need that information anymore anyway.

I turn to leave, but before I can a woman approaches, almost nervously. "Hi?" she says as though it's a question. "Are you . . . you're Camden's wife, aren't you?"

After Libby's bitchery, this woman's kind eyes are a balm, so I'm probably too enthusiastic as I reply, "Yes! Hi!"

She rolls her eyes in exaggerated relief. "Okay, I thought

that must be you. I hadn't seen you before, but you were talking to Libby, and we heard he was back in town, so—"

"Logical assumption." I nod. "I'm Jules."

"Beth. Lord, Camden McTavish. I thought he was *never* coming back."

I don't miss the way Cam's name sounds in her mouth or the way her expression brightens. It doesn't bug me—look, you don't marry someone who is cute, tall, and comes from money, and not expect other people to have noticed those same attributes—but it's also jarring. A reminder that Cam had an entire life here before me, that he'd forged connections I know nothing about. For most people, this wouldn't be such a revelation, but Cam has always seemed to me like someone who just sprung to life fully formed. I'd liked that about him, honestly. We were both orphans, we both understood what it was like to feel alone in the world. We were the couple with no one but a handful of coworkers at our courthouse wedding. We'd never celebrated a holiday that wasn't just the two of us.

I guess I've gotten used to never having to share him with his past.

"He was always quiet," she goes on, "but nice. Guys who had way less reason to brag than he did could be arrogant pricks, you know? But Cam was sweet. Maybe it's because he was adopted into all that money or something, I don't know."

"He's still quiet," I tell her. "Except when UNC makes it to the Sweet Sixteen. And nice. No exceptions there."

"Good," she says, nodding, and then she looks around before leaning in, lowering her voice.

"Between you and me, Camden is the best thing that ever came out of that family. Whole town knows it. I think if you two decided to stay, we might throw a parade."

I laugh. "Always love a parade."

"And," she adds, her voice a whisper now, her dark eyes bright, "if you threw every other member of that family out on their tails? Well, hell, girl, you'd probably get a statue in the town square."

It feels like fate. Providence. A sign from God.

See? *This* is why we had to come back. It's not just about us, it's a whole *town* that would be better without the rest of the McTavishes lurking around.

So how can anything we do to make that happen be bad?

I head back up to Ashby House later in the afternoon, stopping by the little grocery store at the base of the mountain for a few things first.

When I pull up in the drive, the sun is low in the sky, a glow settling in over everything, the gray stone gone fiery orange.

I'm practically skipping inside, paper sacks in my arms.

Camden is in the kitchen when I come in, and there's something about the set of his shoulders that makes me wonder if he had a run-in with Nelle. I tense up, too, waiting for him to say something, waiting for the questions, but instead, he just comes over to take one of the sacks from my arms, pressing a quick kiss to the side of my head.

"There's my girl. Thought about sending out a search party."

Whatever it is that's bugging him, it's not about me, and I breathe a silent sigh of relief.

"I met an old friend of yours today," I tell him, my tone teasing as I set my bag down near the sink.

Hands on the counter, arms spread wide, Cam raises his eyebrows. "Oh? Who?"

"Beth? Dark hair, shorter than me. Really good skin."

Cam screws up his face for a second, thinking, and I shoot him a wry look.

"Killer body despite dressing like a third grader."

His expression clears, and he nods. "Bethany Sullivan."

Rolling my eyes, I toss him a bag of brown rice. "I thought that detail might jog your memory."

"You don't need to buy things."

I swear to god, Nelle must be made of bone dust and Shalimar perfume because I never hear her enter a room, and yet there she is, just inside the kitchen.

"Cecilia purchases all our groceries," she goes on, and I make myself smile brightly at her. Another tartan skirt today, I notice, but a red cardigan this time.

"I figured I'd just pick up some stuff while I was in town."

"But it's not necessary."

"But I wanted to."

"I see why Camden chose you," she says, and it is definitely not a compliment. Her eyes are too mean for it to be anything other than a put-down.

Luckily, I have plenty of experience with mean.

"Because I don't take any shit?"

Her mouth purses. I'm not sure if it's the attitude or the four-letter word that bothers her, or maybe it's both. Maybe it's me.

In any case, she gives another one of those haughty sniffs.

"Ben wants us to have dinner as a family tonight in the formal dining room," she informs us. "We have business to discuss. Camden, I trust you remember the dress code."

"Didn't exactly pack a suit, Nelle."

Holy shit, this is a formal-dress-for-dinner household? I guess I probably shouldn't be surprised, but still.

"You and Benjamin are close enough in size. He'll let you borrow something of his."

Her gaze turns to me. "And Libby can find something for you, I'm sure. I'll tell her to bring something to your room. Seven o'clock. On the dot."

She starts to leave then and I turn to pull a face at Cam. "On the *dot*," she says again, but he's already turning away, and as he does, I see something in his face I've never seen before.

Fear.

March 25, 2013

Andrew understood people. More than that, he *saw* them. Better than they could see themselves, I think. It's what made him such a brilliant artist. There's a reason his portraits still hang in all those museums even when the subjects themselves weren't always particularly interesting people. But Andrew *made* them interesting because he could recognize something in them that no one else could. You see it in the portrait he painted of me, I think.

I'd felt so remote at that point in my life, cut off from normal society, an island of a woman whose head was filled with far darker thoughts than anyone guessed. But Andrew saw that there was still something human inside of me, something warm and worth loving.

And he did love me. He loved me so much.

So you can see where I thought he might understand.

Ten years is not all that long to be married to someone in the grand scheme of things. Nelle and the Dreadful Alan were married for forty-two years, a worse punishment than even I would've dreamed up for her, but still, a marriage people would point at and say, "That's a lifetime together."

But those ten years with Andrew *felt* like a lifetime. In the best way.

They were the happiest ten years of my life.

I wasn't used to happiness, and certainly not happiness that lasted so long. It made me soft. Stupid.

Worst of all, it made me think I was safe.

It was 1980. I had just turned forty, an interesting point in a woman's life, the age at which she finally begins to feel like she might have finally become the person she was meant to be. I certainly felt that way.

Daddy had died not long after Hugh, just a few months later, and if he harbored any suspicions about Hugh's death, they weren't strong enough to make him change his will. McTavish Limited was mine, every holding, every investment, every zero.

Oh, Nelle got a lovely little nest egg, thanks to money Mama had put in trust. It was certainly enough to keep her happy for all her days, but when was Nelle ever happy? Besides, it was never the money that she cared about. It was the house, and that—every brick and board of it—belonged to me.

Daddy had put a caveat in the will that Nelle could never be cast out of Ashby House, that she was entitled to live there for the rest of her life. Still, I'd assumed that, with him gone and me and Andrew firmly installed, my sister would take Mama's money and buy her, Alan, and Howell their own place.

I'm very rarely stupid, my dear, but when it comes to Nelle, I somehow always underestimate what a goddamn pill she can be.

She stayed on at Ashby, her and her horrid little family. By that winter of 1980, Alan was hardly ever around. He'd moved on from Violet to some other woman in town, and we all pretended he was busy with work. Howell was sixteen and had already crashed the gorgeous little Corvette Nelle bought him for his birthday, crushing it against a tree just at the base of the mountain. Wonder he didn't break his fool neck, and in my darker moments, I often thought, *Not a wonder. A shame.*

But none of it was all that bad because I had Andrew.

He had a way of turning all these irritations and frustrations into funny little anecdotes. Oh, god, his impression of Nelle was a thing to behold! He could get that way she holds her mouth *just right*. And he was so good at poking fun at Alan's cheerful blandness, Howell's teenage entitlement, and things that would usually aggravate the fire out of me became things that, through Andrew's alchemy, were funny.

He was the one who made me love the woods around Ashby as well, those woods I'd always had such a distaste for. But holding Andrew's hand, seeing the leaves and the trees through his eyes, I fell in love with the land that surrounded my home. I even had new trails made, and we would wander them together, cut off from everything but each other.

You and me against the world, he would sing underneath his breath sometimes.

And so it was.

That's how it felt that night in 1980, curled up on the sofa in the den with Andrew, watching the fire crackle in the fireplace. It was January, a wet mix of sleet and snow pattering against the windows. Andrew had one arm around me, idly stroking my hair, the other holding a book, one of those spy thrillers he always loved. I didn't want him to lift his other hand from my hair, so every once in a while, he would murmur, "Turn," and I'd reach up and turn the page for him, both of us amused every time, him joking that who would've thought a poor Yorkshire lad would one day have the lady of the manor flipping pages of a book for him.

I don't believe in an afterlife—I'm sure you can understand why such an idea is abhorrent to me—but if there is a heaven, and through some mix-up of celestial paperwork I actually got to go there, this moment is where I'd want to spend eternity. Andrew's hand on my hair, the fire before us, the snow outside, the crackle of pages turning and his soft chuckle in my ear.

"How's your book?" I asked.

"Horrible," he replied. "I've counted at least three plot holes, and the author has had to describe blood so often that he's beginning to run out of synonyms for 'red.' I expect the next death to involve the word 'vermilion' at this rate."

"And you're loving it."

"Very much."

I smiled and settled back against his side, and to this day, I can't say what made me say what I said next.

"When Duke died, I thought his blood looked almost black. But it was dark and there was so much of it."

Andrew's hand stilled on my hair, but the words kept coming out of me. "That's why I can never read those thrillers of yours. They never seem to get it right. What it feels like, what it looks like, when someone dies violently. How much blood there is, the sounds they make. When Duke died, there was this rattling noise in his chest like nothing I'd ever heard before, but in those books, it's always silent."

I sat up then, looking at him, and he watched me with his sad eyes, interested, but not alarmed.

Not even when he said, "I thought Duke was already dead when you found him."

And so I told him.

It was—more or less—the same version of events I told you, so you can go back and reread that letter if you want to. I can't imagine what your face looked like as you learned the true story of Duke's death, but Andrew's never changed. I waited for shock or horror to sink in, for those dark eyes I loved so much to shutter closed to me, but he just listened and when I was done, he leaned over, his hand a warm weight on the back of my neck as he kissed my forehead.

"You brave girl," he murmured, and it cracked something open inside me.

Not a monster. Not a murderess, a liar, a lunatic.

Brave.

The love I felt for him overflowed from that crack in my heart, the understanding in his face a balm I hadn't known I needed, and I felt almost drunk with gratitude, with the freedom that came from saying it all out loud.

Like I said.

Soft. Stupid.

Stupid enough to get greedy, to want that same love and understanding poured over Hugh's death as well, for both of my darkest sins to be washed clean.

If I hadn't been so giddy with the relief of it all, maybe I would've found better words or known to soften the story. But it felt so good, you see, spilling all this darkness into a welcoming vessel, and so I didn't catch the shock—the horror—that I had been waiting for when recounting Duke's death slowly slide into his eyes as I described Hugh's.

I didn't notice how the fingers of his left hand, resting on the back of the couch near my head, began curling tightly inward like he was afraid he might touch me accidentally.

I didn't realize I'd lost him until it was too late.

The silence stretched between us once the story was over, and he tried to smile at me, but it wobbled on his face. He cleared his throat and said, "What things to keep in your heart."

Then he sat back, his book sliding off his lap and hitting the floor, pages bending. He didn't pick it up. He only rubbed a hand over his mouth, and muttered, "What things to keep in mine."

I knew then that he'd never tell anyone.

I want you to understand, that's not what I was afraid of. I didn't think he'd go running to the police or the press. I didn't think he'd leave me, either.

Honestly, I *wish* he'd done either of those things. That would've been better. It would've been easier.

Instead, we went on as before, like nothing had changed, but everything had, of course. I'd catch him watching me, and the look in those eyes that I loved so much—the very first thing I had noticed about him—became worse than any prison sentence. Worse than a hangman's noose.

I hope you never have to watch the one person you love most in the world, the person who loves you just as fiercely in return, lose that love, day by day, bit by bit, a steady draining away until there's nothing left. Until they're just a person who sleeps inches from you at night, and eats meals across a table from you, and reads books at your side, even smiles at you or laughs with you, but whose heart has shut you out forever.

Andrew was a good man. Truly. I think he loved me very much, and even after he knew the worst of me, he still *wanted* to love me. I think he tried.

But he couldn't.

And if he couldn't, I realized, no one could. No one ever *would*.

I waited for him to leave me. I would've let him go. I want you to understand that, before we get to this next part. If Andrew had only left, if he'd only told me he couldn't stay married to me knowing what I'd done, I would have signed any papers he wanted, given him all the money in the world.

But he didn't leave.

Not physically, at least. Spiritually, emotionally, mentally . . . oh, he left me in those ways. But he stayed in the house, stayed my husband, and the longer that went on, the more unbearable it started to feel.

Even now I ask myself why he stayed. I've had over thirty years to wonder over it, and I think he was waiting to get past it. To love me again. Or maybe that's just what I want to believe.

At the time, however, those darker thoughts crept back in. Duke had wanted my money and my body and my fear. Hugh had wanted some idealized version of me, a woman on a pedestal. Andrew had, I believed, wanted me for me. But what if I'd been wrong? What if it was the money, the easy life in Ashby House, the heightened attention on his art that came from being the husband of a wealthy woman?

When I first started slipping the ant killer into his morning tea—just the smallest amount, never enough to kill—I didn't actually want him to die. I just wanted to bring an end to the torture for us both.

Surely, he'd realize what was happening, and he would tell someone. Part of me even hoped he'd call the police, and I'd be forced to face some punishment for my sins. At the very least, he'd finally leave me, end the charade that we were both stuck in.

As he got sicker, thinner, I waited. For him to drive down that mountain and never return, to tell someone what I'd done to Duke and Hugh, what he now thought—what he must have known—I was doing to him.

But instead, I watched Andrew sit there in Dr. Donaldson's office, nodding as he said the symptoms might be from all the years of exposure to his paints and their chemicals. Or, perhaps it was some kind of rare infection, or an autoimmune disease they had yet to detect. There were all kinds of ideas and theories thrown his way, charcoal tablets prescribed, sleep studies scheduled, and never once did Andrew say, "Or, perhaps my murderous wife is killing me."

Not once.

I've never understood that. Even when he was retching in agony, even when I got more and more reckless—with bigger doses in his lukewarm tea and oatmeal, the only things he could keep down—he never said a word, never took those fucking tablets that might have saved him.

He just looked at me with those sad eyes of his, and I wanted him to die and I wanted him to live and I wanted someone to stop me, to march into Ashby House with handcuffs, a straitjacket, even, and finally—*finally*—put an end to it.

But no one ever did.

The worst thing, the thing I can't even bear to think about all these years later, is that, in the end, I stopped.

No more ant killer, no more tea or oatmeal. Andrew had proven to me that he was loyal, that even if he didn't love me anymore, he couldn't bring himself to hate me despite all I'd done to him.

But it was too late. His kidneys, his liver, they'd endured too much damage over that long year.

The longest year of my life.

Andrew died on another wintery night, late December of 1980, snow falling outside, as soft as his final breath.

No rattle this time. Just a gentle sigh, then nothing more.

How unfair I'd been to all those novelists and their quiet deaths.

There was no autopsy because I said I didn't want one, and by that point, what I wanted, I got, at least where Tavistock County was concerned.

Harlan Jackson Sr. took my check and patted my hand, telling me he'd handle everything.

Judge Claybourne was so appreciative of my donation to his reelection campaign.

The town was grateful for its new arts center the following year, Andrew's name emblazoned above the doors in metal letters.

My home and my name closed around me, protecting me, shielding me, their queen in her castle who was secretly the dragon.

Well. Not a secret any longer, is it, my darling?

Not to you.

-R

CHAPTER TWELVE

Camden

There are plenty of rooms in Ashby House that are comfortable. Cozy, even. The den is fairly modern with its earth-toned furniture and cream-colored rugs. There's a sitting room in the east wing that actually has a flat-screen TV and a couple of gaming systems from when Ben and I were kids. And the kitchen was totally renovated to Cecilia's specifications right before Ruby died.

But Ashby's formal dining room hasn't changed since 1904, and as I take my seat next to Jules at the teakwood table Ruby's grandfather had shipped over from what was then Siam, I find my eyes landing on all the other bits of McTavish family history in this room.

There's a black lacquered sideboard holding crystal bottles of expensive liquor that even Howell had never dared to touch without Nelle's or Ruby's blessing. The walls are covered in silk, deep green with a swirling gold pattern, and the chandelier overhead glimmers, despite the cobweb I can see clinging between several of the crystals.

At one end of the room is a huge bay window, but it's too dark to see the view outside, so I find my eyes drifting to the painting that hangs on the opposite wall. It's a hunting scene, featuring gently rolling fields and men in jaunty red jackets. It would be positively serene if it weren't for the deer in the foreground, getting its throat ripped out by hounds.

I hated that painting as a kid, always wondered why anyone would hang it in a room where people eat, but it feels appropriate tonight.

I'm that deer, and as the other McTavishes settle around the table, I have no doubt they're the hounds.

Jules reaches over and takes my hand where it rests on the table, giving it a little shake. I make myself give her a quick smile, squeezing her fingers in return but, in truth, I can hardly look at her.

Libby had done as Nelle asked, and sent up a dress in a heavy black garment bag. I'd assumed it would be typical Libby— bright, probably sexy, maybe a little *too* sexy for a family dinner—and had braced myself for the weirdness of seeing my wife dressed like my cousin.

And then Jules had come out of the en suite.

"What do you think?" she'd asked, standing in the doorway to the bedroom, her arms held out to her sides. "Fancy enough for family dinner?"

She looked beautiful—she *was* beautiful—but the words had frozen in my mouth, and Jules had laughed.

"Wait, so good you're literally stunned speechless?"

"Clearly," I'd said, shaking my head ruefully and taking her hands, kissing her forehead, and thinking, *Libby, you sick bitch*.

Jules would've fit into one of Libby's dresses easily, but that's not what Libby brought her. No, Libby gave her one of Ruby's old dresses. Not just any dress, either, but one of her favorites, the one she most often wore when we did these dinners when I was growing up. She'd had it made in the late sixties and was always so proud that it still fit so well.

Same figure at twenty-eight and sixty-eight, she'd preen, throwing a look to Nelle, who always glowered back, her own body thinner, more wizened as she aged.

It's a gorgeous dress. Even now, from the corner of my eye, I can see the way the chandelier sparkles off the crystal beading along the neckline, how the color of the fabric—not white, not beige, something Ruby called "candlelight"—makes Jules's skin glow.

But it just adds another layer of unreality to the scene. I'm back in Ashby House, back at this table, back with these people, and my wife is wearing my dead mother's dress.

Christ, I hate this family.

They're all seated now, Nelle at the head of the table where Ruby used to sit, Ben at her right hand, where Howell always sat, Libby on the left.

Ben is cheerful, his tie loose and shoulders relaxed. Nelle is almost smiling, which, in her case, means she's not actively scowling. Only Libby seems a little unsettled, her eyes darting again and again to the sideboard, her nails drumming the edge of the table.

I wonder if she feels guilty for the stunt with the dress, but guilt is not something I've ever known Libby to be familiar with. She's probably just bored.

Still, that sense of unease lingers, potent as the smell of the gardenia-scented candles lit in the sconces on the walls.

"Ben, why don't you pour the wine?" Nelle suggests, and he gets up to do just that. As he fills each of our glasses with a rich cabernet, I watch Nelle, sitting proudly in Ruby's place.

How she must love this, queen of the castle at last.

"That contractor come by today?" Ben asks, and it takes me a second to realize he's talking to me.

"He did." I take a sip of wine. "He said the ceiling on the second floor isn't as bad as we thought. Didn't think it was rain damage, though. Did a third-floor bathroom flood or something?"

Ben waves a hand, topping off his own glass even though it's already pretty full. "Who knows? This house is as twisted as the people who live in it."

He gives a hearty laugh, one that no one echoes, and I think we're all relieved when Cecilia starts bringing in steaming dishes of food. I hate that she's had to stay late for this, and I find myself thinking about hiring more staff for the house. Ruby had a paranoia about people working here, never wanting the maids or handymen that were so common on other estates like this. When I was a kid, I'd wondered if it was because of what happened to her. The kidnapping. That guy, Jimmy Darnell, had been an itinerant worker, so Ruby had good reason not to trust strangers in her space. She had a cleaning crew come out once a month, but Cecilia had done everything else, and as I watch her wince slightly while putting down a heavy tureen of soup, I realize she's got to be in her mid-sixties by now. Ruby hired her not long after adopting me.

Maybe she'd like some help or—

No. Thoughts like that are for someone who plans to stay here, to take actual ownership of the house, and that's sure as shit not going to be me.

No one really talks as we fill our plates and pass around platters of food. I'm sure whatever Cecilia prepared is delicious, but I can't taste any of it, and when the dishes are cleared away, I couldn't tell you what we'd just eaten.

I've just sat there, going through the motions, waiting.

Part of me wants to get up now, tell them to drop the bullshit, and let's just get this over with. The production, the drama . . . Ruby could pull it off, but they can't. They're all sitting there, practically wiggling in their seats with anticipation, and when Ben leaves the table for a minute and returns with a bottle of champagne, I hate myself even more for not telling Jules we walked into a trap.

"Okay, Benji," Libby says admiringly. "The good shit."

"Language!" Nelle snaps, but Ben only laughs, the cork popping out of the bottle with a practiced twist.

"Oh, it's fine, Nana Nelle," he says. "She's not wrong. This is indeed 'the good shit.' The 1959 Dom Pérignon Rosé, a favorite in this house."

Ruby's favorite, actually. I had my first sip of it on New Year's Eve when I was nine, and thought it tasted sour, the bubbles making me want to sneeze. She always had it around for special occasions, and it was only after I left this house that I learned those bottles run you around thirty grand.

If I had any doubt that I was completely fucked, Ben opening the 1959 Dom put that to rest.

Once we all have our flutes, Ben takes up a position next to Nelle, raising his glass, his eyes trained on me. He's gleeful, like a little kid on Christmas morning, and I think again about that vision I had, his head cracked on the parquet by the front door.

"A toast," he goes on, and everyone raises their glasses but me. At my side, Jules falters a little bit, her glass lowering slightly, hesitant.

"Cam?" she murmurs, placing her other hand on my arm.

But I'm still watching Ben, waiting.

"To family," Ben says, gesturing around the table with his glass. "To the McTavishes. The real ones."

I smirk at that, and his smile turns poisonous. "And to at long last evicting the interloper."

There's a loud slap as Libby tosses a folder on the table.

Had she been holding that in her lap the whole dinner? Just waiting for this moment?

If so, she fucked it up because she throws it just a little too hard, and it slides across the slick surface until it reaches the edge, papers spilling out onto the floor to my left.

"Fuck's sake, Lib," Ben mutters, but Libby just throws her hands up and says, "Look, just tell him already."

"Tell him what?" Jules asks, and I take a deep breath, keeping my hand steady as I lift my glass of champagne and finally take a sip.

"They're going to tell me," I say, surprising myself with how calm I sound, "that the woman I knew—that we all knew—as Ruby McTavish wasn't Ruby at all."

Another swallow of champagne, but it might as well be acid sliding down my throat. "They're going to tell me that she was really Dora Darnell."

From the Desk of

Ruby A. McTavish

March 29, 2013

Roddy Kenmore was a drug-addled fool who I never should have married in the first place, and the only regret I felt when I watched him slip under that dark salt water was that I hadn't shoved him sooner.

There. That's the last husband sorted, and, frankly, that one sentence is more effort that I want to expend on him.

Oh, fine. I suppose I can give you a *little* more information.

After Andrew, I was as lost as I'd ever been. I left Ashby House for over a year, unable to bear the giant rooms, the rural seclusion, without Andrew by my side. Nelle was thrilled, of course, finally Queen of the Castle. I thought about letting her keep the damn thing, just signing it over to her and never darkening its door again, instead making my own way in the world without the McTavish name. I had no idea what that would look like, though. I'd gotten so used to life there at Ashby, in Tavistock. Out in the rest of the world, my money still opened doors and smoothed paths, but it wasn't the same. I liked the power of the name, the safety it implied. Being the latest in a long line, a person with roots that ran deep.

It's no surprise to me that Roddy Kenmore found me when I was floundering like this. The Roddys of this world have a sixth sense for homing in on the vulnerable, the lost, the rudderless.

I actually met him at one of those clubs I'd bought back in
the sixties, the one in Miami. When I first invested in it, it was
called "The Palma Palace," and then in the seventies, it was just
"Palma" for several years. By 1985, it had become "Paloma," and
it was making a rather staggering amount of money. (Lucky
for you, I sold it in 1989 for a mint. Two years later, I believe
there was some mess with drugs and maybe a murder? I don't
remember. Perhaps you now understand why I wouldn't be all
that interested in murders I did not commit.)

So, there I was at the Paloma, dancing in a Halston dress,
the music so loud it drowned out any rational thinking, which
must be why I found myself dancing with a man who was
little more than a boy, really. Twenty-six, but he seemed even
younger with his long red hair and his bright smile.

Roddy was always the husband that didn't make sense.
Duke was an obvious choice at the time, Hugh was a logical
second husband, and anyone could see Andrew and I were
mad for each other. So why did I marry a spoiled brat who
said "irregardless" and thought Tiffany lamps had all belonged
to someone *named* Tiffany?

For one, he was a good time. At least at first. Roddy had
one goal in life, and it was to have as much fun as possible.
There was no past with Roddy, no future, only the present,
only *now, now, now,* and, with a past like mine, can you blame
me for wanting a taste of that?

For another, Roddy was filthy fucking rich, darling. Yes,
yes, I am, too, but remember, at this point in my life, I was
giving serious thought to leaving all things McTavish behind
me. Roddy's money—or really, his father's money—would
allow me to do that.

As for why he married me, well . . .

I could flatter myself here. I did still look very good at

forty-five, my figure unchanged, my hair just as dark and lustrous. I was exciting and good in bed (sorry, darling), and I suspect there was a little dark glamour clinging to me with that trail of dead husbands, and that was definitely the sort of thing Roddy would have been drawn to.

But again, we're being honest here. While the above attributes probably didn't hurt, the real draw was the eight-figure trust fund Roddy could access once he was married.

One flight to Los Angeles, a short cruise down to Mexico, and I became Mrs. Roddy Kenmore. It was the first of my marriages to make national news, do you know that? A little feature in *People* magazine, me in that off-the-shoulder white dress with the floppy sun hat (it was the eighties, darling, don't roll your eyes), Roddy in a white suit with a shirt unbuttoned to his navel and all that red hair blowing in the breeze.

Did I think we'd be happy? Did I think it could last?

I'm not sure I was thinking at all, honestly. I know Roddy wasn't. It's hard to think of much when you're coked out of your mind every waking hour.

I'd known he enjoyed the occasional sniff recreationally. Everyone he hung around with did. What I *hadn't* known was how finally having access to all that money would make Roddy decide that every single dollar of it should go straight up his goddamn nose.

Christ, it was irritating. A nonstop party *sounds* all fine and good until you're faced with the reality of it. The sweaty nights, the late mornings—afternoons, really—waking up with strange people still in the living room, the constant headache at the base of my skull from too little sleep and too much noise.

Now, you're reading this and thinking, "Yes, that all sounds annoying, but surely *this* one you could've divorced."

That's fair. I could have, yes. It would have been a hassle, and the money would've been a nightmare, but you're right that I did not *have* to kill Roddy Kenmore.

I wanted to.

Why? I still wonder myself. I think there was a part of me that felt that after killing Andrew, it would be disloyal to let Roddy live. How could I kill the man I'd loved so much and then just divorce someone who hadn't meant anything to me?

What can I say? It made sense at the time.

So. A midnight sail. My idea, whispered in Roddy's ear at dinner on Avalon.

Wouldn't it be nice, just the two of us?

For all his faults, Roddy really was a beautiful boy, and I can still remember the sleepy smile he'd given me there tucked into our red leather booth, the flickering votive on the table playing along his freckles.

Just the two of us and Captain Bart, he'd replied, and I'd looked over at the bar where the man who actually did the sailing on the *Rude Roddy* was pushing his sun-bleached hair out of his face and attempting to buy a deeply uninterested brunette a drink.

We don't need him, I'd purred in his ear. *You can sail us around just a little bit, can't you?*

Oh, the arrogance of rich young men. It's far more fatal than I've ever been, if you ask me.

So we left Captain Bart to his fruity drinks and his bored brunettes, and headed out into the night.

I didn't expect it to be quite as easy as it was, but Roddy was, as usual, out of his mind on something or other. He was also possibly the most impatient person I've ever known, the kind of man who hated to sit still, so when the wind wouldn't cooperate, he'd marched to the stern of the boat where the engine was.

I can still see him there, shirtless and wearing jeans with holes in them, his foot bare where he braced it against the side of the boat.

"Fucking piece of shit!" he yelled as he yanked at the pull start, the motor spluttering.

Worse last words than Duke's, darling.

A push. That's all it took.

I can still see it so clearly. The sky overhead spangled with stars, the water below black and murky, Roddy precariously balanced, and me in a Pucci caftan of all things, wedding rings glimmering as I placed my hands on his bare back and shoved.

He couldn't swim, you see, despite wanting to sail the *Rude Roddy* to Australia at some point in the near future. Or maybe Thailand? I can never remember. I never quite understood why someone who couldn't swim took up sailing as a hobby, but then his father had sent him to some boarding school in Maine, so that may have had something to do with it.

An aside: I'm still irked about all that "Mrs. Kill-more" nonsense. I wouldn't have even gotten the fucking nickname had I not married a man named Kenmore, and now his name and mine are linked forever by something even more binding and eternal than wedding vows—gossip.

Roddy is the one I thought I wouldn't get away with, if I'm honest. It was hardly all that sneaky or subtle, my husband of two months drowning off the coast of Catalina Island and me, his new wife, the only other person on board. (This was in 1985, by the way, only a few years after that poor actress also found herself in those same dark waters, so Roddy's name is often linked with hers. That I *do* regret. No one deserves such a fate.)

(To be linked with Roddy for eternity, I should clarify. As has been previously implied, there are some people who I clearly believe deserve drowning, although she was not one of them.)

But as it had with Andrew, the McTavish name and fortune wrapped around me, buttressing me as I glided through the inquest, the interviews, the implications. Before I knew it, I was back at Ashby House as though nothing had changed.

I had changed, though.

If Andrew's death had proven to me that I was as monstrous as I'd always feared, Roddy's made me decide it might be time to find out why that was.

Why did dealing out death come so easily to me? Why, with the exception of Andrew, had I never felt true guilt over it? Duke, I could justify to myself. He had abused me, no doubt would have continued doing so, and in that initial moment, I had genuinely been fearful for my life. But Hugh had been nothing more than annoying; Roddy, a mistake I could've easily undone without ending his life. And Andrew . . . even Andrew, I could've left, though it would have broken my heart. We could have split amicably; I could have set him free to wander the world with my secrets, secrets I knew he wouldn't tell.

And yet.

It was then that my mind once again turned to autumn 1943, when I was snatched from the woods surrounding Ashby House to spend eight months with the Darnells of Alabama.

I couldn't remember any of it, but it was a trauma that had to be locked inside of me, and might, I thought, be the explanation for this darkness in my soul. Had something happened to me in those eight months, something that had

turned me into this woman without a heart? Or—that old
buried fear, resurfacing yet again—was it because I *wasn't*
the real Ruby? Could I possibly be the lost Dora, just like the
Darnells had always claimed?

I decided to find out.

It took longer than I'd thought, darling, and it's a long story
to tell. Too long for tonight, in any case.

I know, I know. This is the bit you're the most interested in,
but patience, darling.

As I told you, that was one of the qualities Roddy was most
lacking in, and you see what happened to him.

-R

TRAGEDY IN CATALINA

- *Roddy Kenmore, heir to the Texas oil fortune, DROWNS off coast of Catalina just TWO MONTHS after marrying NOTORIOUS HEIRESS Ruby McTavish Callahan Woodward Miller!*

- *Friends claim Cursed Heir was sailing buff who, ironically, NEVER learned to SWIM.*

- *"Roddy was FUN, but he was kind of a dumb-a**," says University Chum who wishes to remain ANONYMOUS.*

- *Only RECENTLY WED to Mrs. McTavish (20+ years his senior), the OIL HEIR had purchased a yacht that was regularly the scene of WILD PARTIES and RUMOURED DRUG USE, according to sources in the Catalina Island area.*

- *The TRAGIC NIGHT unfolded just a few miles from shore with no one save MR. AND MRS. KENMORE on the ship at the time.*

- *"Ruby really wanted Roddy to settle down," claims a friend of the MUCH WIDOWED HEIRESS. "I think that night was really about giving them a chance to be alone, just the two of them. She couldn't have known what would happen."*

- *Other friends wonder just how one woman could be SO UNLUCKY in love!*

- *"Mrs. Kenmore? More like MRS. KILL-MORE," says one marina employee!*

—The National Enquirer, July 10, 1985

CHAPTER THIRTEEN

Camden

For a few seconds, just the space of a couple of heartbeats, really, a stunned silence hangs over the table. It feels good, watching the wind visibly slip from their sails, and I savor it more than the expensive champagne in my glass.

Then I feel Jules's hand on mine.

Her expression is stricken, her skin pale, and any satisfaction at getting one over on the McTavishes drains out of me in an instant.

I should have told her. I know that. I had plenty of chances before now, and ever since Nathan's phone call this afternoon, I've known this was coming. But something held me back.

No, not something. Some*one*.

Ruby.

"You knew," Ben says, and I squeeze Jules's fingers, pleading with my eyes for her to understand before I turn to look at Ben.

He's still standing at the head, his face almost as pale as Jules's except for two red flags of color on his cheeks. Both fists are planted on the wooden tabletop, his body practically vibrating with anger. I take a deep breath, make myself have another sip of champagne before I answer.

"When I turned eighteen," I say, looking at Nelle and Libby, both of whom are frozen in their chairs. "She brought me into her office—"

"My *father's* office," Nelle says, the words brittle, and I ignore her.

"And she told me that she'd had some lab run a DNA test. She used your hair to do it, Nelle," I say, nodding at her as she seethes in her chair, her knobby fingers tight on its arms.

I can still remember how it felt that afternoon, the winter sunshine coming through the windows, a fire crackling in the hearth, making the room too warm, and the scent of Ruby's lavender hand lotion kicking off a sick, pulsing headache behind my eyes.

Or maybe it hadn't been the scent. Maybe it had been her words, so calm and cool, so classically Ruby.

Anyway, it's the sort of thing I think you should know, she'd said, like she was telling me what the code to her safe was, or which funeral home I should call when she died. Just a normal bit of business, mother to son, matriarch to heir.

"It's funny," I go on, tapping the edge of my knife against the table with one hand, Jules's cold fingers still clutched in the other. "You're actually the reason she got the test done." I nod at Nelle. "Well, you and Howell. She knew, by the way. About the two of you taking *her* hairbrush, sending it out for testing. She was just smart enough to get ahead of you."

She'd actually been amused by it, chuckling as she'd shaken her head.

Science, darling. Who knew it would come for me in the end?

Nelle's mouth works, lips trembling as little flecks of spit appear in the corners. "I knew it. I knew she'd interfered somehow. Howell said I was being paranoid, that she couldn't have done such a thing, but he never knew Ruby like I did. None of you did. A snake in the grass from the day she slithered into this house."

Honestly, this might be the first time I've liked Nelle, Ruby had said. *No idea she had it in her.*

I still don't know how Ruby figured out what Nelle and Howell were up to, or who she paid off to make sure that particular DNA test came back declaring that she was just as much a McTavish as they were. Ruby only ever shared what she thought was necessary.

Still, to her credit, she decided it was necessary for me to know the truth she'd hid from the rest of the family: that she'd had her own testing done, and there it was, in black and white. She had no biological link to Eleanor McTavish, no miraculous recovery for Baby Ruby after all. Just a child stolen from poor parents to replace the one the rich parents had been too careless with.

Or at least that was the story Ruby had told me then. I had always suspected there was more to it, but what did it matter now?

My mouth is dry, but my glass is empty, so I clear my throat before saying, "Nathan called me this afternoon. He'd gotten a call from someone at First Carolina Bank, saying that a McTavish had been in with the key to a safety-deposit box that Ruby had set up in 2010. You, I'm guessing?"

I nod to Ben, who is now almost purple with rage.

"You *knew,*" he says again. "You've known for the past fourteen fucking years that she had no right to give *any* of this to anyone. She had no right to it herself."

"She had every right," I fire back, my own temper sparking. "Blood doesn't fucking matter, *Benji*. Mason left it all to her. Not to the eldest surviving McTavish, not to the 'heirs of his body' or whatever bullshit term you want to pull out of your little legal hat. He left it all to *Ruby*. Who then left it all to *me*."

"You grasping little bastard," Nelle says, rising shakily to her feet, one hand still clutching her chair. "Waltzing around here these last few days like lord of the manor. No wonder she loved you. Like calls to like, and you were both trash."

"Nana," Libby says, reaching over, but Nelle shakes her off.

"I won't have it!" she goes on, her voice breathless and shrill.

"You really thought you'd uncovered something, didn't you?" I say, almost laughing now. "Let me guess," I continue, turning to Ben. "When Howell died, you started going through his things. His office, right? Which used to be Ruby's. You found that key taped to the back of a drawer. Which your dad never did because he wasn't nearly as diligent as you. Or as desperate."

I remember Ruby putting it there, tapping the handle once she was done.

First Carolina Bank, Box 1306. I'll ask you to keep this information between us, but once I'm gone, do with it what you will.

Another burden, another responsibility bequeathed to me that I'd never asked for, never wanted.

And now you know my biggest secret, Ruby had said, her eyes twinkling, and then she'd given a little shrug.

You could destroy me with it if you ever wanted to, I suppose.

I wouldn't, I'd said, and I'd meant it. Wouldn't do it, wouldn't want to.

She'd smiled at that, and reached over, squeezed my hand, her fingers cold, the skin papery thin. *You and me . . .*

Against the world, I'd finished.

Because it really had been the two of us against everyone, against it all. And even after everything that had happened, there was still a part of me that was instinctually loyal to Ruby, that had sworn to keep her secrets and had chosen to do so, over and over again.

Even from my own wife.

THE LAUGH DIES a bitter death in my throat, and I swallow hard. "And then what? You go to the bank, you find the safety-deposit box. You read the DNA report. You learn the truth about Ruby. You must think you've really blown the case wide open, don't you? You're certain you're going to find some kind of loophole in the will now. Something that yanks all this shit away from me and hands it back to you, right?" I pause, staring intently at Ben. "I mean, I assume that was your big reason for becoming a lawyer. And not just any lawyer, but one who specializes in *estates.* You've spent the past decade trying to figure out a way to screw me out of my inheritance, but there isn't one, is there?"

When he doesn't answer, I shake my head. "No. I *know* there isn't, because I had Nathan Collins go over every bit of that damn will with a fine-tooth fucking comb a decade ago. Ruby was too smart for you."

I look around the table, at everyone but Jules, who I can feel staring at the side of my face.

Later. I'll apologize. I'll make her understand.

"She was too smart for all of you. Still, you wanted to play out this little scene. You figured I'd be shocked, figured I hadn't done my own homework because—what is it I am again?"

I swing my gaze to Ben. "'Hillbilly trash'?"

Back at Nelle. "A 'grasping little bastard'?"

"Okay, can we all just stop talking about this now?" Libby says, dropping her forehead into her hand, and I pluck my napkin off my lap, throwing it onto the table.

"I have nothing left to say." I shrug. "Except, go ahead. Tell the world Ruby wasn't a McTavish. Make a big thing about it, if you want. Tangle us all up in court for a million years until every dime of your precious fucking money is in lawyers' pockets."

I stand, bracing both hands on the table and leaning in. "Meanwhile, I thank God every goddamn night that I'm not related to any of you," I say. "And honestly, I think Ruby did, too. So if we're done—"

"We're not!" Nelle all but shrieks, thumping the table with one fist, and now Libby gets up, going over to her and putting an arm around her shoulders.

"Nana Nelle," she says, her voice sharper. "You shouldn't upset yourself, your doctor said—"

"Your doctor said you had to be careful with your health," Ben finishes, but he's still looking at me. He's not nearly as purple now, and there's a light in his eyes that has something cold settling in the pit of my stomach.

"Your mother died young," Ben goes on, speaking to Nelle but watching me. "And your father wasn't all that old, either. Ruby, of course, lived to be seventy-three, but then she wasn't actually your sister. I wonder how long she might have lived if she'd had a . . . natural death."

Next to me, Jules stands, her hand curling around my

elbow. "Camden, let's go upstairs," she says, but I feel frozen to the spot.

Even my lips feel numb as I say, "Is this what we're doing, Ben? Rewriting the past? Ruby died in her sleep. Doesn't get much more natural than that."

I say it so easily, another lie that slips off my tongue.

Another one of Ruby's secrets, locked inside my chest.

The memories are there, pushing against the back of my eyes, threatening to drown me, but I've had a lot of practice keeping things hidden over the years, and even as Ben smiles at me in a way that has my teeth clenched and sweat dripping down my back, I meet his gaze.

"Thing is, Cam," Ben says, shoving his hands in his pockets and rocking back on his heels in a way that reminds me so much of Howell it's eerie, "things weren't great with you and Ruby at the time, if I remember. You weren't even speaking to her, were you?"

I don't answer, and Nelle sinks back into her seat, still trembling, but her gaze is turning triumphant now. I think of Howell's email again, Nelle insisting Ruby killed herself, the only one who ever suspected the truth.

Libby stands there in her pink dress, her lower lip pulled between her teeth.

"And of course," Ben adds, "you were here at the house that night. The night she died."

"Yeah, I was," I say, fighting the urge to curl my fingers into a fist. "You know that. I came back to get some more of my stuff. But I never even saw her that night."

I've repeated that lie so many times that I can almost believe it's true, can almost see myself at twenty years old, sullenly putting X-Men comics I hadn't read in years and an old clock radio in a duffel bag, rain howling outside and Ruby far away in her own bedroom.

"It's weird, though," Ben says. "I mean, I wasn't here that night, and Nana Nelle was up in her room asleep early. But Libby was here. And . . ."

Trailing off, Ben shakes his head. "Man. I hate to say this. Hate to even think it. But Libby says she saw you coming out of Ruby's room. Thought it was weird you told a different story to the police when they came, but hey."

Ben flashes that grin, but his gaze, when it meets mine, might as well be stone. "We're family, right? We keep each other's secrets. Until we don't."

Time feels slow now, my heartbeat a steady thud in my chest, my ears ringing.

I look over at Libby.

She *wasn't* here that night. I remember. Her car passed mine coming down the mountain as I was going up, the window barely cracked because of the rain, but the firefly glow ember of the tip of a cigarette catching my eye. We'd looked at each other, her mouth twisting into a sour scowl, and then she'd flown past me, tires skidding a little on the muddy road.

"Isn't that right, Libby?" Ben says, a little too loud, and she presses her lips together, twists one of her bangle bracelets around her wrist.

"Yeah," she says at last, the words coming out as a sigh before she straightens her shoulders and says it again, firmer. "Yeah. You came out of Aunt Ruby's room, and you were really upset. Shaking. I thought you'd been crying."

She's warming to the story now, looking over at Jules, who I still can't bring myself to face. "It freaked me out, honestly, but like Ben said, we're family, so . . ."

Libby shrugs. "But now I guess we're not."

"Plan B, huh?" I say. I'm actually smiling, but it's like there's broken glass in my throat. "Can't scare Camden off with the big Ruby reveal, so we threaten to accuse him of murder instead?"

"Okay, this is officially insane now," Jules says, the first words she's spoken in what feels like ages, and Ben cuts his eyes at her.

"You wanted to be a McTavish, right?" he says. "Well, this is what it looks like, sweetheart."

She scoffs, about to fire back with her own retort, but I don't give her the chance.

"Fine," I say. "You know what, Ben? You win. Keep your money. Keep this house. It's worth it never to have to see a single one of your faces again. Fuck all of you. And fuck Ruby for ever bringing me here."

With that, I reach for the bottle of champagne, still half-full. I snag it with one hand, and reach for Jules with the other.

She lets me lead her from the room, and as we make our way to the staircase, I can hear the others all start talking at once, but I ignore it. My only thought is getting upstairs, packing our bags, and heading back to Colorado as soon as humanly possible.

I've already got one foot on the bottom step when I realize Jules is tugging at me, her feet planted.

"Camden," she says, and I turn, bottle of champagne still in hand.

"Can you believe that shit?" I ask her, gesturing with the bottle. "Now do you get it? Now do you see why I never wanted to come back here?"

"They're assholes, I know," she says, dropping my hand.

"No disagreement from me on that score. But ... you're just going to let them win?"

I stare at her. Some of the adrenaline is wearing off now, and it's making me feel muddled, confused.

"They'll always win," I tell her, but she shakes her head.

"No. No, they don't have to. Jesus Christ, Cam, you can't think this plan of theirs would actually *work*? That anyone would believe them?"

"It doesn't matter," I tell her, wishing she weren't wearing Ruby's dress, wishing I didn't feel Ruby's eyes boring into my back from her portrait at the top of the stairs. "I mean ... what do you want me to do, Jules? Fight them? Spend the next decade tangled in legal shit with people I hate? People who hate me?"

"Of course, I don't want that," she says, but the words come out too fast, and she keeps glancing back toward the dining room.

Any relief I was feeling starts to drain out of me as I look at my wife, planted at the foot of the stairs.

"You do," I say, slow. "You do want that. You want me to fight it. You want this place, and everything that comes with it. Even after that display. Even after what they accused me of."

Jules climbs a couple of steps, her hand resting on the banister, the simple wedding set I bought for her catching the light. "I just don't understand why you're giving in so quickly. And why didn't you tell me about Ruby? About knowing she wasn't a McTavish?"

A headache is starting to pound behind my eyes, and I want to fall asleep almost as badly as I want to get in the car and get out of here.

"It didn't matter. They're the ones obsessed with blood,

about some kind of clannish bullshit and who has the right to what."

"But *you* have rights, Camden," she fires back. "And a damn good lawyer. Call Nathan. Tell him about the shit they just pulled, what they're accusing you of—"

"It's not fucking worth it, Jules! How many times do I have to say it?"

I have never raised my voice to her since the day we met. I've hardly ever yelled at anyone, and now my words seem to echo around the cavernous hallway as she lifts her eyes to mine, her expression turning stony.

"Fine," she says, moving past me. "Fine. Let them have it all. We'll go back to the rental, and you'll go back to teaching, and they can live the sweet life because two hundred years ago, their ancestors did a thing and ours didn't. Got it."

"Jules," I say, all the fight gone out of me now, but she just keeps moving up the stairs, and I watch her go, eventually hearing the distant slam of our bedroom door.

Sighing, I trudge up the stairs, too, but instead of making the turn to our room, I go down the other hallway, almost without thinking.

I'm at Ruby's room before I quite realize it, and when I push open the door, that familiar scent hits me. Lavender and cedar, still preserved just as I remember it, like everything else in this bedroom.

Her dressing table, her tiny watercolor paintings that she'd bought at a yard sale and proclaimed "delightful," plopping them down alongside a genuine Degas sketch in a silver frame.

The Belgian lace bedspread that scratched the back of my legs when I'd sit in here after soccer practice. She always insisted I come in and tell her about my day.

I sink heavily onto the bed now, setting the champagne bottle on the nightstand with a thunk before dropping my head into my hands.

The real reason I can't stay and fight is because I got lucky tonight. If I leave now, if I cut every string tying me to my past, I might be okay. But if I stay here, if I go toe to toe with Nelle and Ben and Libby, those strings are only going to get tighter and tighter until they finally choke me.

And I can never tell Jules why.

I look back to the champagne, but then I think of something else, sliding open Ruby's nightstand drawer.

I expect it to be empty, but her things are still there. Reading glasses, an old *Reader's Digest*, a pot of lip balm.

And her pills.

She had dozens of them, all kept in a little silver pillbox, and I close my hand around it now.

Even in the darkness, I know the shape of the one I'm after.

I've never taken anything to help me sleep, figuring I deserved whatever bad dreams or sleepless nights I got, but tonight, I want oblivion.

A bitter white square under my tongue, a swig from the bottle, and I curl up on Ruby's bed, still in Ben's suit, only my shoes kicked off, and let the blackness take me.

I SLEEP LIKE the dead, waking up in the gray light of dawn, my head stuffed with cotton, my mouth dry, and it takes me a second to become aware that something is happening outside.

I hear running feet, a slammed door, and I sit up, trying to blink away the fog, wishing I hadn't taken the damn pill in the first place.

I've just managed to sit up when there's a sound that pierces that haze like a bullet, sending me shooting to my feet even as the room spins dizzily around me.

It's Jules.

Screaming.

March 30, 2013

Now, where were we?

Ah, yes. My biggest secret. The family shame.

All of that.

The Darnells had not had an easy time of it since 1944, the year I was reunited with my family, and Jimmy Darnell was shot trying to escape the local jail. His wife, the woman who claimed she was my mother, had moved away from Alabama shortly after, and had gone back to her maiden name.

It took some doing before I was able to track her down. When I did, it was only to discover that she'd died in 1984.

God, how that frustrated me. So close! A year earlier, and I could've met her. It sounds silly, probably, but I was so sure that if I simply *saw* her, I would know immediately whether she was in fact my mother. Finding out that she was dead made me almost abandon the whole enterprise altogether.

But then, the very discreet—and even more expensive—detective I'd hired called to inform me that while Helen Darnell had died, her daughter, Claire, was still alive and living in Tallahassee.

Claire.

I remembered seeing the name all those years ago in Daddy's office, thinking how pretty it was. It was even prettier to me now because Claire might be my salvation.

A side note—one rarely finds salvation in Florida.

Claire was forty-two in 1985, just three years younger than me, but she looked much older when she opened the door of her little apartment in an ugly square building surrounded by other ugly square buildings. I'd tried to dress down for the visit, knowing better than to swan in wearing Chanel, but my Gloria Vanderbilt jeans and Halston blouse were still entirely too much as I saw very clearly on Claire's face.

She was wearing a T-shirt over cutoffs, her face bare, her hair—the same deep brown as mine, I noted—scraped back into a messy ponytail. Her expression grew wary as she stared at me from her doorway.

"Is this about Linda?" she asked.

I had no idea who Linda was, so I shook my head, sweat already sliding down my lower back, my sunglasses—which, I realized too late, *were* Chanel, goddamn it—fogging up in the humidity. "No, I . . . my name is Ruby McTavish."

Her expression cleared then, lips curving into something that would've been a smile if there hadn't been such a mean edge to it. "No," she said. "You're Dora Darnell. I wondered if you'd ever turn up one day."

With that, she turned to go back into the apartment. I stood there, stunned, and she waved a hand for me to follow her. "Come on in. Sit down."

The apartment was cool, a window unit rattling in the living room. A little girl sat on the green carpet in front of it, two Barbies in her hands. She looked to be about eight or so, her dark blond hair neatly braided, her pink overalls and clear jelly shoes meticulously clean. The whole apartment was clean, I noticed. Small and shabby, but neat as a pin.

Claire poured me a glass of sweet tea, and we sat down at the kitchen table, studying each other.

"Linda, baby? Go play in your room," Claire called, and the girl pouted.

"It's too hot in there."

"Then go in my room. You can watch TV."

Magic words, apparently, because Linda happily trotted off toward the small hallway, opening the first of three doors.

After a moment, we heard the muted blare of music, and Claire shook her head. "She's not supposed to watch MTV, but it's a special occasion, I guess."

She turned her head to me. "You have kids?"

"No," I said, my mouth dry, the tea so sweet it made my teeth ache.

Claire tapped her fingernails on the side of her glass, right over the grinning face of some cartoon character. "I didn't think I would. Have kids. I was thirty-four when she was born. One of those things, not quite on purpose, not quite an accident."

She flashed me a smile, and I sucked in a breath, thinking about Andrew's portrait of me hanging at Ashby House. The smile on Claire's face was the same as mine. "Her dad ain't worth shit, but he was good-looking at least. So she's got that going for her."

"She's a very pretty child," I said, the words prim in my own ears, and Claire smirked, leaning back in her chair.

"When did you figure it out?" she asked, and I didn't bother pretending to misunderstand.

"I haven't yet. I've always been curious, though. I'd read the stories, and I suppose I—"

"You suppose you started to wonder if my mama wasn't a liar?" Claire finished, and I wondered how I was already so helplessly on the back foot.

"Something like that."

She tilted her head, looking at me for a long time before saying, "If it makes you feel better, you were pretty expensive."

The room had felt too cold earlier, but my skin flushed hot at that, and I took another sip of my tea, my throat so tight that I nearly choked.

"I don't know how much, exactly. The number changed a lot over the years, but the story stayed the same. Little girl missing, rich family in North Carolina. They saw her picture in the paper, Mama and Daddy, and Mama said it tore her heart up because she looked so much like you. And later she said she wished she'd never said that because if she hadn't, Daddy might not have ever thought about it."

She rattled the ice in her glass. "But he did. She never knew how he got in touch with your family, but your daddy sent someone down in a fancy suit to look at you, and then he came himself."

I pictured Daddy—*my* daddy, with his big mustache and his Acqua di Parma and his white suits that never got dirty—sitting across a table from Jimmy Darnell, and suddenly I could see that table.

No, I couldn't just see it. I *remembered* that table. One leg just a little shorter so that it always wobbled when someone leaned against it.

"His wife was beside herself, he told Daddy. Or that's what Mama said he told Daddy anyway. Mrs. McTavish blamed herself, I think. She was the one who told Ruby to go find the nanny, to leave her alone for a little while. Said she saw her walk up the hill and out of sight, but thought the nanny was just on the other side. Only the nanny had already started packing things up and carrying them back to the car, and she didn't know Ruby was headed her way."

I could picture that, too. The little girl, toddling along the forest path, her eyes searching for a familiar figure, but not seeing any. Her little brain whirring, her legs carrying her deeper into the forest, thinking her nanny—*Grace*—must be there.

I waited for that image to have the same whiff of memory, but it didn't. It was just my imagination. And my imagination kept going, carrying the child deeper into the forest, until there were too many trees, until she was confused and scared, sweating and whimpering, looking around for Grace, not seeing the drop ahead . . .

"He was afraid it was going to eat her up," Claire continued, and my mind, still fixed on Baby Ruby, conjured up a bear now instead of a steep cliff; a mountain lion, maybe. But then I realized she meant Mama, and her guilt.

No, not my mama. Not if what Claire was saying is true. Anna. Anna McTavish.

"Mama never would've let you go," Claire said, and the air-conditioning clicked off, the room suddenly quiet. "Even after it was all agreed on and the money was stuffed under the mattress, she kept telling everyone you were hers. Nobody listened, though. Not with Daddy confessing."

She lifted one hand off the table, zooming it through the air. "So off you went to North Carolina, Daddy right behind you. Only you went to a mansion and he went to the county jail."

A headache started behind my eyes, sweat soaking through my silk blouse. "And what? That was your father's grand plan, to just go sit in jail? Go through a trial for something he didn't do?"

"Of course not," Claire scoffed. "McTavish told him he'd fix it. Said if Daddy confessed and just sat tight in the county jail for a couple of days, he would make it so that Daddy could 'escape,' and get him back to Alabama. He'd given us enough money to start a brand-new life somewhere else. Mama said Daddy kept talking about Mexico, maybe South America."

She scoffed again, took another sip of tea. "That would've been nice, I guess. Growing up down there. Wasn't in the cards, though."

"The escape was planned, then," I said slowly. "And went wrong."

The look Claire gave me is one I've never forgotten. In part, because she had my eyes, a dark hazel that changed from green to nearly black in the light.

But mostly, because it was the first time in my life anyone had ever looked at me with such pity.

"There was no escape plan," I said, understanding washing over me.

Claire made a gun of her finger, fired it at me. "McTavish had what he wanted. He had you. He didn't need some Alabama farmer who could barely read holding a secret like that over your heads for the rest of his life."

I told myself there was no way Claire could know that for sure. She was a baby when all this happened; plus, it was coming to her from her mother, a woman who'd had her life shattered by Baby Ruby's disappearance. Of course, she'd think the worst of Daddy. Of all the McTavishes.

But here it is, darling: I knew it was true. I felt it, as certain and primal as I'd ever felt anything. And I knew that Daddy had that man killed. I could practically see Jimmy Darnell dashing through the dark woods of Tavistock County, thinking to himself that just through the trees, he'd find a car, ready to take him home to his wife, his baby girl, and all that money.

I bet the last thing that went through his head before that bullet hit was a vision of crystal-blue water and white sands.

And the reason I knew? It's exactly what I would've done, if I were Daddy.

"The real kicker," Claire said, sighing as she rested her elbows on the table, "is that Mama had proof of the deal. She had all that cash. Like I said, I never really knew how much it was. Thousands of dollars, for sure. But the night they took you and Daddy, she burned every last bill. Big stacks of cash, going up in smoke in the yard."

Claire pushed a loose strand of dark hair behind her ear. "'What kind of mother would I be if I took that money?' she always said. 'What kind of mother sells her own child?' Sometimes, I'd be like, 'Well, hell, Mama, probably a bad one, but at least you would've been a rich one!'"

She laughed, but the sound faded quickly, her smile dimming. "That was before I had Linda, though. I understand it better now."

Heaving a sigh, she stood, the chair squeaking across the linoleum. "We've managed okay, as you can see, but Mama never got over it. She died last year, but I sometimes think she'd been dead for forty years before that. She was just marking time."

"I'm so sorry," I said, and Claire looked at me, eyebrows raised.

"You didn't do anything," she said. "You were just a kid. Although I admit, I used to be jealous of you when I was younger. We didn't get much North Carolina news down here, but sometimes you made the bigger papers, and I used to dream about what it would be like to live in a big house and have all that money. It wasn't very nice of me, but when your first husband died, I thought, 'Well, that's what she gets, isn't it? Her daddy had my daddy shot, and now someone's shot her man.'"

She kept looking at me, her gaze steady. "And then I read about your second husband, and thought, 'Shit, maybe God really does dole out vengeance.' And when the third died, I thought, 'How is one woman *this* unlucky?' It wasn't until the fourth one that I understood."

The sweat prickling on my skin suddenly turned cold. In the bedroom, the TV clicked off, the door opening as Linda dashed out, crying, "Debbie's outside, I'm gonna go play!"

"Stay by the building!" Claire called back as the front door opened and slammed shut, but she never took her eyes off me.

"You may have been born a Darnell, Dora, but they made a McTavish out of you in the end."

I didn't know what to say to that.

I stood abruptly, my hands fluttering nervously in a way they never did. "It . . . it sounds so crass to say this, but I'd like to . . . if there's anything I could do, or . . . your child might need . . ."

Claire let me ramble on, making me feel smaller and smaller until finally my words came to a stop. I didn't even manage to get out a full sentence.

"That's really sweet of you to offer, Mrs. McTavish," she said after a long silence. "But I think this family's done with y'all."

I nodded meekly. "Thank you," I said. "For the tea. And . . . well. Thank you."

I moved to the door, but before I opened it, slipped my hand into my pocketbook, pulling out one of my calling cards. It looked ridiculous, made me *feel* ridiculous, that heavy eggshell card stock with its swirling black print, *Mrs. Ruby McTavish, Ashby House.*

Scribbling a number on the back, I said, "In case you change your mind," then laid the card on top of a wicker and glass table by the front door.

"I won't," Claire replied, but I pretended not to hear.

I thought it would feel better.

Knowing at last. The true story, the one that made the pieces click into place. Mama's weeping and drinking, her face sometimes crumpling when she looked over at me. In her heart, she must've known. Daddy had thought the loss of Ruby would eat her up, and it had. My presence only made those teeth sharper.

And Daddy. My beloved father, ruthless in business and now, I knew, in everything.

His wealth and his family name were supposed to protect him and his own from tragedy. Parents lose children in a myriad of ways every day, but Mason McTavish was not supposed to be like ordinary people. He was supposed to be blessed.

Special.

He couldn't accept his loss, so he did the only thing he knew how to—threw money at it until it went away. Until his world was right again.

No matter who got chewed up in the process.

I might have had my answers, but I didn't know what to do next.

Amends felt called for, but Claire wouldn't take my help, and I couldn't blame her for that. Besides, if I had given her money, it would've made me just like him, like Mason (I couldn't bear to think of him as "Daddy" for some time after that).

There had to be some way, though, something I could do.

Something that would, if not right the wrong, then balance the scales of the universe somehow.

It would be almost ten more years before I'd figure it out.

I couldn't give the Darnells back what they'd lost, but I *could* take from the McTavishes. What's more: I could take *and* give to someone else, someone more deserving.

Claire's question, about if I'd had children, kept coming back to me. I had never gotten pregnant despite my many husbands—the fear I'd had in Paris had proven unfounded—and I suspected I wasn't capable of it. And by that point, I was in my midforties with no intention of marrying again, so that door was firmly shut to me.

It was yet another sign of my strangeness within my own family—well, not my family at all, I knew that now—that the question of who would inherit after me had never really raised its head until that moment. The money, the house, everything that came with being a McTavish . . . I had been happy enough to embrace it for myself with little thought to what would happen after I died.

Why would I care? Like Roddy, I had begun to live only in the present, terrified to look back, indifferent to what the future might hold. But Claire's revelations changed things for me.

When I died, everything McTavish would go to Nelle. And if she died before me, then it was Howell's. Cruel, stupid Howell, who had Daddy's eyes and Nelle's pinched mouth.

Howell, a real McTavish, as I was not.

It irked me, darling. The Darnells had given up everything for a shot at something more, something bigger. In a twisted way, I was the result of all of that, and it seemed . . . I don't know. Unfair, I suppose. Unjust. Daddy had won, and when I died without children, the McTavishes would slowly reclaim what had always been rightfully theirs, the same way kudzu climbed the trees around Ashby House.

But there were other children out there. Children like me, without families.

And the more I thought of it, the more I became sure it was the way forward.

I would adopt a child, make him or her my heir. Mason's will had been an exacting, exhausting thing, leaving it all to me, every last cent, every stick of furniture. At the time, I thought it was about preserving the fortune, that he didn't want to see it divvied up into smaller shares, and that he trusted me to take care of Nelle and hers.

Now I wonder if it wasn't his own form of penance, or else some sort of delusion? Maybe he'd convinced himself I *was* Ruby, and that the whole sordid business with the Darnells had never happened. Maybe leaving everything his family had built over three hundred years to me made that lie feel real in his own heart.

In any case, once this idea took hold, I couldn't think of anything else.

But it couldn't be just any child. I would have to *feel* it was the right one.

And of course, I'd keep an eye on them through the years. If their soul showed any signs of curdling under the influence of all our largesse, then I'd rethink the plan.

I know this must sound insane to you, but you have to understand, the sins of my family—my sins included—were too great for reasonable measures.

The rot had to be cut out, and this was the only way I could think to do it.

Took ages, though.

I became convinced that I'd know the right child when I

saw him (and I knew it would be a boy by then. I can never decide if that was intuition or some sort of internalized sexism, but there you have it. I was born in 1940, I do the best I can).

I'd almost given up until the adoption agency I'd hired called. Until I looked into a pair of eyes, one blue, one brown. Sad eyes, like Andrew's.

Camden. My beautiful boy. The one good thing I've ever done.

Oh, my darling.

I can't wait for you to meet him.

-R

CHAPTER FOURTEEN

Jules

I'm at the top of the stairs, staring up at Ruby's portrait.

It's dark, the house quiet, and I'm still in that fancy dress, the crystal beading digging into the skin of my collarbone. Those crystals glitter in the dim light from the sconces lining the wall, but Ruby's eyes are shining brighter, and as I watch, they begin to move.

She's looking directly at me now, and her painted lips curve up even more, a smile that reminds me of Camden, and I know I should be scared—paintings aren't supposed to come to life—but all I feel is relieved because she's here now, because I can finally talk to her.

I need her help.

"Tell me what to do," I whisper, but she doesn't answer. Instead, the painting shifts, color bleeding away from her dark hair, her green dress, and now I'm the one in the portrait, still wearing this dress, my hands folded just like hers had been.

No, not like hers. Hers were pale and elegant, a discreet emerald ring on one finger, and mine, mine are red.

Dark crimson drops fall from my painted hands, soaking into the skirt of my dress, and I look down at my bare feet on the carpet to see that the blood is seeping out of the frame now, snaking along in a viscous river, warm when it reaches my skin.

I stumble back in horror, but the stairs are there, and I'm falling until fingers wrap around my wrist, pulling me up short.

Camden looks at me with those eyes, the eyes I love, one blue, one brown, both cold as he says, "I told you we shouldn't have come here. Why did you make me come back here?"

I look over his shoulder at the painting, and it's Ruby again, she's laughing, and then Cam is letting me go, and I'm falling again, falling into nothingness, falling—

I startle awake to arms wrapped around me, to a voice in my ear and warm breath at my temple.

"Jules. Jules, wake up."

For one dazed and horrified moment, I struggle in Cam's arms, pushing him away, remembering that cold look, the feel of his fingers slipping from my wrist, but when I look into his face, there's only concern.

His palm rests against my cheek, warm and real, and the last bits of the nightmare finally let go of me, making me sag, exhausted, against his chest.

"I haven't had a nightmare since I was in fourth grade," I stammer against his shirt—he's still wearing his suit?—and he holds me tighter.

"This is what happens when we sleep in separate rooms."

It all comes back, then: dinner, that scene with the papers, Ruby's DNA test, the panic flooding my system as I realized what was happening, the fight with Cam . . .

No wonder my dreams were haunted.

Now I let Cam hold me, breathing in his familiar scent, reminding myself that he's here and he's real and that cold-eyed man in my nightmare was just a figment of my imagination.

We sit there for a long time, arms around each other, the mountain waking up around us. I can hear birdsong as the light in the room goes from gray to orange, the sunrise lighting up all that red, making it garish.

It reminds me of the blood dripping from Ruby's portrait, and I shiver, closing my eyes.

Cam is stroking my hair, rocking me slightly, and I think I could almost fall back asleep right there, exhausted as I am, when he suddenly goes still.

I can feel tension tightening his muscles, and I look up, frowning, to see him staring at the window.

There's another sound now, tires on gravel, and Cam lets go of me, slowly rising from the bed and going over to that window, the one that faces the front of the house.

Confused, I follow him, stepping on Ruby's dress where I left it last night, crumpled on the floor. The beading bites into the sole of my foot, but I ignore the slight sting, going to stand next to Cam.

A police car sits in the drive. There are no sirens, no flashing lights, and for some reason, that makes it feel much more ominous. And then another car appears, a sleek dark blue BMW, parking just behind the cruiser.

Cam is watching as the cops get out of the cars, followed by the man in the BMW, his hair snow white, belly hanging over the belt of his khaki slacks. Then we see Ben, still in his pajamas, coming out to meet them, pointing back at the house.

A muscle ticks in Cam's jaw, and when he turns away from the window, I follow him out into the hallway.

Ben is coming up the stairs, the policemen trailing him, and when he looks up at us, I see that his face looks slack, his eyes bloodshot. He looks awful, and after last night's bullshit, that should be satisfying. But right now, I'm more concerned with those men behind him, their solemn expressions, the guns on their waists.

"What's going on?" Cam asks, and Ben pauses, running a shaking hand over his jaw.

"It's Nana Nelle," he says, and then he and the police make their way past us, the two in plain clothes giving us tight nods.

"Nelle?" Cam asks. "What about her?"

Ben turns at the top of the stairs, his face flushing red. "She's dead, that's what."

The words are flat, but his voice cracks just the littlest bit on that last word before he makes his way to the second staircase, the one that leads to the third floor where Nelle's bedroom is.

"Lordy lordy," the man with white hair says, huffing as he holds on to the banister. "I told her she needed to move to the ground floor years ago, but she wouldn't hear of it. Said her room had the best views in the whole place."

When we follow them into Nelle's bedroom, I see immediately that she was right. The large windows behind the bed frame the forest outside, the mountain below, and other peaks in the distance, soft gray smudges against the sky.

I want to keep my eyes on that view because otherwise, I'll have to look at the small, shrunken figure in the bed.

They look like they're sleeping.

That's what I've heard about dead people. That's what I've seen in movies—someone walking into a bedroom, calling cheerfully for the person in the bed to wake up, only to be concerned when they don't move, that concern slowly turning to panic as they realize the person is never waking up again.

Maybe that's true in some cases, but Nelle is unquestionably dead. Her skin is a waxy yellow, her eyes open and cloudy, mouth agape.

Next to her on the sheets is a doll, an old one if the flaking paint and yellowing lace dress are anything to go by. One of its eyes is half-shut, making it look as dead as the woman in the bed, and a shudder runs through me, making me chafe my arms as a bitter taste floods my mouth.

"I found her just before I called you," Ben says, and I think he's talking to the police, but it's the white-haired man who nods, his wrinkled face creased with sympathy.

"Hell of a thing, Benji, hell of a thing. But her heart had been bad since . . . what, 'fifteen? 'sixteen?"

"Sometime around there," Ben says with a sigh.

One of the police officers is holding Nelle's thin wrist in his hand, but that's clearly a formality, and he nods at his partner, who steps out of the room, pressing the radio on his shoulder as he goes, the static crackle loud in the quiet room.

"At least she got to pass here at Ashby," the white-haired man says, clapping Ben on the shoulder. "It's what she wanted."

"She was tired last night," Ben says, almost to himself. "She said so. Went to bed early."

Trailing off, he swings his gaze to Camden, his jaw clenching. "It was too much for her. That little performance at dinner. Wore her out."

Like "that little performance" was all Cam's doing. Like they hadn't all licked up the drama of it eagerly, Nelle herself in the starring role.

Honestly? It would serve her right if that shit is what finally made her heart give out.

"So. I came up here early this morning to see how she was feeling, and—what the hell are you doing?"

He barks the words, and the other cop, the one still by the bed, drops his hand from Nelle's face. He's young, probably barely in his twenties, and a flush actually rises up his smooth cheeks, like he's been caught with his hand in the cookie jar. Like Ben is the authority, not him.

"I was just . . . I thought I could see some bruising on the inside of her mouth, and I wanted to check."

"Now, now," the white-haired man says, stepping forward and laying his hand on the younger officer's shoulder. "This is an old woman who died in her bed, Officer Jamison. No need to upset anyone with that kind of talk. And Miss Nelle certainly wouldn't want strangers pawing over her in her own bedroom."

I wait for the officer to tell him that it doesn't matter what Nelle would want, she's *dead,* and he's a cop, doing his job.

But instead, he mutters, "Sorry, Mr. Jackson. Mr. McTavish," practically doffing his cap to them.

I've seen the house and the wealth and the way people in town respect the McTavish name, but until this moment, I don't think I fully realized the kind of power this family wields around here.

It's their own little kingdom, and everyone else is simply a servant bowing to their commands.

God, no wonder they're all so fucked up.

The cop steps back into the room, skirting around me and Cam, still frozen just inside the doorway, and walking over to Ben. "The coroner is on his way. I guess you want her taken to Thornton's?"

Ben nods, and the white-haired man makes his way over to us, giving me a broad smile with teeth that are just a little too big and a little too white. "Harlan Jackson," he says, offering me his hand. "Family friend, foremost, but also family attorney. You must be Mrs. McTavish."

"Jules," I murmur, shaking his hand, and then he looks over at Camden.

So do I, and what I see makes my heart almost stop.

Cam looks nearly as pale as Nelle, his face gone gray, his expression shuttered, and Harlan gives him a sympathetic frown, resting a hand on his arm. "I forgot you were the one who found Ruby," he says. "Hell of a thing."

I'm guessing that's his go-to phrase for anything bad that happens, but when Cam just nods robotically, swallowing hard, I get the sense he's in his own hell right now.

I take his hand, his fingers icy, and when I squeeze, he doesn't return it. Doesn't even look at me.

His gaze is locked on Nelle in her bed. When Harlan turns back to Ben, Camden drops my hand and strides out of the room.

I stand there for a beat, suddenly remembering that I'm wearing nothing more than an oversize T-shirt that used to be Cam's and a pair of sleep shorts, my bare legs cold in the chilly room, my hair a sleep-tangled mess. I murmur something about getting dressed, and hurriedly excuse myself, making my way back to our bedroom.

But Cam isn't in there.

I stand in the hallway, unsure of what to do next, when I hear a sound from the other end of the hall.

The door is ajar, and I push it open to see Cam sitting on the edge of a lace-covered bed, elbows on his thighs, head in his hands, one foot jiggling up and down so hard that his whole body shakes with it.

Closing the door behind me, I hurry over to him, crouching

between his knees, my hands reaching up to take his face. "Hey," I say softly. "I'm so sorry. Not about Nelle, honestly, fuck her, but I didn't know about Ruby. That you were the one to find her . . . that must have been so hard. And, Jesus, they had the nerve to say all of that to you last night, to accuse you of . . ."

Pushing myself up onto my knees, I wrap my arms awkwardly around his shoulders, feeling him trembling, but he doesn't make a move to hug me back, the top of his head pressed against my chest.

I've never seen him like this, and I don't know what to say, what to do, to make this better, guilt almost choking me.

I'd told myself that I could make things right here, that I could heal this place for him, and instead, I've let it break him wide open.

My eyes are hot with tears as I say, "I'm sorry. This is all my fault."

He shakes his head, hair tickling my chin. "Don't say that," he replies, voice thick, and finally his hands drop from his head, coming to rest on my ribs for a moment before he lifts his head.

I let him go, sitting back on my heels and looking up at him. His face, his beautiful face that I've loved from the first time I saw him, is anguished, tears wetting his cheeks, and there's a twisting pain in my chest that makes me understand why people say a heart breaks. That's what it feels like now, and I know how much I must love him because if I could take this away from him, if I could feel whatever agony is inside of him so that he wouldn't have to, I would.

"It brought it all back, didn't it?" I ask, stroking his calf. "Seeing Nelle. You can tell me, Cam. You can tell me anything. You know that, right?"

He's staring somewhere over my shoulder, his hands clasped

in front of him, knuckles white. I can see where he's picked at his cuticles, the skin raw, and I touch one of those red places gently, once again wishing I could take the pain he's feeling and hold it inside of me instead.

"I know things with you and Ruby were complicated," I say, my voice low and gentle, like I'm talking to a wounded animal. That's what he reminds me of right now, jittery and tense, his eyes haunted. "But still. It must have been such a shock, finding her like—"

Cam gets up so fast that I rock back in surprise, almost knocked over by his long legs as he strides away from me, one hand on his hip, the other rubbing his mouth.

He stands there in the middle of the room, and something starts to go cold inside me, sinking into my veins, my heart.

"It wasn't a shock. Finding her," he says as I sit there on the plush carpet of Ruby's bedroom and wait for him to say what my sick stomach and dazed mind somehow already know.

"I knew she was dead when I opened the door," he goes on, and he turns, our gazes meeting, and I want to tell him to stop there, not to say the next part, the part that he won't be able to take back, the part I won't be able to unhear.

"I knew. Because I killed her."

CHAPTER FIFTEEN

Camden

I killed her."

The words hang in the air, words I've never said out loud before. You'd imagine it would feel good, getting something like that off your chest, even if you know it's about to ruin your fucking life.

But it doesn't feel like anything. It's just a fact, one I've tried to run from, though I've now learned you can't run from these kinds of things.

They always catch you in the end.

Jules is still sitting on the floor, her legs twisted to one side, her eyes wide in a pale face. Her legs and feet are bare, her toenails turquoise. I flash back to her painting them in the bathroom of our little house in Golden, singing softly to herself as I lay in our bed and watched her, warmth in my chest, contentment in my bones.

How fucking stupid I was, thinking I could have that forever.

"I, uh. I'd come back from college. I was going to UNC then, but I'd already started the paperwork to transfer. Do you know why I picked CSU San Bernardino?"

She shakes her head, and I rub the back of my neck, a humorless laugh harsh in my throat. "Neither did I. I just searched 'colleges in California,' and told myself I'd choose one at random. It didn't matter where, just so long as it put the whole country between me and this place. Because I knew by then. I knew what Ashby House did to people. How it twisted them. It's not just the money. I mean, the money is part of it, but it's more than that. It's what happens when you live in a place that never expects you to . . . well, leave, I guess. To go out in the world and actually do something with your life. Ruby, her family? They might as well be gods here. It's why they all stay. They're so used to everyone knowing who they are, to their last name opening doors and greasing wheels, and . . ."

I blow out a shaky breath. These secrets have been stuck inside me for so long, and now they're all tumbling out. "When nothing has ever been hard for you. When you've never had to do the normal shit everyone else does to get through their day, you start thinking maybe you *aren't* a normal person. Maybe you *are* better. Which means you can do what you want. Anything you want."

Jules hasn't moved, but I can see her chest moving up and down, her lips parted, and I wish there were some way to make her understand, to pour all these experiences into her head, all the years of living in this house. To make her see how confusing it was to be simultaneously the coddled Golden Boy and the outsider, the orphan.

"Ruby used to say that to me," I continue. "'You're a McTavish now, Camden. That makes you special.' But I saw what being 'special' looked like to this family."

It looked like Ben wrecking a boat on Beaver Lake, slamming into some poor kid on a Jet Ski who never walked again. No matter that Ben was drunk, no matter that he should have been arrested. The kid lost his legs, but thanks to the McTavish fortune, he had a full bank account for life.

It looked like Howell's wife, sunglasses hiding black eyes, but new diamonds always appearing in her ears, around her neck, before the bruises even faded. Howell was a mean drunk but a regular at Tiffany's.

It looked like Nelle, placidly watching the police haul away one of the cleaning crew on robbery charges. Then, later that same evening, appearing at dinner wearing the very same bracelet she'd claimed had been stolen. "I found it in my jewelry box," she'd said with an elegant shrug, and nothing more. There was no phone call down to the station, and certainly no guilt at having jumped to conclusions.

It looked like Libby sitting on the edge of my bed, expecting me to be enthralled, assuming I'd be seduced.

And yeah, you know what? It looked like Ruby, picking some poor kid out of the foster system and hanging a golden anchor around his neck just to piss off her family.

"She hated it," I tell Jules, sinking down on the bench in front of Ruby's dressing table. "The idea of me leaving. I think it was the only time she ever raised her voice to me."

You're a little old for teenage rebellion, Camden, and frankly, I'm tired of this discussion. Transfer to Duke, transfer to Wake Forest, but you have responsibilities to this family, and I will be damned if you abandon them!

"I stopped taking her calls. She stopped paying my bills. I got a job working at a restaurant in Chapel Hill only to have the manager call me into his office after my first shift and say that he needed to let me go."

I laugh bitterly, shaking my head. "It took two more jobs that shitcanned me after only a day to realize what Ruby was doing. As long as I was in North Carolina, I was within her reach. In trying to make it hard for me to leave, she only proved why I couldn't stay."

"Is that . . ."

Jules's voice is whisper-thin, and she stops, takes a deep breath. "Is that why? So that you could be free?"

It's not an absolution, but it's not a condemnation, either. She hasn't gotten up, hasn't run out screaming, and fuck knows I shouldn't be dumb enough to hope for anything more, but that's what the little spark in my chest feels like right now.

"I don't know," I tell her truthfully. "Maybe? I didn't . . . it wasn't something I planned. I didn't come here that night to . . . to do that."

But I'd just lost another job, my credit cards were frozen, my bank account was locked. I'd told myself I didn't need her money, I could make it on my own. I didn't care if I slept in my car and ate cheap hot dogs and canned chili for the rest of my life, though of course, I didn't realize how naïve that was. For one thing, the car wasn't mine, and a phone call from Ruby would've had it on the back of a tow truck within the hour. And if I couldn't keep a job for more than two days, I couldn't make enough money to buy hot dogs, much less a new car, and the more jobs I lost, the harder it would be to get new ones. Everywhere I turned, there was some new, Ruby-shaped roadblock in front of me. Every path of escape had slowly been cut off.

"I didn't realize how hard it would be," I tell Jules now, and when she blanches, I lift a hand, shaking my head.

"No. No, I don't mean that . . . part. I mean, just *leaving*. I didn't understand how every part of my life was tied to Ruby.

To what she'd given me. To what she could take away. When I came up here that night, all I wanted to do was talk to her, to see if we could find some kind of compromise. I thought there had to be a way, you know? I thought . . ."

I thought I could find the right words to make her see reason, to let me go. What I didn't get was that there was nothing *reasonable* about any of this to Ruby.

That Ruby would *never* let me go.

I breathe in through my nose, knowing I have to finish this.

"It was raining that night. Ben was off at college and Libby was in town." I laugh, but there's no actual mirth in it. "So, yeah, she was lying at dinner, but she was also telling the truth in a fucked-up way. Howell was doing some guys' fishing weekend down in Georgia. Nelle was upstairs watching TV—she got really obsessed with *Downton Abbey*. A rich family in England, that big house, World War One? Classic Nelle."

I'm stalling, I know I am, but I make myself say the most important part.

"And Ruby . . . Ruby was waiting for me in her room. In here."

She'd been sitting on this bench, dressed in her pajamas, but even those seemed like formal wear on Ruby. She was seventy-three by then, but looked younger, her dark hair turned silver, and as I stood there, dripping rain onto her carpet, she rubbed that fancy cream of hers into her hands, watching me in the mirror.

Have you finally come to your senses?

"I begged with her. I pleaded. I swear to god, Jules, I actually got down on my fucking *knees* right there."

I point to where she's sitting.

I can't stay here. Please. Please, let me go.

"She got up, and she crossed the room, and she put her

hands on my face. They were cold. Almost . . . almost slimy. From the cream she used. She was smiling at me. I was crying, and she was *smiling*. And then she said, 'Do you remember Tyler Hayes?'"

Jules slowly draws her legs up, wrapping her arms around her knees, her brows drawn tight together. "Who was that?"

I shake my head, swiping at my face. I hadn't realized that tears were streaming down it, just like they had that night.

"This asshole kid I'd gone to school with. In tenth grade, we got in a fight after a soccer game. Just stupid teenage boy shit, I don't even remember what it was about. But he got in one really solid punch and it broke my nose."

I touch the slight bump on the bridge, remembering. "Hurt like a motherfucker. Ruby met me at the ER, and held my hand while they reset it. It was the only time I'd ever seen her be maternal in my life. So, there I am, with my nose throbbing and my stomach grinding because I'd puked from the pain, and we're driving back up here, and she goes, 'That Tyler boy. His father works for me. Well, for the company. He runs that little hotel on Main Street.' And I knew that, of course, but I didn't really care what his dad did for a living, so I think I just grunted or something. And then she said, 'If you want, I'll fire him.'

"I laughed because I thought she was joking with me. Like it was one of those, 'Want me to kill him?' things. Just something you say when a person hurts someone you love. Not something you actually *do*. But she was dead serious. 'I can have the whole bed-and-breakfast shut down, actually,' she said. 'And the bank that has the mortgage on their house is obviously very keen to keep my business, so that's another avenue to pursue. If you want.'"

Jules's arms tighten around her knees, and I smile wryly. "I said no. In fact, I said, 'It was a stupid fight, Ruby. You don't ruin a guy's life over that.'"

You *might not,* Ruby had said, her eyes staring straight ahead. *Others would.*

"And that's when I remembered there had been other instances like this. Times when something shitty would happen, and she'd offer to use various weapons at her disposal to right the scales, and I always said no."

The girl who dumped me right before my first homecoming dance. The guy who dinged my new car in the parking lot of the Food Mart, then acted like it was somehow my fault.

"I'd seen Howell pull similar strings for Libby and Ben, and I had no doubt Nelle had done the same for Howell, but it always felt gross to me, you know? So, I just thought Ruby was doing what this family did. I didn't realize it was a test."

You didn't want me to make Tyler Hayes pay for what he'd done to you. You're a good person, Camden, Ruby had said, moving to the bed and turning down the covers. *At your core. I have given you every privilege, every advantage, everything that every McTavish has had since the first one showed up here three hundred years ago. And every McTavish since then has grown more self-centered, more uncaring. Not a one of them should have this. But you, my darling boy?*

She had gotten into the bed, folding her hands on top of the sheets.

You are my redemption.

"Redemption," I echo to Jules. "That's what she called me."

Jules is frowning now, but she's still listening.

"And then," I say on a sigh, "she told me about the pills."

MY REDEMPTION, SHE repeats. *And I'm going to prove it to you.*

Her face looks beatific, skin almost unlined despite her age.

You want to be free of me, from all of this, but I've made that impossible for you. If I were to die, though . . . well, then you'd have what you wanted. Money, which you say you don't care about, but also freedom. An entire fortune at your disposal, and no one to stop you from doing what you see fit with it.

But she doesn't say "see," exactly. The *s* slides, s-s-s-s-see, a hiss almost, and I notice one eyelid drooping.

I've made it . . . so easy for you.

Her words are slowing down, and she waves one hand lazily at her nightstand.

Not even sure what all I took. Think . . . think some pills still left from . . . from Duke, things they-they don't . . . sell the-ese days-s-s. As soon as I s-a-saw your . . . your car. In the drive. Swallowed them down w-with a glass . . .

She smiles then, hazy.

A glass of the 1959 Dom.

My stomach lurches and I rise to my feet.

What have you done? What the fuck have you done?

You could let me . . . let me die and get all you ever wanted. B-but you won't. Just like . . . like you never told th-them. About Dora Darnell.

Her smile widens, teeth glinting. *About me. You wouldn't . . . wouldn't do that. And you're not going to do that. Not going to do this. You're . . . you're going to call . . . call the . . . ambulance, the siren . . .*

Her eyes open and close, the lids heavy, then lifting quickly, her thick lashes blinking against her pale cheeks, chest heaving.

B-better than me, she says on a wheezing breath. *I made you better th-than all of us . . . I made you . . .*

She keeps smiling at me, and then her smile starts to change. *Camden.*

Confusion on her face, then something that would be panic were the drugs not pulling her under. A jerky movement, a thin hand slapping at her nightstand, nails tapping the acrylic of the French phone by her bed, and suddenly I find my legs.

I don't even think, I don't let myself think.

I pick the phone up, unplugging the cord from the back, and clutching it to my chest, I begin to back away from the bed.

Ruby watches me, panting now, fighting to keep her eyes open, her mouth opening to scream, but all that comes out is a breathy sort of moan, and I keep backing up, backing up, backing up until my heels hit the wall, my head thumping back, my eyes never leaving her.

As Ruby McTavish Callahan Woodward Miller Kenmore slowly dies in her bed, I sink down against the wall, holding on to the phone so tightly that later, I'll find red grooves in my palms, a bruise making a purple line against the skin of my chest.

I sob as she finally stops struggling, sitting there on the floor as her breathing slows, steady at first, like she's sleeping.

But there are gasps after that, and then, for a long time, so long I can feel my mind cracking inside my skull, there's a rattling, guttural noise.

And my mind must crack because that's when I get up from my spot against the wall, the phone clattering out of my grip, and grab a pillow from her bed and press it over her face, just wanting her to stop, stop making that sound, she needs to stop . . .

She does.

Later, I put the phone back into place, plug it back into the wall. I wipe it down with a washcloth from Ruby's bathroom that I shove in my back pocket and, later, throw out the window of my car somewhere near the Georgia border.

I'm in my bedroom that next morning when Cecilia knocks, her face tearstained, her hands reaching for me.

Oh, honey, she says, and I let myself be hugged and wonder how soon I can leave Ashby House forever.

WHEN I'M FINISHED, I've stopped crying, but Jules had started somewhere around the part with the phone, tears dripping onto her gray T-shirt, leaving dark splotches.

"She gave me everything," I say. "And she trusted that I'd save her. She took all those fucking pills because she believed I was a good person. But I wasn't. She was right. If she died, I was free, and I . . . I chose that. Chose it over her. I let her die rather than stay here."

Jules gets up then, moving across the carpet on silent feet, and stands in front of me.

She cups my face in her hands, and then leans down and kisses me.

"I love you," she says when we part, and I didn't know until that moment how much I needed to hear that. "I love you, and you are a good person, Camden. The best person I know."

I shake my head, wanting to deny that, *needing* to, but she won't let me. "You were a kid," she says, her grip tightening on my face. "And she threw you into this . . . this fucking snake pit to prove something to herself. She let Nelle and Howell and even Ben and Libby treat you like shit just to see what you could take. She killed *herself,* Cam."

Jules is right, I know she is, but I still want to deny it, am already opening my mouth to protest when she pulls me to my feet, her hand firm in mine.

"You need to see something."

She pulls me out of Ruby's room and down the hall, back to our bedroom, and picks up a sheaf of paper from the nightstand. Even without her letterhead at the top, I'd know it was from Ruby's desk. I'd seen that heavy, cream-colored vellum my whole life, done my fucking algebra homework on it.

"The other day when I was in Ruby's office, looking through photo albums, I . . . okay, I took the snooping a little too far, and went through her desk. I found these."

Letters. Not addressed to anyone, but I can hear Ruby's voice as my eyes scan the first line.

Well, darling, here we are.

"I took them out because I thought they must be to you, but I didn't read them until last night. I couldn't sleep, and after I read them, well . . . then I *really* couldn't sleep."

Pages and pages, written in Ruby's careful, neat hand, all dated in the days just before she died.

I've never seen them before.

I don't want to read them, I don't want Ruby's voice in my head, and I try to hand them back to Jules. "It doesn't matter," I tell her, but she patiently shoves the papers back at me, her hazel eyes imploring.

"It does, Cam," she says softly. "I promise you."

I'm exhausted, drained, but I sit on the edge of the bed, willing to humor her.

I read the first page, then the second. Three more, five more.

Page after page, confession after confession, Ruby's familiar, chatty voice, and then all these nightmares, all this death. I feel heavy with it, weighed down with the knowledge of who this woman, the only mother I'd ever known, really was.

But right behind all of that?

Relief.

Because now I know. The rumors, the whispers, the secret Google searches at the library, the guilt for suspecting that the woman who raised me was a murderer making my palms sweat and my stomach ache.

All of it was true.

What's more, I feel like I understand her better now. She did these things, and she wanted to tell me about them because I was her son, and she thought I deserved to know.

And then I get to the last letter and remember that nothing was ever that simple with Ruby.

CHAPTER SIXTEEN

Jules

I watch as Cam reads Ruby's letters, waiting for him to say something, but when he's finished, he just places the last page facedown on the growing stack beside him on the bed, his expression far away.

"It's heavy, I know," I say, and he rubs his hands over his face.

"That's one word for it," he replies, the words muffled.

"Do you have any idea who she was writing to?" I ask him now. "Because I thought they were to you, but then that part at the end about wanting someone to meet you . . ."

Cam presses his hands onto his thighs, standing with a wince. "No clue. And honestly, I don't care. If you found them, she never sent them to anyone."

He looks back at the papers. "For all we know, this was just another mind fuck of hers. A trap to spring further down the line. You said these were in her desk?"

I nod, and Cam shakes his head, blowing out a long breath.

"Thank sweet fuck Ben and Howell didn't find them first," he says. I wait for him to ask the obvious question—how could Ben have found that key to the safety-deposit box, but missed these letters?

But he doesn't, just keeps staring at the papers in his hand, and my fingers itch to pick up the pages again, to hunt for more clues. I think of Ruby saying that she kept replaying scenes from her life, looking for some hint of what was to come, and now I understand that impulse, because I'm sure there's more to her story.

It doesn't feel finished yet.

But our story here at Ashby, mine and Cam's, that's over.

I know that now. I thought that love would be enough to chase out the darkness, and in her own twisted way, I think Ruby thought that, too. I think she *believed* she loved Cam, but I don't know if she really knew how to love anyone, no matter what she said.

But I do. And I love Cam too much to make him stay here.

"Let's go," I tell him. "Right now. Back to Colorado or . . . fuck, Timbuktu, I don't care, just not here, okay?"

He looks at me, his fingers brushing mine. "I'm sorry," he says. "That I couldn't give you what you wanted."

I step close to him, grabbing his shirtfront and pulling him in tight. "Don't ever say that to me again. You have given me everything, Camden. Way more than I ever should have gotten."

I mean it, and I hope he feels that in my kiss when I lift my face to his.

When we pull apart, he rubs my upper arms and says, "All right. Timbuktu it is. But there's something I need to handle first. Can you manage being here on your own for a few hours?"

"Of course," I say. "I can pack up while you do whatever it is you need to do. I'm sure the rest of them will be busy making arrangements for Nelle, so they probably won't even notice I'm here."

Cam nods, but his mind is already somewhere else, I can tell.

"I'm going to shower and change, and then I'll head out. I should be back by dark."

I blink, shocked to realize that it's already noon. Time had stopped meaning anything once we'd gone into Ruby's room and Camden told me what had happened there ten years ago.

I want to ask Cam where he's going, but, more than that, I want him to tell me himself.

Instead, he kisses my cheek and makes his way to the bathroom.

I start folding Ruby's letters, and he pauses, turning back around. "Do me a favor while I'm gone? Get rid of those. Burn them, shove them down the garbage disposal, whatever. But I don't want anyone else to see them. Ever."

ONCE CAM IS out of the house, I take my own shower and change, then start gathering our things. It's hard to believe we've been here less than a week. I feel like a different person than the Jules who rode up here, full of anticipation and plans, excited to settle into her husband's home.

It doesn't take long until the room is clear of all our things. Except for Ruby's letters.

I hold them in my hand for a moment, remembering Cam's instructions to destroy them, and I hesitate for a moment before shoving them into the bottom of my bag.

Just one more thing to do now.

Ruby's office is quiet and dim, the door barely creaking as I push it open and make my way over to the desk.

The whole house is quiet, in fact. The coroner came for Nelle while Cam and I were in Ruby's room, and Ben had followed them to the funeral home. Libby had been so upset that she'd taken an Ambien and gone back to bed.

That was hours ago, but I haven't heard anyone return, and when I glance out the window, I see that Cecilia's car isn't in its usual spot.

It's possible that I'm completely alone in the house, but I still try to be as quick and as quiet as I can as I slide open the top drawer of her desk.

My heart leaps at the sight of that familiar paper, but the pages are all blank, and the other drawers are nearly empty, like I'd known they'd almost certainly be.

Fuck.

I straighten up, looking around the office for another hiding place. But the thing with fancy offices in mansions belonging to homicidal heiresses is that *everything* looks like a hiding place. For all I know, I could go pull one of the books on the far wall and an entire room would open up.

Still, I move in that direction, my fingers dragging along the spines, looking for anything likely.

I've just picked up *The Rubáiyát of Omar Khayyám*—Ruby strikes me as both vain enough and potentially crazy enough to choose something that sounds like her own name as a hiding place—when a shadow falls across the shelf.

"Stuffing your pockets with valuables before you slink out of town?"

Ben stands there, still in the suit he'd worn to accompany Nelle's body to the funeral home, that blinding grin on his face.

"Just looking for something to read," I lie, and he winks at me.

"I liked you, you know. Thought you had spunk."

Of course, he did.

"I didn't like you. I thought you were a dick," I reply, and his grin widens as he points at me.

"See? That's what I'm talking about. A straight shooter!"

If he does finger guns at me, I swear to god—

"Kapow!"

He blows imaginary smoke from the tip of his finger, and I grit my teeth.

"Really cheerful for a man whose grandmother just died," I tell him, and finally, he drops some of that Good Ol' Boy bullshit.

"She lived a long life and died happy in her bed. None of us could wish better for someone we love."

"Right, because love is in such abundant supply in this family."

I head for the door, frustrated and anxious. This was my one chance, and now it's gone. It's already late in the afternoon, Cam will be back soon, and then we'll never step foot in this house again. This will become Ben's office, probably, and what if he finds—

"I'm guessing you're looking for this."

He pulls a tight rectangle of folded papers from his suit jacket, and my mouth goes dry.

Still, I make myself say, "I wasn't looking for anything."

"Oh, you weren't?" He raises his eyebrows. "Huh. Well, I'll be damned. Because I found this not long after Daddy died. Right before you got in touch."

He nods at the bookcases, specifically at a jeweled box

nestled onto one of the shelves, glittering dully in the low light. Its top sits at a drunken angle, the hinges broken.

"Didn't make much sense at the time," he goes on, "but I hung on to it anyway. Just in case."

What a stupid fucking mistake I'd made, assuming Ben was annoying, but harmless. A toothless Doberman. How many other people had been suckered by his surface charm covering simple meanness, not knowing that he was smarter than he let on?

"And then, of course, when you got in touch after Dad died, Camden's sweet wife Jules, just wanting to see his family home one time, promising the *moon* if I would just tell him we needed him here . . . well, some things, you just don't forget."

Still holding the papers in one hand, he lifts them and snaps his wrist, the pages unfolding in front of his face as he makes a show of squinting, scanning through the lines until he gets to the one he wants.

"Right, here it is. 'I think your idea of using another name is very smart, dear girl, and of course I can help with the paperwork. Julianne is a lovely middle name, so I agree, use that.'"

I'm shaking, my vision going gray around the edges, and I think of Camden, wherever he is right now, coming back to me, coming back to *this*.

"'And besides,'" Ben goes on, his voice a high, syrupy imitation of what Ruby sounded like, grating over my ears. "'You can go by Jules. Ruby, jewel, do you see? Clever of us, isn't it?'"

Ben looks at me over the top of the paper.

"Clever, indeed." His voice is his own again, dripping with menace as he moves closer. "Guess she never got around to sending this before she died, but I'm guessing there were others, weren't there? Because there's all this talk of 'confessions.' Confessing to what, Mrs. McTavish?"

"I don't—"

"Don't try to brazen this out," he says sharply, cutting me off. "You can't, although I admire the effort. Like I said. Spunk."

He bites the ending of the word off between his white teeth, and I grimace.

I try another tactic. Licking my lips, I say, "What's the point of this now? Camden's agreed to give you everything. You don't have to go to court over it, you don't even have to hire lawyers. All he wants is to be free from this, from *you*. You're getting everything you want, so why would you even bother to show this to him?"

But he doesn't have to answer.

As soon as the words are out of my mouth, as soon as I look into his eyes, I know the answer.

"Right," I say softly. "Because it will hurt him."

Because Cam had the gall to exist alongside them, even though he wasn't one of them. Because for all the petty cruelties they threw at him, they couldn't break him.

Because he made them afraid that the life they'd known would someday be taken away from them.

Of course, they can't forgive that.

Of course, even now, with everything they want stretching out in front of them, it's not enough.

It will never be enough.

The anger that floods through me is hot. Clean. Maybe the purest thing I've ever felt.

"What won't you people do?" I say, my voice still barely above a whisper. "Every opportunity in the world, and you turned out like this. These ... these sad, grasping, *pathetic* fuckers who'd kill each other just to get a bigger piece of the pie."

I'm not thinking of Nelle when I say it, truly. It's just a figure of speech.

But maybe you've figured out by now that I think fast on my feet, and while Ben may be smarter than I thought he was, that still doesn't make him smarter than me.

I see the way he blanches, see the vein that ticks in his forehead, his eyes sliding from mine just for a second, and I almost start laughing.

"Fuck me," I say, shaking my head. "You did. You *did* kill your own grandmother."

If Camden relinquished his hold on the McTavish inheritance, Nelle was next in line for the whole thing. Sure, she was almost eighty, and bound to kick it sooner rather than later, but Ben couldn't wait even that long.

"Shut your mouth, bitch," Ben growls, and now I do laugh.

"Oh my god, that's why you didn't want that cop looking at her mouth, right?"

Cam's confession, that horrible story, Ruby seizing on the bed, his sobs, the pillow over her face . . .

I knew that after ten years in the grave, there wouldn't be any evidence left if someone decided to exhume Ruby, if Ben decided to follow through on his threat and actually accused Cam of murder. Nevertheless, I still found myself frantically Googling on my phone after he had left.

How to know if someone has been smothered.

Apparently, the evidence is usually in their mouths.

Bruising inside their lips, from their teeth pressing hard against the skin.

"And yet you tried to come in here, and hold it over my head that I lied?" I say to Ben now, my voice growing louder.

"Yeah, I did, okay? I lied, and I schemed, and I wanted Cam to throw all of you out. I wanted this house, and to be a McTavish, but I am *nothing* like you. And neither is Cam. We're better than all of you, and that's what you can't stand."

I snatch the letter from his limp hand, the pages almost tearing. "Get fucked, Ben. Sincerely. I'll DVR your episode of *Dateline*."

And then I make one last, stupid mistake.

I turn my back on a man with nothing to lose.

CHAPTER SEVENTEEN

Camden

I used to make this drive a lot when I first got a car.

Two hours to Knoxville, almost on the nose.

Ruby never asked where I went, maybe didn't care, but if she had, I think I would have told her the truth.

It wasn't that hard, finding my birth mother's name. Ruby could be careless with paperwork, leaving sensitive things in places where anyone could find them.

I was fourteen when I saw the name for the first time.

Penny Halliday.

It didn't even bother me that in the space for Father's Name on my birth certificate, there was just one stark word: Unknown.

And I never planned on seeing her, on making these borderline-creepy drives to Knoxville, but as soon as I had my license, that's where I'd found myself heading.

I've never spoken to her, never tried to make any contact with her. It wasn't about that.

It was about reminding myself that whatever it is that runs

through the McTavishes—whatever made them cruel like Howell, or dangerous like Ben, or even benignly neglectful like Ruby—was nothing that lived inside of me.

And hell, it was possible that Penny Halliday was all those things, too. But for some reason, I didn't think so.

For one, she taught art at a community center for under-privileged kids, a place I couldn't imagine any McTavish ever stepping foot inside. And when I parked my car outside that building, watched her walk out the front doors that first time, she'd been smiling. Laughing with another woman, in a carefree way I'd never seen from anyone at Ashby House—even though no one had more reasons to be carefree than they did.

I stopped making the drives when I was eighteen. I started feeling weird about it, like I was intruding on her life, even if I never talked to her. And anyway, what did it matter?

She'd given birth to me, but she was only my mother in the biological sense.

Ruby McTavish was my true mother.

For better and for worse.

So I don't know exactly why I'm making this drive now, or why I looked Penny up on Facebook to see whether she still teaches these classes.

But I am, and she does, so I park where I used to park, and I wait for her to walk out of the building. For the sight of her to remind me that there's another side to me, a part of myself that Ruby had nothing to do with.

Penny Halliday was only sixteen when I was born. I learned that the same day I learned her name, and I remember think-ing, on that first drive over here, that I was the same age as she had been. How foreign it felt to me, the idea of being a parent.

I never resented her for giving me up. I understood it, hon-estly. She simply did what she thought was best. But I wondered if she ever learned what happened to me, if she saw those pictures in that magazine and her heart swelled and broke all at once seeing me called "The Luckiest Boy in North Carolina."

The doors open across the street, and kids pour out into a courtyard, excitedly chattering. I wait for the adults that follow.

Penny is one of the last ones to leave, but there she is, wearing a red shirt and jeans. She's only forty-eight, and she hasn't changed much in the last decade, her brown hair, the same shade as mine, tucked behind her ears.

She has other kids now, I learned on Facebook. I have a half brother and a half sister. They're twenty and eighteen, and the boy, Brandon, has my eyes.

One blue, one brown.

I'd looked at his picture forever, waiting to feel something, a connection, a link.

But he was just a stranger. A boy with my eyes, but a different nose, a different smile, and as I look at Penny now, I realize she's a stranger, too.

"Family" is a complicated word—more complicated for me than a lot of people, I'd guess. I've spent so much of my life trying to figure out what that word even means to me.

Sitting there in that parking lot in Knoxville, though, it all becomes clear. Simple, even.

Jules is my family.

Jules, who sees the darkest parts of me, the worst thing I ever did, and loves me anyway.

Just like I see the darkest parts of her, the worst thing she's ever done, and love her, too.

She doesn't know it, though.

Oh, she knows I love her. It's the rest of it.

The darkest parts, the worst thing.

It took me awhile to put it together, I can admit that.

When she first slid into my life, I mostly thought how stupidly lucky I'd gotten, this gorgeous girl who wanted *me*, even though I was still the human equivalent of a locked door when we met.

And then, once the sex haze wore off and I started paying a little more attention, I thought maybe I was just being paranoid. Ruby was dead, after all—she couldn't have had anything to do with this pretty-eyed girl in my bed, in my heart.

But Jules knew things about me she shouldn't have, things I hadn't told her. Things that would slip out, like the name of the soccer team I'd played on in middle school, or that I was allergic to cats. I'd thought about how desperate Ruby had been to keep me tethered to her, how no one hedged their bets quite like she did, and how, when I looked into Jules's eyes, I saw that same deep green, dark enough to seem black, fathomless.

I tried to use the money Ruby had left as little as possible, but you need cash to pay for the best and most discreet private detectives, something Ruby had known when she found Claire Darnell.

My guys found Claire Darnell, too. She was dead by then, but she had a daughter, Linda.

Tragedy stalked the Darnells, though, because Linda had also died—in a car accident in 2011, which had left her nineteen-year-old daughter an orphan.

Caitlin Julianne Darnell.

A real mouthful. Didn't blame her for switching to Jules, although I still can't tell you where Brewster came from. Never did figure that part out.

Did Ruby reach out first? Did Jules?

I don't know.

What I do know is that the great-granddaughter of the man accused of kidnapping my adoptive mother showing up at the shitty wing place where I worked seemed like too big of a co-incidence to explain away.

I could tell you that's why I stayed with her. That I was wait-ing to see what she'd do. If Ruby had put her up to this, that plan had to be fucking toast now, given that Ruby was dead.

I admit, I was curious.

How long could she keep it up?

Trouble was, I did the dumbest thing I could have, given what I knew.

I fell in love with her.

And then she did the dumbest thing *she* could've done.

She fell in love with me, too.

Sometimes I want to ask Jules if those feelings surprised her, like they did me, but that would mean telling her I knew the truth, and I've never been able to make myself do that.

Because if there's one thing I learned from the deep, dark se-cret that Mason McTavish killed to hide—in the end, it doesn't matter. The truth isn't some finite thing, it's what we all choose to believe. Ruby was Dora Darnell, yes, but in the end, wasn't she Ruby McTavish, too? And Jules might have been born Caitlin Darnell, but she was *Jules*. My wife. She loves bad puns and can quote just about every line of the movie *Labyrinth,* and when she has more than two beers, she'll dance to any music playing.

And she's the woman I fell in love with, the woman who fell in love with me.

That's the truth.

Ten years. A decade together, born out of fucked-up cir-cumstances, yes—but despite all that, what we have is real.

How could it not be when she heard the story of Ruby's

final night, and not only did she not run from me, she walked straight into my arms?

I don't care what—or who—brought her to me. I only care that she's here, with me, now.

It's the only thing that matters.

I watch Penny Halliday get into her car, and in my mind, I know this is it. I won't see her again; I'm saying goodbye for good. I hope her life makes her happy, and if I hadn't decided to give the whole fucking inheritance to Ben, I'd write a big check for this community center right now, fund it into the next century.

Instead, I start the car and head back home to Jules.

I told her I'd be home before dark, but the sky is a deep navy by the time I take the exit to Tavistock, and I push the gas a little harder, the needle ticking toward ninety.

The sooner I'm back, the sooner we're gone, away from this place, just the two of us.

Just as it should be.

The sky is lighter when I make the turn up the mountain, and for a moment, I'm confused, looking at the clock, glancing back over my shoulder, trying to figure out if the sun is still setting in the western sky.

But no, the compass on the SUV's dash tells me I'm headed northeast, and the glow in the sky is an odd color, not the soft pinks and purples of Blue Ridge sunsets at all, but a brighter orange.

Fire.

My heart is in my mouth, my hands choking the steering wheel, and the back tires slide as I slam on the gas, climbing higher and higher as the sky gets brighter and the thick smell of smoke starts seeping into the car.

The gates are open, and I tear through them so fast that I

hear roots scraping the undercarriage, a distant metallic thunk that can't be good, but I don't care because now I'm rounding the last bend, then I slam on the brakes as I raise my hand against the glare.

Ashby House is burning.

Every inch of it is lit up with white-hot flames. The fire engine I now see at the side of the house is blasting water, creating clouds of steam in the night sky. But the steady stream is no match for the blaze.

When I stumble out of the driver's seat, the heat almost has me reeling back, but I can't, I have to keep moving toward the house, toward Jules.

"Jules!"

Her name is a harsh scream in my throat, and I call it again and again, eyes frantically searching, but the house is so damn bright, and the few dark figures I see are all in heavy gear.

Firefighters, spraying their hoses, wielding their axes, and I stand there, watching Ashby House burn, imagining Ruby's portrait inside, those painted eyes somehow intact, watching as flames lick at Jules's skin, her hair, burning her to ash.

If only you'd been the man I thought you were, Camden. If only you'd picked up that phone.

My knees are weak, and I'm fighting the urge to sink to them when I see white lights off to the other side of the house.

An ambulance, doors flung open, and a figure on a stretcher.

Sitting up. Gesturing toward the house.

Blond hair glowing.

I'm running toward her before I know it, and when she sees me, Jules pulls the oxygen mask off her face. She's streaked with soot and tears, parts of her hair crisped away, but she's alive, and already reaching for me.

"Cam!"

I wrap my arms around her, hardly believing it.

"You're okay," I say, and one of the EMTs, a redheaded woman I think I went to high school with, gently pushes me back.

"She's not okay. She's got a nasty lump on the back of her head, and she's inhaled a lot of smoke."

"I'm okay," Jules argues, then turns to me, insisting again, "I'm okay."

Her face clouds then, cold fingers tangling with mine. "But Cam . . . Ben was in there. I don't know about Libby, but . . ." Her voice breaks, a sob mixing with a hacking cough.

She tries, she really does.

And it's good, I have to give it to her. Good enough to fool anyone else. My girl wasn't a theater major for nothing.

But she can't hide from me.

Maybe one day she'll tell me the truth.

Maybe not.

Maybe she'll wait until she's in her seventies, and then she'll write me a long stack of letters, letters that are actually for *me* this time.

That's fine.

For now, I just hold her hand in mine and together we watch the McTavishes burn.

March 31, 2013

Surprise! Another letter.

I'm sure you thought I was done after the last one. Honestly, so did I. I'd given you everything, darling, so what else was there to say?

But then I got your reply—now thrown in the fire, just as you asked, how very clandestine we're being!—and, since I have some time tonight, I thought I'd jot one final missive.

Besides, I have some questions for *you* now, questions I somehow neglected when we met.

Have you always been this clever? It's just that cleverness does not seem to run in the family, no offense. (And how could I offend, given that it's my family, too? Insulting your bloodline is insulting mine, let's not forget, darling.)

Although, I suppose my father/your great-grandfather had a certain kind of low cunning. You have to be pretty ruthless to sell your toddler, after all. But then my mother, your great-grandmother, had the integrity to burn thousands of dollars when she could barely keep a roof over her head.

Do those two impulses balance out in you?

In any case, you were right to contact me. I had assumed your grandmother threw my card away back in 1985, and that I'd never hear from any of you again.

Imagine my delight when I got your message!

Well, I wasn't *completely* delighted. I do wish you'd been a little nicer, and a little less . . . threatening, let's say, but still, a bit of intrigue always livens up one's day.

I don't think I told you the night we met, but you were very good in that play. I've seen *Arsenic and Old Lace* many times—it was one of Andrew's favorites—and I did not have especially high hopes for a community college production in Gainesville, Florida, and yet there you were, impeccable as Elaine. Far better than the boy playing Mortimer Brewster, I'm afraid.

But then, I'm sure you already knew that. You strike me as a girl who knows her worth.

To be honest, I'm not sure I fully believed I was a Darnell until I met you. Your grandmother certainly resembled me physically, but we were miles apart spiritually. *You*, though, Miss Caity.

You're a girl after my own heart.

As I told you in that horrible diner you insisted we go to, it's always been my dearest wish to somehow repay the Darnell family for their loss. Not that anyone ever could replace such a precious thing as a child, but I've longed to make amends for some time.

Camden helped with that, a bit. He's such a sweet boy, the best I've ever known, and I'm sure you'll agree.

But it wasn't quite the same, was it? I could take from the McTavishes, but how to give to the Darnells?

And then you!

You fell into my lap with your strange phone call and your rather unsubtle hints at blackmail, and I suddenly understood why it couldn't be your grandmother or even your mother who showed me the path to making things right.

It had to be you. You, and my Camden. Born in the same year, you know. In 1992. Just two months apart.

Fate, one might say!

Now, like I told you, Camden is being a *bit* difficult. I'd
hoped he'd stay here in North Carolina, but he continues to
insist on going to some college in California. Not even one of
the nicer ones near the beach, either, but in San Bernardino.
He's just doing this to upset me, some kind of delayed
rebellion, I assume, but fair warning, our plans may need to
shift a bit. He's coming to see me tomorrow evening, though,
and I think I have just the thing to make sure he's right where
we need him when you're ready to make the drive up here.

You'll need to be subtle, I should warn you. Camden is
naturally suspicious, and I'm afraid I may have only made that
worse over the last few months. But I have faith in you, my
darling!

My great-niece.

What a thing.

I think your idea of using another name is very smart, dear
girl, and of course I can help with the paperwork. Julianne is a
lovely middle name, so I agree, use that. And besides, you can
go by Jules.

Ruby, jewel, do you see? Clever of us, isn't it?

And thank you for your response to that packet of letters.
It was a difficult thing, unpacking all of that after all this time,
but you were right that night at the diner. (About the need for
absolute truth between us, *not* the hash browns. Smothered,
covered, fluffed, buttered, I have no idea, I just know I couldn't
sleep that night from the heartburn.)

You're a tough cookie, but you understood what I was
telling you. You had compassion for me in spite of all of it.

And yes, I have heard that tale about the scorpion and the
frog. The poor little frog agrees to carry the scorpion across
the river, even though he worries that the scorpion will sting

him. The scorpion promises he won't, but sure enough, he can't resist, sinking them both beneath the water.

"Why did you do it?" the frog asks before he drowns. "Now we'll both die."

"Because it is my nature," says the scorpion.

Yes, darling. If that's the story that my confessions made you think of, I think you might understand all of us better than you know.

You'll be good for Camden. He'll be good for you.

And I will sleep well at night, knowing I've left Ashby House in the very best hands—the only hands—I could.

-R

September 3, 2013

Ruby,

Well, this is a first for me: writing a letter to a dead lady.

But honestly, I wasn't sure what else to do. I guess this is the kind of thing normal girls would journal about, but when have I ever been a normal girl? When were *you*?

You can't answer that, I know.

Still, I liked writing with you, and I miss it. I miss *you*, which is strange since we only met that one time. But I guess once someone has shared their murder confessions with you, you feel a certain *bond*.

Or maybe it's a family thing. I mean, you're my great-aunt after all.

Were my great-aunt.

It was a gut punch, reading about your death online. Heart failure, huh? Don't you have to have a heart for it to fail? (You should imagine a little cymbal crash here, by the way. Or was that joke too mean? I guess it doesn't matter, what with you being dead. Anyway, I still think you'd laugh.)

For a month or so, I waited for . . . I don't know. Something. Like, maybe someone would find my letters to you and would know to get in contact with me. Or that there'd be one last secret bequest in your will, and I'd get to show up all dramatic and in a black veil to whispers of, Who is she? (It's possible I watched a lot of soap operas with my mom as a kid.)

Instead, there was nothing but silence.

It's so weird that for the last year, you've been such a big part of my life, and I'd like to think that I was a big part of yours, and yet nobody knew. Now nobody will ever know.

Except me.

When it became clear that no one was getting in touch with me, that you didn't have any other tricks up your sleeve, I figured I should probably abandon our whole plan. What was the point if you were gone? I mean, sure: I knew that Cam was cute and rich, but I figured there were other cute and rich guys out there, maybe even ones with less fucked-up families (although I'll admit, probably not any with a house as amazing as Ashby).

Still, I'd already been thinking about moving to California, and I had that money you gave me when we met, so I thought, "Why the fuck not?"

(I'll try to stick to only one "fuck" in this letter, too. It was a good rule, and I'm sorry my first letter to you probably sounded like a Quentin Tarantino script. You probably don't know who that is. And it *doesn't matter* because I am writing *to a dead person who will not read this.* But that's hard to remember sometimes. I guess it's because I've got your letters here in front of me. When I read them, I can see you and hear you so clearly, it's like you're in the room with me.)

(But also, please don't be in the room with me—this situation is weird enough without adding ghosts to the mix.)

Anyway. California.

I wasn't going for Cam, I was going for me. Might as well try out the acting thing for real, right? And I had a friend from high school in San Bernardino, so off I went.

I'm not gonna lie, so far, it kind of sucks. California is expensive, for one thing, and also San Bernardino is *not* L.A. I'm not exactly getting discovered babysitting for my neighbor's kids, you know? So it has not been the best time, and I was honestly thinking about heading home.

And then tonight happened.

God, Ruby, I wish you were really here. I wish you'd really read this. You probably wouldn't believe me, but that's okay. You'd laugh, at the very least. You'd spread your hands wide and say something like, *Fait accompli, darling,* and I'd wonder yet again if in addition to being a murderess, you were a witch.

Because it had to be magic, Ruby. It had to be *something.*

I met Camden.

Not on purpose! I didn't seek him out. I wouldn't have even known *how* to, since he seems very committed to never appearing on any social media, ever. But tonight, I walked into this place called Senor Pollo's, and there he was, behind the bar.

I recognized him from the pictures you sent, and for a second, I'm pretty sure I just stood there with my mouth hanging open because *how*, right? Of all the wing places and all that.

He smiled at me. He poured me a beer. We talked, and we . . .

You know what? I'm gonna preserve a little mystery there. I feel like you'd understand.

Was it fate? Destiny?

Ruby, was it *you?*

EPILOGUE

Jules

Eight Months Later

Mountain views are overrated.

Watching the morning sun break through the clouds over a navy-blue sea, whitecaps foaming, I sip my herbal tea and let that familiar contentment sink into me, wiggling my toes in the warm sand beneath my chair.

I keep thinking I'll get tired of it eventually, sitting here just after sunrise, another gorgeous day unfurling before my eyes. But it's been five months since we bought this place on a tiny spit of land off the coast of South Carolina, and I still feel my stomach flip with happiness every morning.

Or maybe, I think, resting my hand on the firm curve of my stomach, that's just my little freeloader here.

Yes, it might be a little emotionally manipulative of me, telling you I'm pregnant, hoping you'll forgive me for everything else, but hey. We use the gifts God gave us.

Ruby had it right, I think, in that last letter.

My great-grandfather sold his own child for a buck (okay, a lot of bucks). My great-grandmother burned that money to a crisp.

My grandmother turned down Ruby's offer of cash. My mother once stole everything I'd saved from a year of babysitting so that she could buy a bunch of lottery tickets.

We're made up of many different types of people, is my point.

Good ones, bad ones. Most of them, like me, probably fall somewhere in the middle.

That gives me hope for the little girl currently floating around inside me. Camden is good, through and through. Me? Only middling.

But surely that gives her a better chance than most.

I hope so, at least.

Are you frowning right now, thinking to yourself, *Bitch, didn't you set a house on fire? Didn't you murder two people? In what world does that make you* not *a bad person?*

That's fair.

Libby was an accident, though. I didn't know she had taken an extra Ambien that afternoon, once they got back from the funeral home. She never even woke up; she simply breathed in all that smoke until she never breathed again.

That's not my fault.

Ben, though . . .

After I turned to leave Ruby's office—after he'd cornered and tried to threaten me—he struck me from behind with a paperweight from Ruby's desk. The pain stunned me, made me stumble, literal stars in my vision. (I always thought people made that up! But nope.)

It makes you crazy, that kind of pain. That kind of *fear*.

For the first time since I'd read her letters all those years before, I understood what had made Ruby pick up that gun and go after Duke Callahan on that hot Paris night.

For the first time, I felt like we must share the same blood.

Was that what made me curl my fingers around the fireplace poker, the first thing I laid eyes on?

Was that what made it feel so goddamn *good* when I swung, hard, at his head?

I don't know. I wish I could have asked Ruby.

Of course, once Ben was dead, I had to do *something*.

This is the part where I'm supposed to say I didn't think I'd get away with it.

But I knew I would.

Ruby had showed me how.

No one in Tavistock liked the other McTavishes anymore. They were cruel, and petty, and ungenerous, and Cam still held every purse string.

And I was Cam's wife.

Mrs. McTavish.

The *only* Mrs. McTavish.

It didn't hurt that Officer Jamison hadn't been as easily dissuaded from looking more closely at Nelle's death as I'd originally feared, and ultimately found those telltale marks on the inside of her lips.

My story of finding Ben burning something in the office, of asking him what he was doing, his sudden rage, an attack, and then a fire spreading out of control . . .

It made sense.

Or at least, people accepted it.

The sun breaks through the clouds, and I shade my eyes with one hand, glancing down the beach. Cam is nothing more than a speck, but I know it's him, wrapping up his morning jog, and I smile to myself, patting my belly.

"That's your daddy," I tell my daughter, heaving myself out of my chair to make my way—slowly, very slowly—back up the steps to the deck and the sliding glass door leading into the open kitchen and den.

"Morning, Ruby," I call.

Her portrait was the one thing that survived the fire. All of Ashby House was in ruins, but Andrew Miller's painting was somehow mostly intact. The frame was too badly burned to save, and the edges of the canvas were stained with smoke and water damage, but Ruby herself had been no worse for wear.

"That happens sometimes," one of the firefighters had said. "A whole house can be destroyed, but the paintings are virtually untouched."

He said it was because the heat tended to snap their hanging wires early on, so they fall face down, protecting them.

Another story that made sense, sure.

But when I meet Ruby's eyes over the fireplace of this new house, I wonder if there's more to it.

I'd told Camden we could get rid of it if he wanted. I would understand. Now that I knew the full extent of what she put him through I wouldn't have blamed him.

"We can donate it or something if you feel weird about throwing it away," I said. "Any museum would be happy to take it, I bet."

That had been in the early days, before we bought this place, when it was just the two of us (well, three, but we didn't know it then) in a hotel room in Asheville.

He'd thought about it, but in the end, he'd shaken his head and said, "It's all that's left of her, really. Only thing left from Ashby House."

Not the only thing, I think now, my hand once again going to my stomach. Ashby House may have been reduced to a dark rectangle of earth on a mountaintop miles away, but one night in that red bedroom gave us a permanent reminder of our time there.

And Ruby's portrait, professionally repaired and reframed, was the first thing we hung in our new house.

I wondered if I'd feel differently about her, now that I fully understood all that she was, all that she'd done. She'd seemed like my savior, all those years ago. A woman who wanted to ease her conscience by fixing everything that was wrong in *my* life? Setting me up with her handsome son, ensuring that I would ultimately inherit her estate? What wasn't there to like?

But she'd hurt Camden. Oh, I know that in her own way, she'd thought she was doing the right thing by him. I even think she had known she might die that night, had made her peace with it. She was giving Cam one final test, but in her mind, either outcome would mean that her project had been successful. He'd call the ambulance and prove his loyalty—or he'd let her die and prove his independence. Either way, I'd be waiting in the wings.

Still, she'd manipulated him—manipulated *me*—in ways I might never fully understand.

And yet.

I couldn't make myself get rid of that fucking portrait.

Or her letters.

Lost in the fire, I'd told Cam, and that was for the best. Why would we need them now? I knew everything there was to know about Ruby, about her crimes and her schemes and her plans.

I understood her.

And learning the truth about Ruby's past had released something in Cam as well. No more shadows in his eyes, no more guilt.

No, that was my emotion to carry, but I was fine with that. It seemed like a small price to pay.

The sliding glass door opens, and Cam comes in, damp with sweat and sea air. "How are my ladies this morning?"

"The littlest lady is apparently doing some kind of spin class in there, and *this* lady is thinking you should make her an omelet."

"Well, I have my marching orders," he says, dropping a kiss on my forehead and then heading toward the sink to wash up.

I smile and drift into the den as he hums to himself.

He's lighter now, Cam. Finally free, from all of it.

The money, it turns out, was not such a terrible burden once it was no longer connected to that place, those people.

Cam is already using it to do good things. He made a major donation to this community center in Tennessee, and there's a trust his lawyer is putting together in Tavistock that will make sure the town has a sizable endowment for decades to come.

And of course, even with all that generosity, we'll still have more than we could ever spend. The three of us—or four, five, who knows what shape our family will take?—will never have to worry about money.

Somehow, impossibly, we've gotten our happy ending.

I stand in the living room, the soft sound of the waves in the distance a soothing soundtrack as I gaze up at Ruby's portrait.

Only I know that behind her dark eyes, slid between the canvas and its backing, are all the letters Ruby had sent me. The ones I had saved and hidden for years, the ones I'd taken with us to Ashby House because I'd known that once we were there, it would be time for Cam to learn the truth, too.

The ones I'd run through a burning house to save.

Even that last letter, the one hidden in her office and never sent, was now tucked away with the others, the full accounting of Ruby's sins—and mine—hiding in plain sight.

Would she be pleased with how things had turned out? This life that Cam and I have built? She said she wanted good things for him, but did she truly? Or had she always been using him—and me—for her own ends?

Glancing over my shoulder, I see him pull out eggs, butter, and I think—probably for the thousandth time—that I should tell him the truth about us.

I found Ruby's card in my grandmother's things a week after the accident that killed my mother. Grammy had died two years before, and her entire existence had been contained in two cardboard boxes in the back of my mom's closet.

I'd taken those boxes out of the closet along with the few other things I could carry because Dan, my mom's boyfriend, already had another woman moving in and "didn't have room for Linda's shit anymore."

I remember going through those boxes in my dorm room, knowing that next semester I'd have to find somewhere else to live because there was no way I could afford even student housing, not after burying Mom.

I'd been terrified, and more than that, *angry*.

How unfair it all seemed, to be alone in the world at nineteen.

I almost threw that card away, but for whatever reason, I shoved it in my purse, forgetting about it until I was searching for a ten-dollar bill I thought I'd stashed away. Still, it had been another week or two before I was curious enough to google Ruby McTavish.

There was much more to find than I expected. I spent night

after night at my computer, reading about her husbands, about Ashby House. Wondering what in the world my grandmother had had to do with a person like that.

And then, finally, I stumbled on the story about her kidnapping, about her miraculous recovery. About the poor family in Alabama who had stolen this golden girl.

Suddenly, the pieces clicked into place, and the rush I felt as I realized who this woman might be to me—it still sends chills up my spine, just thinking about it.

I somewhat regret that stupid, heedless phone call—but miraculously, it led to me standing here in this house with this man, this child just months away from being born.

I *will* tell him, I promise.

But you'll keep my secret for now, won't you?

I think you will. I trust you.

Here—I'll even tell you one more secret, for good measure.

When I cut that slit in the back of Ruby's portrait to hide her letters, I discovered I wasn't the first person to use it as a hiding spot.

As I'd shoved the papers inside, my fingers had brushed a crinkled piece of newsprint. When I'd pulled it out, it was yellowed with age, the date at the top reading *August 18, 1987*.

The article that had been carefully clipped out was some fluff piece about a parade in some small Iowa town called Bishop, the faded color photo showing people lined up along a flag-bedecked street as an old car drove by, a beauty queen waving from the back.

I couldn't figure out why Ruby had cut it out, much less hidden it, but I knew it had been her handiwork. I recognized her elegant, spidery script in the blank space alongside the photo.

F & L (R & G?) she'd written, and then, underneath, a list.

Iowa, 1987
Missouri, 1970–1987
Ohio, 1962–1970
Kentucky, 1960–1962
Before: ??

It didn't make any sense to me, and I'd turned the clipping over in my hand, hoping for more clues, but there was only an ad for the local Ford dealership. I looked more carefully at the picture, studying the beauty queen. She was pretty, her red hair curled back from her face, but there was nothing familiar there, and my eyes drifted to the crowd.

It took awhile—all the faces were a little blurry, and several were wearing sunglasses—but finally, I saw a dark-haired woman standing just at the edge of the photo, her hand shading her eyes.

Mrs. Faith Carter watches the parade with her mother, Mrs. Lydia Hollingsworth.

Faith and Lydia. *F & L.*

I swear to you, I *felt* Ruby in that crinkled old piece of newspaper. I could almost see one shiny red nail tapping the picture, and those dark hazel eyes—my eyes—settling on those two women.

There *was* something familiar about the dark-haired one, something about the way she stood, the set of her shoulders, the slight purse in her lips as she watched the parade.

She looked, I realized with a dawning horror, exactly like Nelle. The older woman at her side—her mother, according to the caption—was taller, her hair twisted into an updo that was old-fashioned even forty years ago, and her hand was resting on her daughter's arm.

I stared at that picture for a long time, thinking back

through everything I'd read about Baby Ruby and her kidnapping. About the nanny, Grace, who had vanished from North Carolina only days after Ruby went missing.

R & G?

In her letters, Ruby had imagined what must have happened to the other Ruby, thinking of that poor baby sent off to find her nanny, searching the woods for Grace, before stepping off a cliff, plunging into all that dark, thick greenery, swallowed up forever.

But maybe . . .

Maybe there had been another story there all along.

A woman—a girl, really; Grace had been only about twenty—seeing the sickness in Ashby House before anyone else had known to look. A woman who loved a child enough to try to save her from it. Who had found a way to make them both disappear.

Or maybe this was simply another fantasy of Ruby's. Nothing more than a delusional hunch, a wish that the real Ruby, Dora Darnell's spiritual twin, had been a fighter, too. That she had, perhaps, survived.

In any case, it was another one of Ruby's many secrets.

One I decided to keep.

Well, except from you.

That piece of newspaper is still there in the painting, wrapped gently in all of Ruby's letters, and I think about it every time I look into the eyes Andrew Miller so lovingly painted all those years ago.

The love of his life.

And his doom.

Here's one final secret for you.

Sometimes, when I look up at Ruby's portrait, I think

about how happy she was when it was painted. She thought she'd beaten it then, the dark thing that was lurking inside her.

She thought it could be that easy.

And I think about me and Cam, how happy we are.

How easy it is to think the darkness has been exorcised from us both.

Even though Cam pressed a pillow down on his mother's face until she stopped moving.

Even though I swung that poker at Ben without one second of hesitation.

Were we forced into the role of murderer? Did we have any other choice?

I think I know the answers, but sometimes . . .

Sometimes I lie awake at night, our child kicking inside me, half him, half me, and remember that Cam and I are both Ruby's heirs.

Me by blood, him by a different, but no less powerful bond.

And I wonder.

I WONDER.

ACKNOWLEDGMENTS

Camden McTavish might bristle at being called "The Luckiest Boy in North Carolina," but thanks to the amazing team I get to work with on these books, I wear the title "The Luckiest Girl in Alabama" very proudly!

Ruby really put me through the wringer, and I would not have made it through without the guidance of my brilliant editor, Sarah Cantin. Thank you as always for your instinctive understanding of these absolutely wild plots I come up with, and thank you for always pushing me and the book to be as good as we can be.

Thank you also to Drue VanDuker for your sharp eye, smart notes, and truly excellent author care!

I am beyond lucky to have found a publishing home at St. Martin's Press, and I am so grateful to everyone there. Jennifer Enderlin, Kejana Ayala, Marissa Sangiacomo, Jessica Zimmerman, thank you so much for all you do for me and these books.

I also owe a special thanks to the team over at Macmillan Audio. Mary Beth, Robert, Drew, and Emily, it was so lovely to get to spend time in the booth and to see all the work that goes into making these stories as fun to listen to as they are to read!

How delighted it makes me to thank Holly Root for the seventeenth time! As I've said before, and will no doubt say again, landing you as an agent was the luckiest break I ever got in this biz. Thank you also to Alyssa Maltese, for all that you do for so many authors. You're the best!

Thanks to Heather Baror-Shapiro and her team, for helping these unhinged stories find homes all over the world, and thank you as well to Jon Cassir and Berni Barta over at CAA, who work to get these unhinged stories on your TVs/movie screens!

To my family, friends, and cats, thank you for literally everything. All of it.

And to my readers: This year was the first time I really got to get back out on the road and meet so many of you, and I hadn't realized just how much I'd missed that—missed *y'all*. Thank you, thank you, thank you. When you buy one of my books, you aren't just spending your money. You're also giving me your time, and that's the most precious commodity we have. It's an honor to get to entertain you for a few hours, and I hope I've made time in waiting rooms, during hours on flights, or just a simple boring afternoon go by a little faster and a little more enjoyably.

As kids, Emily and Chess were inseparable, but their bond has been strained by the demands of their adult lives. So when Chess suggests a girls trip to Italy, Emily jumps at the chance to reconnect with her best friend.

Villa Aestas in Orvieto is breathtaking, but it has a dark past: in 1974 it was rented by a notorious rockstar, who was joined by up-and-coming musician Pierce Sheldon and his girlfriend, Mari. By the end of the holiday Pierce is dead, and Mari goes on to write one of the greatest horror novels of all time.

As Emily digs into the villa's history, she begins to think that Pierce's murder wasn't just a tale of sex, drugs, and rock & roll gone wrong, but something more sinister – and that there might be clues hidden in the now-iconic works that Mari left behind.

Yet the closer that Emily gets to the truth, the more tension she feels developing between her and Chess. As secrets from the past come to light, equally dangerous betrayals from the present also emerge – and it begins to look like the villa will claim another victim before the summer ends.

Available to order

HEADLINE